# LOVE
### AND
# GLORY

# LOVE
### AND
# GLORY

## ROBERT
## FUNDERBURK

## BETHANY HOUSE PUBLISHERS
### MINNEAPOLIS, MINNESOTA 55438

Cover illustration by Joe Nordstrom

Published by Bethany House Publishers
A Ministry of Bethany Fellowship, Inc.
11300 Hampshire Avenue South
Minneapolis, Minnesota 55438

Printed in the United States of America

**Library of Congress Cataloging-in-Publication Data**

Funderburk, Robert, 1942–
    Love and glory / Robert Funderburk.
       p. cm. — (The Innocent years ; bk. 1)

    1. Married people—Louisiana—Fiction. 2. Lawyers—
Louisiana—Fiction. I. Title. II. Series: Funderburk, Robert,
1942–     Innocent years ; bk. 1.
PS3556.U59L68   1994
813'.54—dc20                    94–27177
ISBN 1–55661–460–8            CIP

To Gilbert Morris,
who taught me to write

# CONTENTS

★ ★ ★

### PART FOUR
### ASH WEDNESDAY

# PROLOGUE

★ ★ ★

Catherine felt that in her own way she, too, had become a soldier after the Japanese dropped their bombs on Pearl Harbor. Instead of a uniform, she wore the pale blue dress with white lace trim across the bodice that Lane had given her the day before he went off to war. And the battle she fought today was against the monthly bills that lay stacked before her on the old roll-top desk that had belonged to her grandfather. Could she use Lane's allotment check to fend them off, or would they overrun her position?

Smiling ruefully at her thoughts of the desk as battleground, she picked up the bill from Thompson's Garage, reading the brief note Walter Thompson had scrawled across the top.

Mrs. Temple,

I know with Lane overseas you're trying to fix things yourself to save money, but with the car it might be better if you call me first before you try.

And remember—never, ever use a hammer on the spark plugs again.

We appreciate your business,

Walter

Catherine lifted the white porcelain cup with the tiny grapevine pattern running just below the rim, taking pleasure in the hot, sweet tea. It was a taste she had developed since Lane had gone off to the South Pacific. *We'll have that small difference between us when he gets back—his coffee and my tea. I wonder how many others there'll be.*

She glanced to her left and saw her three-year-old son, Cassidy, lying on the sofa. A golden swatch of sunlight streamed through the high windows and glinted off his hair, so blond it was almost white. *Mine was the same color when I was his age, but I still think his eyes are a lighter blue than mine. Cass, you look like such a little angel lying there. But, my goodness, what a handful you are when you're awake!*

The long white curtains flowed into the room on the warm breeze of early August, their shadows insubstantial as wraiths on the gleaming hardwood floors.

Catherine worked awhile on the household budget, paying some bills, putting others off until the following month. *I'll be so glad when Lane's back and we have enough money to pay everything off, get some new clothes for the children, and buy enough groceries to fill up the pantry. And a night out at a fancy restaurant up in Memphis—just the two of us. Won't that be fun!* Lost in thought, she heard the radio only as a dull droning noise in the background until the first four notes of the song played.

She placed the top back on the inkwell, laid the pen aside, and listened to the lyrics of "I'll Be Seeing You." The song brought back memories of the early years of her marriage when she and Lane had lived in a small tree-shaded apartment three blocks from the Ole Miss campus.

*I'll find you in the morning sun and when the night is new. . . .*

Outside, the wind stirred the pale, graceful sweep of the weeping willow boughs. The leaves, catching the sunlight in a green-gold radiance, shimmered and swayed and brushed softly against the screen as though sighing an arboreal lullaby to the sleeping child inside.

But Catherine was lost in the melody and the words of the song, taken to another place and another time.

★ ★ ★

*"What a beautiful child!" B.L. Kirkland, the tall, gangly pastor of the little white frame church they had attended since their move to Oxford, Mississippi, took Jessie in his arms. A diffident, unassuming man given to long prayers and short sermons, Kirkland stood in the tiny foyer greeting his congregation as they walked out into the grove of beech trees after the morning service. He smiled benignly at Catherine. "You know, babies can be a source of embarrassment for preachers—not knowing whether it's a boy or a girl. But there's no doubt about this fine boy. He's certainly got his father's brown eyes, doesn't he?"*

*Catherine's mouth pursed slightly with displeasure, but Kirkland was cooing to the child and didn't notice.*

*"Yes, he certainly does, Pastor," Lane answered for*

his wife. "Maybe he'll grow up to be a quarterback just like me."

Catherine frowned at Lane, who was struggling to keep from laughing out loud.

"Well, God bless ya'll," Kirkland offered, handing the baby back to Catherine. He returned to his flock who were still filing out of the church as Lane and Catherine walked down the front steps and out onto the sidewalk.

"A boy! How could he possibly think this beautiful little girl is a boy?" Catherine muttered digustedly, adjusting the blanket around Jessie's face. "And you went right along with it."

"Aw, c'mon, Cath. Give the man a break. He has a tough enough time as it is dealing with people." He put his arm around her shoulder. "I didn't want to embarrass him. Besides, the man's got a good heart."

"You're right," Catherine conceded, glancing up at her husband. "I guess he just offended a mother's pride. After all, she is our first child."

As they walked home along the sidewalk, cracked and tilted by the roots of huge oaks, they greeted friends and fellow church members who were enjoying the unusually mild January weather. Almost everyone congratulated Lane on his performance in the bowl game the week before when he was selected as Most Valuable Player. Catherine realized that, for the moment at least, her husband was the biggest celebrity in Oxford—with the possible exception of William Faulkner.

She had long realized how important Lane's success was to her. Even in high school she thought of herself as Lane Temple's sweetheart rather than as Catherine Taylor. And now he had achieved national acclaim. But as she watched his reaction to the compliments showered on him, it suddenly occurred to her that they held little meaning for him. For Lane, football was merely a *job, a means of getting an education that he would never be able to afford otherwise.*

*They came to a little park near the Oxford clock tower and sat on a weathered bench beneath a stand of tall pines. Lane took Jessie in his arms and leaned back on the bench. High above them, the wind sighed a lullaby through the crowns of the trees, swaying green and graceful against the brilliant winter sky.*

*Catherine moved close to Lane, placing her hand on his as he cradled their firstborn. She gazed at the strong, clean features of her husband, took comfort in his strength as well as the tender way he held their child. In that ordinary moment, she came to know something of what Lane did hold to be important, and it was far more lasting than touchdowns and cheering crowds.*

★ ★ ★

A log truck rattled by the house, bringing the present into sharp conflict with the past. Catherine glanced around the room, almost surprised that she was in her own home years after that bright January morning. She thought again of their awkward pastor and how careful Lane had been not to hurt Kirkland's feelings. It was a habit of his, she had come to realize—the way he dealt with fragile people.

That same dreadful longing she had endured for more than three years seemed to settle in her breast. She ached to touch Lane, to lose herself in his arms. Only in sleep and in memory could she be with him now. She shivered slightly and let herself slide back once more into the past.

★ ★ ★

*The sound of the marching band thundered across the stadium as the Ole Miss football team, the red and* gray of their uniforms recalling other times and other battles, charged through the goalposts and onto the field. The crowd came alive, standing, cheering, roaring its approval for the Rebels.

At the other end of the stadium, the purple-and-gold-clad Fighting Tigers of Louisiana State University trotted out onto the white-striped turf. They were greeted by a few calls and whistles of the staunch supporters who had made the trip up from Baton Rouge to Oxford for the game.

Catherine, very much pregnant with their first child, sat in the student section directly behind the Rebel bench. She wore Lane's letter jacket against the autumn chill. He had told her to stay home and listen to the game on the radio, but she had insisted on coming and he finally relented.

Lane knelt next to the bench. She could see his crew-cut brown hair glistening with sweat, his chest heaving with exertion as he listened intently to his coach. Catherine could almost feel the pressure her husband was under as she watched the intense concentration in his eyes.

The game was a seesaw battle until the last five seconds.

The score was LSU—13, Ole Miss—7. Ole Miss had the ball on their own twenty-five-yard line. All eyes were on the sophomore quarterback wearing number 10 on his jersey as he nodded to the coach, slipped his helmet down over his head, and trotted back onto the playing field.

The stadium was silent as the Ole Miss team broke from the huddle and lined up facing the Tigers. From the shotgun formation, Lane barked the signals. The center snapped the ball and Lane caught it cleanly, holding it above his right shoulder as his receivers sprinted down-

*field. But they were all smothered by the LSU defensive backs.*

*Catherine was on her feet, both hands clasped to her breast. She knew how much this game meant to Lane. His college education depended on his keeping his scholarship, and winning was everything in college football.*

*Lane tucked the ball under his arm and sprinted around the left end for the goal line. The safety hit him and went down under Lane's churning legs. As he stiff-armed the right guard, Lane cut back to the inside. The towering right end had a full head of steam as he charged. Lane lowered his head and popped him in the center of his numbers, stunned the big man, and bounced off him, still headed toward the end zone. The Ole Miss fans roared to their feet, sensing imminent victory.*

*One yard from the goal line, three LSU defenders hit Lane at the same time. The slap of leather pads sounded sharply above the grunts and bellows of the defenders as they buried him beneath a blanket of purple and gold jerseys.*

*The small knot of LSU supporters across the field went wild, yelling and waving their banners in the air. The players who had stopped Lane were hoisted high above the ground, carried shoulder high off the field in a victory parade.*

*Standing among the crowd on the silent side of the stadium, Catherine gazed at her husband, lying face down on the field, then at the stunned Ole Miss fans around her. The Ole Miss crowd still seemed unable to believe their quarterback had failed them. He had always come through in the close ones, all year long.*

*Catherine stared out across the field at Lane as he struggled to his feet. She had felt an almost physical pain every time he had been hit by another player. Now as she watched her husband, beaten and spent, trudging heavily off the field behind his team, her eyes brimmed with tears for his defeat. Pride still rose like a warm radiance in her breast for his courage.*

*Climbing heavily over the low concrete wall that separated the stands from the sidelines, Catherine felt the coach's hand under her arm. He grinned broadly at her ponderous body, helping her down to the ground.*

*In the midst of the crowded stadium, Catherine saw only her sweat-drenched, weary husband, holding his helmet loosely in his left hand, his eyes staring at the ground as he plodded along. She hurried out across the scarred and torn playing field toward him. Catherine met Lane and took his face in both her hands. She used her handkerchief to clean away the blood from a cut above his left eye. Then she kissed him warmly on the mouth.*

*Lane grinned wearily down at Catherine as she embraced him. Defeat had lost its sting.*

*She felt Lane's muscled body beneath the soaked jersey, felt his strong and gentle arms as they folded around her, and couldn't have cared less who won the game.*

*The coach began applauding his quarterback who had been an example of hard work and courage all season long—and never more than in this game. Then Lane's teammates shook off their loss and, almost as a single force, joined in with their coach. Next the entire Ole Miss crowd added more applause and a few Rebel yells.*

★ ★ ★

Catherine still stood with Lane under the towering arc lights on the playing field, listening to the noise of the crowd, when the sound of her mother's Model-T pulling into the driveway snatched her out of the memory of her husband's arms.

★  ★  ★

There are certain times in one's life that imprint themselves indelibly upon the memory. The sound of her mother's car began one such memory for Catherine Temple.

"Hurry! Turn the radio on!" Kate Taylor rushed across the living room toward Catherine. Her blond hair, streaked with silver, hadn't been combed yet and she still wore her housecoat. The blue eyes were wide with anticipation. "The President's going to speak about the war!"

"It's already on, Mother."

Kate sat down next to Catherine, turning the knob on the radio almost frantically until she got the right station. "Listen, he's about to begin."

The flat, midwestern twang of Harry Truman's voice cut confidently through the static. "Sixteen hours ago an American airplane dropped one bomb on Hiroshima. . . ."

Catherine somehow knew it was the beginning of the end for the Empire of the Rising Sun. *No more nights of lying awake in that cold, lonely bed.*

" . . . has more power than 20,000 tons of TNT. It is an atomic bomb. . . ."

*Oh, Lane! Hurry home to me!* Catherine pressed the palms of her hands against her breast as if she feared that it would explode from joy.

"If they do not now accept our terms, they may expect a rain of ruin from the sky, the likes of which has never been seen on this earth."

Kate reached out, taking her daughter's hand in her own. There seemed to be no reason to speak of it now. The two women merely smiled at each other as though words might awaken them from a dream that was too good to be true.

When time had dimmed Catherine's eyesight and left her hair white as cherry blossoms, she would still remember the sound of the President's voice that day . . . the touch of her mother's hand . . . her small son lying asleep next to her . . . and the sighing of the willow outside the window.

# PART ★ ★ ★ ONE

# THE YEARS
# GONE BY

# ONE

# REMEMBRANCE OF WAR

★ ★ ★

The dream came to Lane Temple at the usual time—in that hard hour before dawn. As he lay on his bunk, he did not hear the preparations being made for the ceremony that would end the war. In his sleep, the dream possessed him!

"Throw down your weapons! You don't have to die!" Lane stepped again from the thick jungle of the South Pacific island called Guadalcanal. On both sides of him stood a dozen or more marines—battle-weary, dirty, unshaven—their M1 Garands and Thompson submachine guns pointed toward Sealark Channel; their eyes dark mirrors of souls that had lived too long with war, eyes that had seen the blood of too many friends.

Across the narrow beach, a Japanese officer and his last two men stood knee-deep in the surf, facing the Americans. They were blackened and wounded from days of heavy fighting, a tattered remnant of the Rising Sun. The officer's eyes blazed with hatred as he held his Samurai sword in both hands.

"Let me finish 'em off, Captain!" The platoon sergeant, his eyes as black as his week-old beard, held his Thompson at the ready. "We ain't got time for prisoners."

"Not yet, Sergeant." Lane kept his men in check with a movement of his hand. "Give them a chance."

The Japanese officer barked an order. Both men threw their rifles down as they dropped to their knees. The older of the two men, a grizzled veteran, bowed his head. Suddenly the sword flashed in the sunlight, ending the man's life in the time-honored Japanese fashion.

The marines watched this small tragedy with morbid fascination while they waited for the Japanese officer to do the rest of their work for them.

The officer barked again at the younger soldier, still holding his head erect. His wild eyes stared directly into Lane's, pleading in eloquent silence for a chance at life. Lane tried to turn away, but his gaze was married to that of the young soldier's. *Till death do us part!* He felt that the earth had somehow stopped on its axis. The eyes of the Japanese boy bound him as motionless as the coconut palms rising against the blue Pacific sky.

Lane thought of his own young sons back home, of the thousands of sons who had died in the war. He had been taught to hate the Japanese by the marines *and* by the brutal actions of the Japanese. But this was a helpless boy. He didn't have to die!

"No!" Lane knew it was too late, but he shouted anyway. "No! Don't. . . !"

The gleaming steel flashed again. The boy's eyes changed! In them Lane saw for an instant the disbelief and ineffable horror—and his death suddenly became the sum of all the senseless, brutal deaths of the war.

His work done, the Japanese officer beat his bloody sword against the water, screaming his defiance at the tall Marines who had defeated and humiliated him.

Lane took three quick steps toward the water, leveled his .45 at the man's head, and pulled the trigger. He walked into the surf where the Japanese officer had fallen, stood above him, and emptied his pistol into the body as it washed lazily back and forth on the incoming tide.

★ ★ ★

The roar of the pistol still in his ears, Lane came awake with a start! Throwing his legs over the side of the bunk, he sat up and tried to control the shaking. Sweat poured from his lean six-foot frame. He ran his hands through his close-cropped brown hair, feeling empty and hollow as men do who are awakened in the dark with too little sleep and too many dreams. The shaking slowly subsided.

As Lane sat in the dim light of the ship's cabin, he finally came to believe that the dream tormented him not because of the senseless death of the boy, but because of what it had caused him to do to the Japanese officer—and because of what he had not done for the boy. He had lost a part of himself that day and he hoped desperately that he could get it back.

Lane again saw the corpse, awash in the surf at his feet as the heavy slugs from his .45 ripped into it—felt again the mindless rage that had taken him, possessing him like the dream did when it came. And since that time on the sun-washed shore of Sealark Channel, it seemed that a deadness had begun to settle inside him like a soft snowfall, its drifts growing higher and higher until he was lost in the numbing cold.

Lane thought of the times during the past three years of war when he had wanted to run, to sit down and cry, to just give up and be done with it all—but he never had. He had held men in his arms when they had broken and wept, and he had held them as they breathed their last breaths, but he had kept his own feelings locked inside the cold, away from the pain. And he had gone on to another battle. *Maybe I'm too hard now to feel anything again. What about Catherine—and the children? What if. . . .*

Sitting in the dark, Lane listened to the drone of machinery that gave life to the great battleship. The grimy, sweat-streaked faces of his men appeared to him almost as if projected in sharp detail on a screen. He heard again their rough laughter during the times they were pulled out of the lines or when they moved on to yet another sun-baked, forgotten island in the vast reaches of the Pacific.

Lane thought they were the best men who had ever lived—these ordinary Americans who had done such extraordinary things for their country and for their buddies who fought next to them. In his mind he held and caressed the memory of these men as tenderly as he had held his own children at their birth.

★ ★ ★

"You up mighty early, boy."

The familiar voice brought Lane back to the present. He had no idea how long he had been sitting there, but a faint light now seeped into the room. "This bunk's kinda uncomfortable. Guess I miss sleeping in a muddy foxhole." Lane felt the cold steel plate of the deck against his bare feet. Clad only in his green

24

shorts, he shivered and pulled the rough wool blanket about his shoulders.

A match flared. The rounded face of Walker Jones appeared above the flame as he lit his cigarette. His pale blue eyes looked almost transparent beneath the straw-colored hair. "I know what you mean. I think it's being around all these swab-jockeys that bothers me though."

*How could he know what I mean? He's only been with the outfit three months.* "Most of 'em are all right, I guess." Lane watched the red ember of the cigarette bobbing in front of the dim outline Jones made sitting on the bunk across from him.

"Nothing wrong with *any* navy man that a few months in the jungle wouldn't cure."

Lane thought it amusing how Jones slipped right into the role of the hardened combat veteran even though he had seen virtually no action. "Maybe." Lane shivered under the blanket. "I'm glad I wasn't on one of these tubs when the Kamikazes started hittin' 'em, though. In the jungles we could find a tree to hide behind, but what do you do out on the open sea?"

The red ember glowed brightly. "You blow 'em out of the sky—or you die." As Jones answered, he let the smoke flow out of his mouth. It drifted like a white mist in the dark air. "You want a butt?"

"Don't mind if I do."

Jones shook a Camel out of the pack and handed it to Lane. Then he held his cigarette out for Lane to light his from, a habit picked up from other men who had spent long months of island hopping when matches were hard to come by.

Lane noticed Jones's assimilating the mannerisms of the combat veteran and knew most people couldn't tell he was faking—except, of course, for the men who had been there. He took a long drag on the cigarette Jones had given him, sucking the smoke deeply into his lungs. "You know, I still haven't figured out why they chose us for this little shindig tomorrow."

"Today, you mean," Jones corrected him, tossing the pack of cigarettes on the ledge next to his bunk. "It's almost morning."

Lane glanced at the porthole, filling with the first pale glow of dawn. "Hard to believe it's all over."

"Yeah." Jones leaned back, propping his feet on Lane's bunk. "Well, to answer your question, I *do* know why they chose you. It's pretty obvious. And I can *guess* why they chose me."

Lane had learned that sometimes Jones had strange ideas and sometimes he made relatively good sense, so he smoked and waited for the answers.

"It's 'cause you look like the typical All-American hometown hero. The news cameras are gonna be hummin' for this show and they want the folks back home to be duly impressed. Yes, sir! You're a lean, mean marine fightin' machine—tall, dark, and fearsome. That's what you are. Decorated three times and a lieutenant-colonel to boot."

"You don't have to butter me up anymore, Jones. The war's over."

"Don't I know it! And now for *my* role." Jones dropped his cigarette into the butt can at the head of the bunk. "They picked me 'cause I've got this baby face and these big baby blues. And being five-seven just adds to the whole picture. I'm a dead ringer for that mythical soldier everybody calls 'The Kid.' There's one in every war movie, and today's show is gonna be set up just like a movie sound stage."

"Is that all you think this is?"

"Sure," Jones grinned. "They've even got General

Douglas MacArthur to play the part of John Wayne."

Lane laughed and flipped his cigarette into the butt can. "You got everything all figured out, haven't you?"

"Close as I can cut it, Colonel. Close as I can cut it." Jones stretched his arms over his head and lay back on his bunk. "What kinda plans you got when you get back home?"

Lane knew Jones was baiting him to ask the reciprocal question. "Take it easy for a while, I guess. Spend some time with the family."

"You got kids?"

"Four. One of 'em I haven't even seen yet." Lane remembered the picture of Cassidy as a one-year-old, splashing in a galvanized washtub in the backyard of their home. "He was born two months after I left for Melbourne."

"Four kids!" Jones whistled with surprise. "How'd you ever finish school?"

"Only had two of 'em while I was in college. The football scholarship paid for undergraduate," Lane continued, "but I had to work and go part time in law school. That's why I was twenty-seven when I graduated."

"You didn't get to work very long, did you?"

"I got a couple of years in before I joined up. Not enough time to build up much of a practice in Sweetwater, though." Lane thought of the endless days he had sat in his tiny law office over the dry-goods store, waiting for a client to show up—the times he had had to borrow money from his father to buy food for his wife and children. "People usually stick with the same lawyer till they die—or the lawyer dies."

"Well, I'm glad my job's waitin' for me when I get back," Jones offered, obviously disappointed that

Lane hadn't asked him about *his* plans back in the States. "When you shippin' out?"

"I haven't even figured out my points yet." Lane knew what was coming next.

"Me either," Jones admitted, "mainly because I don't know beans about how the system works."

"How many times have I explained it to you?"

"One less than enough, I reckon." Jones put his hands behind his head and lay back, letting his breath out with a sigh. "Elucidate, Professor."

Lane stretched out on the bunk, closed his eyes, and recalled the formula he had recited for his men for what seemed like the hundredth time. "You get one point for each month in service; one for each month overseas; five for each campaign star or combat decoration; and twelve for each child under the age of eighteen." He glanced over at Jones, bathed in the faint rosy light filtering in through the porthole. "Simple? When you get eighty-five points, you get to go home."

As always, Jones—lost in his own plans—ignored the instructions. "You know what I'm gonna do when I get home?"

"I've already told you I'm not interested in your love life," Lane mumbled.

"No. I mean after that."

"Something to do with your daddy's oil business and a lot of money, I imagine?"

"I mean specifically." Jones raised up on his elbow. "I got a letter from Daddy yesterday."

Even in the dim light, Lane could see Jones glance about the small room in a conspiratorial fashion.

"They're *really* openin' the Basin up for oil exploration now. We're talkin' about *billions* of dollars."

"You should have kept your helmet liner on more

28

out in that tropical sun, Jones." Lane cared nothing for Jones's money-making schemes. "I think your brain's about half baked."

Jones had already told Lane that his daddy would love to have somebody like Lane Temple working for his company. War heroes were good for business and Lane had made the news—even in the Baton Rouge newspaper—for his exploits on Iwo Jima. "This is for real, boy! You oughta come on down and get in on it. We could always use a good lawyer."

"Don't think I'm cut out for the city life. Sweetwater's more my style."

"Aw, Baton Rouge ain't nothing but a big ol' country town. You'd love it. I'm tellin' you, there's gonna be a lot of money made now that this war's over. You might as well come on down and get some of it. The food's good and New Orleans is only eighty miles away."

"I was born and raised in Sweetwater and I expect I'll be buried there." Lane could almost see the little town in the Mississippi hills.

"Now that's a real exciting prospect for a life," Jones concluded. "Well, I guess you just can't help some people."

"I appreciate the offer, but even if I wanted to go, I'd have to harness a team of mules to my family to drag them out of Sweetwater. It's the only home the kids have ever known, except for the time we were up at Ole Miss."

"Well, to each his own."

The raucous sound of sea gulls split the stillness of the early morning. Lane got up and walked over to the porthole. A breeze had come up and the surface of Tokyo Bay rippled with light, tinted pink from the eastern glow.

Jones turned over in his bunk. "Wake me for breakfast, will you?"

"I might catch another quick nap myself," Lane responded with a yawn. "You wake me if there's a Banzai attack."

"Don't worry," Jones mumbled into his pillow. "MacArthur's on board."

Lane lay back down and immediately dropped off into a deep sleep where he floated in a blissful warm darkness free of the eyes of the Japanese boy and the sight of waves turning a frothy pink color as they rolled into shore at Sealark Channel.

★ ★ ★

Lane stepped out of the shower, dried himself, and wrapped the green towel around his waist. Walking over to the mirror of the steamy head where a few stragglers from the ship's company were talking about going home to Boston or Savannah or Dallas, he laid his shaving gear on a shelf and stared into the mirror. He was twenty pounds lighter than his high school football playing weight of 185. *Gaunt* was the word that came to his mind. The bridge of his nose bent a little to the left just below his brow where a rifle butt had caught it a glancing blow. *Just gives it a little character,* he thought, *like the scar.*

Letting his forefinger trail along the white-ridged scar that ran from the right corner of his mouth to a point beneath his right ear, Lane remembered the searing pain of the Japanese bayonet as it sliced through his face. To the left of his navel, another scar marked the entrance spot of a 7mm bullet that had gone completely through the fleshy part of his side.

His eyes looked rounder, darker, larger—still possessing that peculiar glazed dullness Lane had first noticed in other men on Guadalcanal. The "Stare" was the mark of the combat veteran—eyes that look without seeing, eyes that see without carrying any image to the brain.

Lane knew intimately those things that had spawned the "Stare"—little or no sleep for days on end; a bone-grinding weariness that far exceeds mere exhaustion; nights of tension; fear that ravages the body like a disease; and an incalculable misery. It was a look of surpassing indifference to anything else that could be done to its owner.

The "Stare" was particularly noticeable in brown-eyed men like Lane. Their eyes seemed to take on an auburn tint, almost like the coat of an Irish Setter. As he gazed at his reflection in the water-stained mirror, he hoped that he could rid himself of that look before he saw his family.

Lane finished shaving and walked back down the narrow hall to his room. Jones, wearing his suntans rather than the marine dress blues (someone had decided that it would be showing too much respect for the Japanese if the Allies wore full dress uniforms), sat on his bunk, buffing his shoes.

"Ready for the grande finale of World War II?" Jones asked cheerily, spitting on the toe of his left shoe.

Lane went through the motions of small talk with Jones, not fully aware of what was being said as he dressed. What occupied him was the face of his wife Catherine—an image he had formed so many times in his mind and had carried him through those long jungle nights.

He saw first her eyes, blue as cornflowers with the lids drooping just slightly as if she were a little bit drowsy all the time. Her thick blond hair, falling in soft disarray to her shoulders and shot through with streaks that were almost white when the light hit it in a certain way, shimmered before his eyes. His fingertips could almost feel the warm, smooth skin of her face. It had an apricot glow and warmth as if it had been bathed in sunlight.

"I get the feeling that you're not hearing a word I say." Jones straightened his single campaign ribbon, snapping to attention and saluting. "How do I look?"

"Just like a marine-recruiting poster," Lane grinned, the image of Catherine still strong in his mind. "Wait'll the girls back home get a load of you."

★ ★ ★

Lane stood next to Jones on the deck of the battleship *Missouri*. Separating them from the table where the documents would be signed stood a railing made of half-inch steel pipe that had been set up for the official surrender ceremonies. Gazing about the huge ship, Lane saw fighting men from many countries.

The Americans wore their plain suntans, in stark contrast to the British, who turned out in their best uniforms, and the Russians, who sported their stiff shoulder boards. Other Allied forces included the French with their colorful decorations, the Chinese in olive drab, and the Australians with scarlet bands on their caps. The bridges, tripod turret, and all the decks of the *Missouri* were literally swarming with fighting men.

A breeze swept in from the sea, wrinkling the bay's smooth waters. Across its sparkling surface lay the city of Tokyo. Great sections of it were now in ruins, its buildings blackened skeletons testifying to the fiery work of the B–29s.

A gig flying the Stars and Stripes pulled alongside

the *Missouri*. Stepping aboard, the one-legged foreign minister, Shigemitsu, led the Japanese contingent of General Umezu and some minor officials. Waiting for them beyond the peace table stood the imposing figure of General Douglas MacArthur. He opened the ceremony with a brief and generous address.

Shigemitsu limped slowly over to the table and with great dignity signed the English and Japanese copies of the document, followed by General Umezu. Then MacArthur walked deliberately forward, accompanied by General Jonathan Wainwright, left to defend Battaan, and General Arthur Percival, who had been defeated by the Japanese at Singapore. MacArthur signed the documents along with Admiral Chester Nimitz and the Allied delegates.

The noble-looking MacArthur now gave the concluding speech: "We are gathered here . . ."

Lane found himself drifting in and out of memory. ". . . whereby peace may be restored."

While MacArthur was making his mark in history with his speech on the deck of the great battleship, Lane let his mind carry him back to the time he had first met Catherine.

★ ★ ★

*The clear, crisp October air carried a faint scent of woodsmoke as Lane walked along the streets of Sweetwater on the way home from football practice. Ahead of him he saw Catherine Taylor. She had moved to town at the beginning of the school year with her mother, who took a job teaching English at the high school. He had seen Catherine around school a few times, but had paid little attention to her.*

*Catherine, carrying a bag of groceries, was suddenly confronted by Rayford Mott, the six-foot three-inch school bully. She obviously wanted no part of him, but he refused to let her pass. When she tried to get by him, he reached for her, causing her to spill the groceries.*

*Lane dropped his books on the sidewalk and sprinted toward Catherine. "I think you'd better take off, Rayford," Lane warned coldly. "The lady doesn't seem to care much for your redneck charms."*

*"Just listen to me—I sound like Douglas Fairbanks," Lane thought. Even though Mott was three inches taller and forty pounds heavier, Lane knew it was mostly flab and that he would have no trouble taking him if it came to a fight. Mott knew this too.*

*"You keep out of this, Temple," Mott growled, his dark face like a storm cloud. "This is between me and her."*

*"You want him to leave?" Lane asked in his best Fairbanks voice, glancing down at Catherine.*

*"Y-yes."*

*Lane gave Mott an icy stare as he curled his hands into fists and balanced lightly on the balls of his feet.*

*"You gonna push me too far one day, Temple," Mott mumbled as he turned and lumbered off.*

*"He won't bother you anymore." Lane knelt down and began to help Catherine pick up the spilled groceries. As he handed her an apple, he happened to gaze into her soft, drowsy, almost-sad eyes. At that moment, with the leaves tumbling rust and gold in the breeze and making their dry scraping sounds along the sidewalk, Lane thought he could see the rest of his life reflected in those eyes that looked too blue to be real.*

★ ★ ★

"It is my earnest hope . . . that from this solemn occasion a better world shall emerge . . ."

*The Samurai sword, raised above the head of the*

*Japanese boy on his knees in the surf, glinted with a lethal light. The boy's eyes pleaded again with Lane to stop the blade's descent.* Lane shook his head, willing himself to put the thoughts of death from his mind. He caught only a few of MacArthur's words.

" . . . a world dedicated to the dignity of man . . ."

★ ★ ★

The corners of Lane's mouth hinted at a smile as he recalled the birth of his first child. *He had been up all night as he glanced over at the old schoolhouse clock on the wall of the hospital waiting room—4:30 A.M. Getting up from the leather couch with its stainless steel arms, he resumed his pacing, the avocation of any dedicated expectant father. An hour later, Dr. Aubrey James ambled down the hall and found Lane still at his pacing.*

*"You're going to wear this floor out, Lane." Dr. James, his short gray hair glinting in the fluorescent light, gazed over his steel spectacles with a mischievous gleam in his dark eyes.*

*Lane turned quickly. "Well?"*

*"Well, mother and child are doing just fine," James grinned, cleaning his glasses with the hem of his surgical smock.*

*"C'mon, Doc." Lane held his hands out in supplication.*

*James delayed the good news once more. "You know, most all first-time fathers want a boy. Not you, though."*

*"Doc!"*

*"You got your girl, Lane. Catherine's already back in her room and little Jessie's with her."*

*"Thanks, Doc." Lane pumped his hand and hurried down the empty hallway.*

*Occasionally in one's life an unexpected sorrow or*

*joy opens so intensely that it remains as clearly imprinted on the mind as the day it happens. Lane felt a quiet joy fill him as he carefully opened the door to the darkened room. In the amber glow of the bedside lamp, Catherine sat up in bed, leaning back against frosty white pillows. In her arms she cradled the tiny helpless child as it nursed at her breast.*

*Lane was overwhelmed by happiness—transfixed by joy. He watched the timeless scene for a few moments, then walked quietly over to the bed. "I love you." Taking Catherine's hand, he kissed her tenderly on the lips.*

*Catherine whispered, "Not as much as I love you. What do you think of our little Jessie?"*

*"She's beautiful!"*

*"No, she's not. She looks like a red spider monkey," Catherine replied, caressing the child's fine golden hair. "But she will be beautiful soon."*

*Even after the labor, there was a radiance about Catherine that Lane had never seen before, not even on their wedding day. He gazed into her drowsy blue eyes, brushing the silky hair back from her face. "You all right?"*

*Catherine nodded, smiling down at their child, then holding Lane's eyes fast with her own. "You want to have another one?"*

★ ★ ★

" . . . Let us pray that peace be now restored to the world, and that God will preserve it always. These proceedings are closed."

World War II was over. Stunned by the magnitude of what they had achieved, the victors shook hands and congratulated each other in a subdued celebration.

Jones turned to Lane with a broad grin. "Well, what did you think of the performance?"

Lane glanced over at MacArthur. "John Wayne could have done it better."

# TWO

# KUDZU

★ ★ ★

*Love is now the stardust of yesterday, the music of
the years gone by.*

The lyrics formed themselves in Lane's mind as he
listened to an army sergeant across the aisle from him
play a mournful rendition of "Stardust" on his saxo-
phone. He wore a 101st Airborne patch on the shoulder of his Eisenhower jacket and a homesick expression on his lean, tanned face. Tie loosened, campaign
cap cocked at a casual angle, he looked like a com-
posite photograph of all homecoming GI's.

Ten miles outside Sweetwater, the train carrying
Lane back from more than three years at war clicked
along on its steel rails, traveling through the long rolling hills of north Mississippi. He stared out the window at the kudzu vines, imported from Japan to stop
erosion on the banks where the roads cut through the
countryside. Their rich green leaves now turned black
and withered away by the merest touch of frost, the
vines spread out stark and gray like an enormous net-

work of veins and arteries clinging to the deep red clay of the hillsides.

But the kudzu was not satisfied with covering the banks it was imported to protect. It climbed telephone poles and crawled out over pastures where cows grazed unawares. In deep summer, so the legend says, you have to close your windows at night to keep it out of the house.

The sergeant finished his song, laid the sax aside, and turned to gaze at Lane's campaign ribbons. "You must have been in from the first shot."

Lane glanced over at the sergeant. "Not quite."

"I made D-day. They dropped us in them rotten marshes just inland from Utah Beach."

"D-day," Lane mused, recalling that period of the war. "I think I was probably sun bathing somewhere in the Marianas about that time."

"I'll *bet* you were sunbathing! Last I heard, the Marianas weren't exactly a *resort* area." The sergeant held out his hand. "Name's Joe Buckels—I'm on my way to New Orleans."

Lane shook his hand. "Lane Temple, and the next *stop* is my home. Nice to meet you, Joe."

"Sweetwater, huh. Guess the whole town's gonna turn out to meet you," Buckels grinned. "All nine of 'em."

"I doubt that," Lane replied, propping his feet on his duffel bag. "My family probably won't even be there. I'm an hour ahead of schedule."

"There sure ain't gonna be anybody waiting for me in New Orleans." There was a slight hint of melancholy in Buckels' voice. "I never even been there before."

"Where's your family?"

"Never had one that I can remember," Buckels replied, his dark brown eyes taking on a remote expression. "I was brought up in orphanages in St. Louis."

"What's in New Orleans for you?"

Buckels reached over and patted his sax gently. "A job making music, I hope. The French Quarter's the place to be if you got a hankering to play the blues."

Lane felt that Buckels needed all the encouragement he could get. "To me, you sound good enough to make it."

"Maybe, but there's a lot of good horn players in the 'City That Care Forgot.' Did you know that's what they call New Orleans? Hope it's like that for me."

With a hissing of air brakes and a dull banging of the couplings, the train pulled into Sweetwater Station. Lane threw his duffel bag over his shoulder and stood up. *I'm as nervous as I was when I left. That doesn't make any sense.*

Buckels held his hand out again. "If you're ever in New Orleans, look me up."

"Not much chance of that, but thanks for the invitation," Lane replied, returning the handshake. "Good luck with your job. You airborne boys deserve *something* good out of this war."

"Thanks." Buckels stared out the window at the few people scattered on the platform. "Hope things work out okay with your family."

Lane stepped down from the train under a heavy November sky, threatening rain. As he walked toward the depot, he spoke briefly to a few people he knew. His eyes flicking about from habit formed by long months in the jungle, he picked up a movement to his right, far down the platform near the middle of the train. A small boy in a sailor suit, his pale blond hair blowing like cornsilk about his head, was trying to climb up the steps onto the platform of one of the pullman cars.

The whistle shrilled loudly as white clouds of steam hissed out of the engine. It rocked forward slowly, the couplings of the cars jarring down the line as the slack was taken up. The boy dangled from the iron railing of the steps, his grip broken by the train's rocking motion. Dropping his duffel bag, Lane sprinted across the platform. Just as the child lost his hold on the railing, Lane snatched him away.

The child grinned up at Lane. Not a sign of fear registered in his bright blue eyes—no cry escaped his lips. He seemed to enjoy the excitement as most children would a bowl of ice cream.

Lane held the boy in his arms, marveling at his reaction to the near accident. Just the sound of the engine's shrill whistle would have frightened most children his age. "Where's your mama, you little rascal?"

The child grinned and pointed toward the depot. "Inside with gramma."

Staring at the boy's eyes, Lane suddenly recognized their precise color. *He's got eyes just like Catherine's.* "Cassidy! I'm your daddy, Cass!"

The child protested by making a face and pushing against Lane as he hugged him tightly.

At that moment, the door to the depot flew open and Catherine came racing across the platform toward them. She rushed into Lane's arms, smothering his face with kisses. "Oh, Lane! Thank God you're home safe!"

Lane felt the warmth of Catherine's lips and the warm softness of her body as he pulled her close. Then he glanced at his son who looked puzzled by his mother's affection for this stranger.

After all the nights Lane had imagined this scene

over the past three years, it seemed more like a dream now than something that was truly happening. He tried to speak, but nothing would come out. His throat felt constricted and a burning sensation welled up in his chest. *Am I going to cry right here in front of everybody—after holding up all this time?* Through a supreme effort, he managed to control himself.

Catherine felt the rough scar as she held Lane's face in her hands. "Oh, my goodness! What's happened to your face?" she asked, her eyes narrowed with concern.

Lane gave her a crooked grin. "Cut myself shaving. Gives me a little character, doesn't it?"

Letting her fingers trail along the slightly ridged scar, Catherine leaned over and kissed it tenderly. "As long as it's part of you, I just love it!"

Cassidy, still struggling, shrieked, "Put me down! Put me down!"

"Okay, son. Just hold your horses." Lane set Cassidy down on the platform. He immediately ran off toward the depot. "That boy could have been in real trouble if I hadn't seen him in time. Does he always get away from you like that?"

"All the time," Catherine shrugged. "I don't know what we're going to do with him. He's not mean or anything, but he's always getting into something."

"Didn't you ever show him a picture of me? He doesn't have any idea who I am."

"I showed him all your old pictures," Catherine replied. "But you—you look so different now."

"Guess I do at that," Lane agreed. "He does too. Last one I got of him, he was only a year old."

"You must be at least twenty pounds lighter." Catherine put her arm around Lane's waist and they walked together toward the spot where he had dropped his duffel bag. "And such a tan!"

"Yep, the South Pacific's a great place to get a sun-tan." Lane kissed Catherine on the mouth and picked up his duffel bag, throwing it across his shoulder. "The accommodations aren't first rate though."

Catherine took Lane's face in both hands. "There's something else. Your nose is a little bit crooked."

"So's my brain," Lane grinned. "But *it'll* straighten out in a few weeks, I hope."

Catherine hugged Lane tightly, then gazed up into his eyes. She noticed something strange about them, but didn't mention it. *Poor Lane, I'll have him thinking everything about him's changed.* "It's *so* good to have you back!"

Lane kissed her again, glancing at the depot. "I see your mother's with you. Where's everybody else?"

"I just *had* to come on out here without them. Couldn't stand waiting around that house anymore," Catherine explained, touching the scar on Lane's face. "The other children are with your mama and daddy. They're planning to come meet you too, but we'll just go on out there now."

Kate Taylor had picked Cassidy up and held him in her arms as she waited for Lane and Catherine.

"Your mother's a fine-looking woman." Lane waved to Kate, who stood smiling at them. "And I'll bet you're going to look just like her when you're her age."

"Welcome home, Lane," Kate smiled. "We're all so very proud of you."

Lane kissed her on the cheek. "And I'm thankful for what you did for my family. Catherine told me how you practically moved in with them while I was gone."

"That's what grandmothers are for," Kate beamed, glancing at Cassidy, who was beginning to fidget in her arms. "That, and helping to corral runaway boys like this one. I never in my life saw a child so active— or so precious!"

"I'm afraid Mama's picked Cass out as her favorite," Catherine observed, gazing at her mother. "I think it's because he's so much like daddy was."

Catherine thought her mother must surely be replaying memories of her father, who had died twenty years before. Her eyes had that dreamlike, faraway quality always present when she was daydreaming of her late husband. "Perhaps you're right. It was never boring living with your father." She put Cassidy down. "And here's another one just like him that you never get bored with. Exasperated maybe, but never bored."

"Well, we'd better be going," Catherine offered, taking Cassidy by the hand before he could get away. "We'll catch them before they leave for the station."

★ ★ ★

As they drove through the shady streets of Sweetwater, memories of childhood friends passed in parade for Lane as he gazed at each of the old white wood-frame houses with their high wrap-around porches and yards filled with azaleas, jasmine, and sweet olive—all resting in drab autumn slumber beneath the spreading live oaks and ancient gnarled cedars.

The town seemed more like a scene from one of Lane's South Pacific daydreams than something actual that he could hear and feel and touch. He kept reaching over and touching Catherine as she drove carefully along in their '39 Ford, just to reassure himself that he was truly home. Adding to his sense of unreality was the fact that Catherine had never driven whenever they had gone somewhere together—but that was before the war.

They reached the outskirts of town where the houses gave way to pastureland. Across the gently rolling hills, scattered trees raised their dark silhouettes above the dry winter grass. Crossing the old wooden bridge over Seven Mile Creek, they turned right and crunched along over a gravel drive through a stand of tall pines. They came out next to a small lake, its dark surface reflecting the trees and the heavy gray clouds, now crowding down toward the earth.

The house stood on a rise, the highest part of the 400-acre farm, overlooking the lake, the woods, and the cross-fenced pastures scattered with ancient shade trees. As they parked next to a white picket fence, seven-year-old Dalton, with his father's brown hair and eyes, leaped from the front porch and scampered out to meet them.

Lane stepped from the car just in time to lift him high above his head. The boy squealed with delight. Setting him down, Lane knelt beside his son. "Why, you're a real little man now, Dalton. When I left, you weren't any bigger than Cassidy."

Opening the gate, Lane took Dalton by the hand and headed up the brick walkway toward the house. As he climbed the massive concrete steps, Grady Temple, wearing his usual overalls and khaki shirt, rose from the porch swing and came over to greet him.

"Welcome home, Lane." Beneath his close-cropped white hair, Grady's deep brown eyes surveyed quickly the changes in his son. He was a man who had known poverty as well as war in his time and appeared glad to see that his firstborn had endured the latter with his courage intact.

"Thank you, Daddy," Lane grinned. He took his

father's hand, hardened from years of labor and scarred by plows and saws and, more recently, by tractors. "I thought about this place a whole lot these last three years. Even more than my own home."

"That figures. You lived here a lot longer." Grady turned to go into the house. "C'mon, your mama's been having a fit to get down to the station to meet you. Let's surprise her."

As Grady reached for the screen door, it swung outward and Maggie Temple stepped out on the porch. "I *thought* I heard somebody talking out here." She rushed to Lane, throwing both arms around him. "Lane, Lane! My boy, my boy! Oh, thank the Lord you're home safe and sound!"

"I'm fine, Mama." Lane was thrown off balance by his mother's affectionate hugs. "That is, unless you push me off this porch and break my neck!"

Maggie backed away from her son, holding him at arms' length as she looked him over. "Good gracious, Lane! Why, you're as skinny as an old stray dog!"

"The marines don't cook as good as you do, Mama." Lane could see the strain that lingered on his mother's face. Then behind her he saw the screen door push outward again. Jessie, his twelve-year-old daughter, stepped out onto the porch and stood smiling up at him. She looked like an eighteen-year-younger version of Catherine. Lane knelt on the porch, opening his arms wide. "Come here, Princess. Give your ol' daddy a hug."

Jessie smiled and stepped into her father's arms. "I missed you so much, Daddy. Did you get my letters?"

"I sure did," Lane replied, gazing into the bright face of his oldest child.

As Lane spoke with Jessie, Sharon, who was barely two when he had left, walked shyly across to the porch swing and climbed up into it. She had Lane's brown hair and her eyes had the introspective appearance of his, although they were blue like her mother's.

As the family crowded together, talking all at once and exchanging one hug after the other with Lane, Sharon swung slowly back and forth in the swing, studying this tall stranger who had come into their midst.

Then Lane noticed his youngest daughter sitting by herself in the swing. He walked over and sat down beside her. "I'm your daddy, baby. I know you don't remember me, but I sure do remember you."

Sharon gazed up at him, at this man with the warm brown eyes and the warm smile. At that moment her innocent eyes seemed to fully register— more surely than if he had spoken it out loud—how very much this man loved her. She reached out and touched his big brown hand with her tiny pale one, squeezing it gently. "I love you too, Daddy."

"There he goes again, Mama!" Dalton pointed out beyond the white picket fence.

Lane looked around and saw Cassidy scampering across the pasture toward the lake.

"Lane, go catch him before he gets to the water!" Catherine cried in mild alarm.

"I declare," Grady observed dryly, "sometimes I think that boy's a cross between a jackrabbit and a mule. Never saw a young'un so hardheaded."

Lane sprang down from the porch, vaulted the fence, and caught up with Cassidy before he was half-way to the lake. Taking him up in his arms, he chided him gently, "We're gonna have to keep a tight rein on you, young man."

Cassidy giggled and tried to squirm free. "Water—me want to see water."

As Lane walked back up the steps holding Cassidy by the hand, Maggie began ushering her brood inside the house. "Y'all get on in now. Lane, I made all your favorite dishes: black-eyed peas, corn bread, fried chicken, collards, and plenty of ice tea. And for dessert, guess what?"

"Banana pudding!"

"Yessiree!"

Lane found himself basking in the glow of attention he was getting from his family. "Mama, I just might put that twenty pounds back on today."

★ ★ ★

Lane smelled the rain before it reached him. No sharp tang of ozone in the air presaged it as with the violent light and sound shows of the summer thunderstorms. The night wind bore only the heavy wetness in the air that changed slowly into a steady, chill November rain.

The dream had awakened him again and, as always, he could still hear in the first few moments of consciousness the steady pounding of the surf on the shores of Guadalcanal. He swung his feet over the edge of the bed, feeling the cool hardwood floor beneath them. Taking a pack of Camels from the nightstand, he shook one out and stuck it between his lips. Then he took the silver lighter, rubbing the Marine Corps emblem on its front with his thumb. Pushing that memory to the back of his mind, he lit a cigarette, flicked the lighter closed, and let the smoke curl in twin streams out of his nostrils.

The first few drops spatted dully against the tin roof; then the sky opened and the rain settled into the steady drumming sound he had always loved as a child—and still did.

"Lane. . . ?" Catherine mumbled sleepily. "Are you all right, honey?"

"I'm fine." Lane drew the smoke deeply into his lungs, wondering why he enjoyed the burning sensation. He felt the soft warmth of Catherine's hand, heard the sheets rustle as she sat up in bed and began to rub his shoulders and neck, siphoning off the tension in them.

Catherine continued her massage, feeling the tightness leave Lane's muscles. "How does it feel to spend the first night back in your own bed?"

Lane rested his elbows on his knees, leaning his head forward as he savored the touch of his wife's hands. "A bed's just a bed. It's the occupant that made a war worth fighting."

Catherine stopped and moved closer to him, encircling his lean waist with her arms, pressing herself against his bare back. She laid her cheek against the smooth tanned skin of his shoulder.

Lane felt his wife's silky skin against his back, could almost feel her love flowing into him—and it was stronger than the memories; stronger than all the cold night sweats and the thoughts that flooded him by day. He stubbed his cigarette out and turned to her, taking her in his arms. His mouth found hers in the darkness and he lost himself in her warmth and softness and the almost forgotten fragrance of her.

★ ★ ★

The rain had slackened to a gentle pattering on the roof. Lane lay on his back, his arm around Catherine as she rested her head against his shoulder. The house creaked somewhere down the hall, settling in for the night.

Turning slightly, Lane brushed his lips against Catherine's hair, a silky brightness in the dim light of the bedroom. "Tell me about the children."

Catherine laughed softly. "Well, you've seen Cassidy in action. That's enough about him for the time being."

"Wish I'd had him as a running back when I played quarterback at Ole Miss. He's so slippery he'd have gone through those big linemen like quicksilver."

"Cassidy's one reason Mama stayed with me so much," Catherine explained. "She's about the only one who can do anything with him."

Lane thought how terribly fortunate he was to be lying in bed with his wife, to have made it through the war, and he tried to ignore the prickling of guilt for those who hadn't.

"And Jessie," Catherine continued, "has been so busy she's hardly had time to eat and sleep. She worked in our little victory garden, helped with the scrap drive in town, and played the piano and sang like an angel in the church choir. They even let her sing a few solos. I think she's got enough musical talent to really do something with it."

"What about Dalton? Seems like he's *all* boy."

"He certainly is! I bet he's killed more Japs in the war than you did—he and his little friend down the street," Catherine smiled. "His grades are only average, but the teachers say he tries real hard. I think the coach has already got his eye on him for the junior high football team. Must have his daddy's athletic ability."

"I don't think I had that much natural ability," Lane offered. "I just worked hard at it so I could get a college education. Anything to keep from farming for a living. I did enough plowing and picking cotton and hoeing when I was growing up to learn I wasn't cut out for that."

"Your daddy certainly is. Never saw a man love the land as much as he does."

"What about Sharon?" Lane found his youngest daughter to be somewhat of an enigma. "She seems awfully—well, withdrawn, I guess you'd call it."

"She's like that at first, but when she gets to know you she's liable to talk your head off," Catherine explained of the child that seemed less like her own than the other three. "She's going to be the real bookworm in the family, I think. Mama's already taught her to read and she's always trying to get somebody to read her the books that she can't understand herself."

"You think she likes me?"

"Oh, I think she's totally infatuated with you!" Catherine affirmed. "I'm so glad you spent some extra time with her today. She seems to be more sensitive than any of the rest of the children—more than any of us, maybe."

Lane and Catherine talked until their eyes grew too weary to hold open and then they talked with their eyes closed and then they drifted into sleep in each other's arms. The rain had slowed to a slight drizzle, plopping softly outside the window as it dripped down from the tin roof.

# THREE

# THE AMOROUS MR. CAGE

★ ★ ★

"I declare—if groceries get any higher, we'll just have to peck corn with the chickens!" Kate Taylor walked with Catherine down the narrow aisle of the Sweetwater Jitney Jungle store. The blue wool coat she wore over the pearl-colored dress matched the color of her eyes perfectly. "Thirteen cents for a loaf of bread! Last year it was only nine."

"Now, Mama, it's not as bad as all that." Catherine, warmly practical in her tan gabardine slacks and the brown leather jacket Lane had given her for Christmas, could never remember when Kate hadn't dressed up when she left the house. She smiled at her mother as she pushed the grocery cart over the plank flooring of the store. The building was so old that the heart pine lumber was fastened with wooden pegs. "Remember how cheap things were during the Depression? But nobody had any money, so what good did it do?"

Kate hefted Cassidy to a better position on her hip

and took a box of Post Toasties from a shelf. "Twenty-one cents for this little box of corn flakes. That Harry Truman better show he can do something besides drop bombs on the Japs or we'll all be in the poorhouse!"

Catherine allowed her mother this little vice of complaining every time they shopped. She knew it was Kate's way of coping with the loss of her husband, who had always gone to the grocery store with her on Friday. It had been a ritual in their marriage, along with dining out afterward.

Catherine still remembered her father, when he hadn't had time to go home and clean up, greasy and sweat-stained from his day of logging the hardwood bottoms of Lee county, strolling through the aisles of the store beside his petite and properly dressed schoolteacher wife.

This lesson had not been wasted on Catherine, who had come to see how important the ordinary, everyday activities of life truly are when done with someone you love. She tried never to take them for granted and relished this simple time with Cassidy and her mother. "This is 1946, Mama. Things just cost more."

"I reckon you're right," Kate conceded. "I see you're not buying nearly as much as you used to."

"Well, I—I was wasting a lot of money on things we really didn't need."

Kate set Cassidy, who had begun to squirm, down on the floor. "Now don't you go running away, young man."

Cassidy grinned brightly up at Kate, his face glowing with health inside the red corduroy cap with its furry side flaps sticking out like another set of ears. "I won't, Gramma." He grabbed a can of Schoolhouse

pork and beans off a lower shelf and studied the football player on the label.

"Put that back, Cass." Catherine knelt to take the
can away from her son.

"Let him hold it. It'll keep him busy for a while."
Kate touched Catherine's arm as she stood up, looking
directly into her eyes. "I know Lane's law practice isn't
doing very well, Cath."

Catherine immediately went on the defensive.
"Oh, Mama, that's just not true!"

"Baby, this is a small town." Kate said it as though
she spoke some great truth, and had, in fact, of small
Mississippi towns. "Now I've got a pretty decent savings account and you're welcome to whatever you
need."

Tears quickly brightened Catherine's blue eyes,
making them look as if they belonged in a porcelain
doll. "Lane would never hear of anything like that,
Mama."

"Well, I just hate to see the children going to
school in last year's clothes." Kate noticed that Cassidy had begun to edge away from them. She reached
down, grabbed his belt, and pulled him back. He
grinned up at her. "Lane's a good man, but sometimes
we all need a little help."

"Oh, Mama, he tries so hard." Catherine brushed
the tears away. "It just breaks my heart to see what it's
doing to him. There's just not enough business in a
little town like Sweetwater for another lawyer."

"The draft-dodgers got all the business," Kate almost snapped, "while the *real* men went to France and
Germany, and places like Iwo Jima to fight for their
country."

"And the newspapers just make it worse," Catherine added. "Starting all those rumors about the Ma-

rine Corps setting aside some islands out in the Pacific where the *crazed* veterans of the 'killer battalions' would have to stay isolated for the rest of their lives like some kind of animals. As if our boys don't have enough problems already!"

"I heard a worse one than that about the boys who fought in Europe," Kate went on. "The worst cases over there were supposed to be put on ships for priority shipment home. Then our own submarines would sink them out in the middle of the Atlantic Ocean. Never heard such nonsense!"

Catherine placed a bag of Domino sugar into the cart. "I saw a Bill Mauldin cartoon the other day that pretty well summed it up. It showed a couple reading a newspaper with the headline VETERAN KICKS AUNT with the man saying, 'There's a small item on page 17 about a triple ax murder.' "

"I know some of them have problems." Kate noticed her daughter's eyes narrowed with concern. "There was a soldier in Louisville who ran everybody off the streetcar with a German Luger because he couldn't find a seat. Men like that would be nutty, though—whether they were veterans or not. Well, let's just forget about all that now and go check out. You think you've got everything you need?"

"I believe so." Catherine opened her purse, took out a five dollar bill and handed it to her mother.

Kate shook her head and pushed the money away. "Buy Jessie a new dress with it."

Will Cage peered over his wire-rimmed reading glasses as Catherine and Kate walked toward him. He smiled fondly up at Kate as she began unloading the grocery cart onto the check-out counter. Wearing a white apron over his thin frame and a second-rate hairpiece on his narrow skull, he looked dressed for a part in a Charlie Chaplin movie. "Morning, Kate. How's my favorite customer today?"

"On my way to the debtor's prison I expect, Will—after I pay you for these groceries." Kate dropped two pounds of hamburger wrapped in butcher's paper on the counter.

Cage ignored the complaint as usual. "The *Lost Weekend*'s playing over at the picture show—Ray Milland and Jane Wyman," he ventured cautiously. "I thought you might like to go see it with me tomorrow night."

"I can't be responsible for what you *thought*, Will," Kate declared bluntly as she put the last of the groceries on the counter. "Now how much do I owe you?"

Cage slowly and deliberately rang up each item on his big green cash register, placing them in a cardboard Pet Milk box. "That'll be seven thirty-four."

"Well, I guess it could be worse," Kate declared, digging the bills and change out of her black pop-open coin purse. "Some people get shot when they get robbed."

"Can I carry these out to the car for you?" Cage asked as he rang up the sale, ignoring the sarcasm.

"No thanks, I believe we'll get some of your *free* hot chocolate before we get back out in the cold." Kate turned to Catherine. "That all right with you?"

"Sure. We've got plenty of time."

Catherine and Kate left their groceries under the counter and walked over to the far corner of the store where Cage had set up a small refreshment area next to the plate glass window. Two round linoleum-topped tables sat near a side table holding an urn of coffee and one of hot chocolate. Kate settled Cassidy into one of the wire-backed chairs and took another for herself, while Catherine brought them three heavy mugs of steaming hot chocolate.

"Now you let Gramma cool it for you, baby," Kate cooed to Cassidy, blowing on the chocolate.

"Mama, why do you treat Mr. Cage so ugly?" Catherine ventured, sipping the rich dark liquid. "He's always seemed harmless enough to me. I know he's getting on up in age, but anybody can see he's just crazy about *you*."

"Well, you're half-right. He is *crazy* if he thinks I'm going out with him," Kate muttered, holding the mug to Cassidy's lips. "But he certainly isn't harmless."

Catherine glanced at the stooped-over, white-haired Cage checking out another customer. "You *must* be wrong. He looks as if he's going to keel over any minute."

"Don't let that dried-up old lecher fool you." Kate wiped Cassidy's mouth with a napkin. "The last time I was in here, he pinched me where no man but your daddy ever pinched me—and that wasn't the *first* time. I think he must be going into his second childhood."

Catherine smiled. "Who would ever have thought it?"

"Well, that certainly isn't the only reason either," Kate remarked with a sly grin.

"What do mean?"

"Just look at that hairpiece!" She glanced over her shoulder at Cage. "Looks like an old stray cat crawled on top of his head and died."

Catherine almost choked as she laughed while she was trying to swallow. "You ought to be ashamed of yourself!"

"Oh, I am," Kate replied with a deadpan expression. "I'm simply mortified." Then she asked, her brow wrinkling with concern, "How do the children seem to be getting along with Lane back home?"

"What way do you mean?" Catherine watched a tan-colored Stetson hat tumbling along the sidewalk in the February wind. Chasing after it was a fat, white-haired man in a heavy denim jacket and cowboy boots.

Kate smiled at Cassidy, who now wore a chocolate mustache. "Well, you kept telling them how great things were going to be when their daddy got home from the war—and things don't seem to be that great at all."

"They're doing all right, I guess—except maybe for Jessie." Catherine felt almost as though she were betraying her husband by talking like this, but she knew that her mother would never broach the subject idly. "I can tell she's disappointed—not having all the new clothes she thought she would get."

Kate shook her head slowly. "You'd think after all Lane's been through, it wouldn't be so hard for him when he got back home. I expect he's not the only one either."

"That reminds me," Catherine asked almost absently, "have you heard from Sidney lately?"

Kate frowned as she thought of the last time her twenty-year-old son had been home on leave and how he had come in at four in the morning drunk and vomiting all over his navy dress blues. "He's still in San Diego."

"Well—is that all you know about him?" Sidney was a sore spot with her mother, but Catherine was concerned about him, and Sidney never got in touch with her.

"I wish that's all I *did* know about him," she replied flatly. "He seems to *enjoy* telling me about his sordid life."

Catherine sipped her chocolate, waiting for her mother to continue. The wind moaned softly in the eaves outside the plate glass window.

Kate took a deep breath, letting it out with a sigh. "He married that barmaid, what's-her-name. Bangles, Bubbles, Burpie—something like that."

"Brooksie, Mama," Catherine smiled, knowing that her mother deliberately mispronounced the name.

"Well, anyway, he married her," Kate mumbled with more than a trace of disgust in her voice. "Can't you just picture that wedding? *Dearly beloved barmaids, pimps, and fellow drunks, we are gathered here today . . .*"

"Oh, Mama, that's awful!"

"It is, isn't it," Kate blushed slightly. "Lord, forgive me! That boy *does* try my patience!"

"Do they have any plans yet?"

Kate suppressed another sarcastic remark. "Sidney's staying in the navy as far as I know."

"Well, at least he'll have steady work," Catherine assured her mother.

Kate seemed to shake the worry off. "By the way, how'd Jessie do in the school talent contest?"

A gust of wind rattled the plate glass in its casing, sending a brief, sharp chill into the room through the narrow crack.

"That's another disappointment," Catherine admitted. "Some boy from Tupelo took first place. Jessie got second."

"I didn't think anybody in this whole district could play and sing as well as Jessie," Kate remarked in mild surprise. "She makes a piano sound the way it ought to."

"Well, this boy was good, all right." Catherine remembered the dark-haired ten-year-old who seemed so shy after he left the stage. "His name is Presley. Melvin Presley, or something like that, and he played the guitar and sang *Ol' Shep*. Jessie said he's a real nice boy. Told me she liked him even if he did beat her out of first place."

★ ★ ★

Lane walked through the sodden, black leaves of late winter, making little more noise in his marine issue combat boots than the early mist. Shrouding the trees like damp, white smoke, it curled in wisps from the creek bottom and floated out over the pasture. At the edge of the woods, he stopped, the double-barrel 20-gauge cradled in his arm as he watched his father approach the briar patch from the opposite side. Grady Temple, wearing his faded blue overalls and red wool shirt, began kicking at the edges of the tall briars, brittle and gray in the cold.

A rabbit bolted out of cover on the opposite side from where Grady stood. As Lane raised the shotgun to his shoulder, the rabbit, heading directly toward him, bounded abruptly to his right and stretched out in a flat run toward the treeline on the other side of the pasture.

Lane let his instincts take over. He had learned from years of hunting (*For three years I hunted men . . .* )—the thought never reached the conscious level of his mind—things happened too quickly to think about them.

The rabbit, flying low over the wet grass at an oblique angle from where Lane stood, was merely a brown and white blur in his vision. The barrels seemed to move of their own accord to a point in front of the rabbit's flight. Lane felt the kick of the gunstock against his shoulder. The hollow boom of the shotgun sounded as though from some great distance.

The rabbit's soft fur erupted in a red blossom just behind the left foreleg as the number five shot slammed into it. It tumbled head over heels three times, skidding to rest thirty feet from the shadowy refuge of the woods. As father and son walked together across the pasture, sunlight sparkled in the dewdrops of the tall grass where the rabbit lay.

"He'll look real good in a skillet full of brown gravy," Grady smiled, holding the rabbit up by its hind legs and stuffing it into the rear pouch of his hunting vest.

Lane stared at the blood dripping from the torn side of the rabbit. He felt queasy. *It's just a rabbit. I've killed hundreds of them.*

Grady noticed the change in his son's face. "How about some coffee? This chill's soaking into my old bones."

"Sounds good to me." Lane walked beside his father through the dew-wet grass to the trees the rabbit had so desperately tried to reach.

*Go! Go! Get off this beach! We've got to make it to that grove of palm trees!* Lane heard again the clatter of machine-gun fire and the flat *whump* of the heavy mortars as he made the gut-wrenching, knee-churning, breathless charge across the sand to the safety of the palm trees.

Grady saw the sweat break out on his son's face. "You feel all right, Lane?"

"W-what? Oh, sure! Just a little cold, I guess."

They scraped the wet leaves away and sat down together under an ancient oak, leaning back against its massive trunk. Grady unscrewed the red top of the Thermos bottle and poured it full of steaming black coffee. "Here you go, son. This'll heat your blood up a little."

Breaking open the breech of the shotgun, Lane extracted the two Remington shells and dropped the spent one into the side pocket of his field jacket. The other he inserted into the loop on his belt. "Thanks, Pop," Lane replied, raising the cup to his mouth. He took two sips of the coffee and handed it back to his father. Looking up through the maze of bare limbs, he watched a red-tailed hawk riding the thermals against the hard blue sky.

Lane remembered his first hunt. The first frost of October glistened on the bare limbs. A thin skein of ice formed on the surface of the little slough he stood next to, watching a fox squirrel's lofty and final journey through the oaks. After the shot, he stood over him as his back legs jerked spasmodically, twitched slightly a few times, and then became profoundly still.

Grady had thought for weeks about how he could begin this talk with his son, finally deciding there was no easy way. "Lane, you just might have to leave Sweetwater."

Surprised, Lane jerked his head toward his father. He stared at him speechless for a moment, then broke the silence. "I never thought I'd hear you say that."

"I didn't either," Grady confessed, squinting his eyes as he sipped the hot coffee. "And it's the last thing in the world I want." He gazed sadly at Lane, then looked out across the pasture toward the distant blue hills. "But you have to think about your future—and your family."

Lane took a deep breath, letting it out slowly. "You're right. I'm glad you had the guts to come out and say it. I might have just stayed here and starved."

"I hate to see it happen, our little town just drying

up like it is. It's all I've ever known—your mama too. About the only thing a lawyer's good for here is to make out wills for us old folks. All the young people are leaving for the big cities." Grady swallowed another sip of coffee and handed the cup to Lane. "Makes me feel like an old, old man."

"You're not old, Pop," Lane assured him, gazing at the deep creases at the corners of his father's dark eyes. He looked weathered and worn from all the years in the blistering Mississippi sun and the icy winds of winter.

Grady glanced over at Lane, a half smile on his face. "I spent the first six years of my life in the last century. That makes me feel old."

Lane gulped the last of the coffee and put the top back on the bottle. "What do you think I ought to do?"

"I've studied on it a lot lately. You'll have to move to a good-sized city to get anywhere with a law practice," Grady offered solemnly.

"Any ideas?"

"Memphis, maybe. That might be the place. Your brother's doing pretty well there."

"Maybe so, but James knew somebody with the police department. That's how he got the job. There's a whole lot of veterans looking for work and it sure helps to have a connection somewhere."

Grady stretched his legs out, crossing them at the ankles. "Catherine did real fine while you was overseas, Lane. Kept the house running and took good care of the young'uns—with a lot of help from Kate and a little from us. With you gone, she had to." He held Lane's eyes with his own. "But she's the kind of woman who needs for the man to shoulder most of the load—she's not as strong as her mother."

"She has seemed a little worried lately," Lane

mused. "But she hasn't said anything."

"I think she's worried that you won't be able to provide for your family. I know different—that you'll do whatever it takes—but women ain't like that. It's time for you to put this little hick town behind you and get on with your life. You got too much sense to waste away here."

Lane had a sudden recollection. "You know, there was a fellow named Jones in my company told me I ought to move to Baton Rouge. His daddy's in the oil business down there."

"What do you know about Baton Rouge?"

"Well, for one thing, Jones said the Cajun cooking is great and for another, Jimmy Davis is governor," Lane smiled. "I've always liked his music."

Grady shook his head slightly. " 'You Are My Sunshine' made him a lot of money, but it ain't likely to do much for you."

"Guess I better take this a little more seriously," Lane conceded. "The economy's supposed to be pretty good with that big Standard Oil plant down there. There's some other big companies, too, like the Ethyl Corporation, and the oil business is taking off. Lot of rednecks like me moving in and a lot of the Cajuns coming up out of the swamps."

"Sounds like an interesting town," Grady said, trying to sound encouraging. "I couldn't handle all that excitement, but you and Cath might like it."

"Guess we could always come back and move the whole family in with you if we don't like it, couldn't we?" Lane grinned at his father.

Grady stood up and held his hand down to his son. "I'm not *that* good a daddy, boy. Let's go skin these rabbits and get 'em in the pot."

★ ★ ★

An orange sunburst flared behind the steeple of the First Baptist Church as Lane drove the Ford sedan down Main Street. He waved to Mrs. Wescott, who had taught him sophomore English. She still wore her gray hair in a bun, and the high-topped black shoes looked like the same ones he had seen her wearing that first day of class. A few stragglers lingered along the sidewalks as the shop owners began closing down for the day.

Passing Thompson's Garage where he had gotten his first summer job, Lane gazed into its murky depths and could almost smell the ancient layers of grease that permeated the floor and the pungent odor of a freshly painted fender. *That three months sure killed any ideas I might have had of becoming a mechanic*, he thought, recalling the sweat and drudgery of the work. *Old man Thompson was a good boss, though.*

Since their conversation that morning, Lane had agonized about his future. *How could I leave this town? All my friends? People I've known all my life. It'd be rough on the kids—changing schools, having to make new friends. And Cath? Hmmm—kind of hard to say how she'd take it. I guess having to leave her mother would be the worst part for her.*

Lane thought of the past few months of sitting alone in his office after he had hung out his shingle. Then there were the times of hanging around the courthouse, trying to look confident and friendly with everyone knowing he was just hoping to stumble into some business. *I've got to make a change. Daddy's absolutely right about that. There's nothing left for me in this town as far as work goes.*

Lane swerved to avoid a big redbone hound that ambled across the street in front of him. "Get on home, Purvis," he yelled out the window of the Ford.

The dog gazed back at Lane with a downcast look on his long face, tucked his tail between his legs, and disappeared from sight behind a manicured box hedge.

Pulling into his driveway, Lane saw Dalton race across the front porch, leap down into the yard, and run out to greet him. Lane lifted him high into the air, spinning around and around while his son giggled with glee.

"How many rustlers did you catch today, cowboy?" Lane asked, setting him back down.

"A whole bunch, Daddy!" Dalton beamed. "Watch this!" He drew both his shiny cap pistols from their holsters, firing at a gang of make-believe cattle thieves.

"Pretty good shootin', partner."

Lane saw Catherine walk out onto the front porch. She had on a simple cotton print housedress and wore her hair pulled straight back from her face. He thought she looked as pretty as any of the Hollywood starlets they saw at the movies together.

Lane smiled broadly as he walked up the front walk, thinking of something witty to say, but his mind was blank. Words seemed to come harder and harder for him since he had gotten home. "You sure look pretty today." He didn't have to think about that. Catherine's smile was the only reply he needed.

"There's a phone call for you."

"Who is it?"

"Somebody named Walker Jones. Do you know him?" Catherine replied. "Says he's calling from Baton Rouge."

# PART TWO

★ ★ ★

# DIXIE

# FOUR

# STRANGE COUNTRY

★ ★ ★

In the fall of 1755 an American diaspora began in the conquered province of Acadia, now called Nova Scotia. The French farmers, fishermen, and trappers refused to become British subjects, give up their language, and deny their Catholic faith. For this effrontery to His Majesty's sovereignty, the British governor sent them into exile.

Some of these Acadians were drowned at sea. Some were sold into slavery in Georgia and Maryland. A remnant traveled inland, following the Ohio and Mississippi rivers down to the swamps and prairies of south Louisiana. There they found fertile land and rich waters, people who spoke French—and refuge from their British enemies.

These people with names like Hebert and Thibodeaux and Bertrand—bound together by their faith, their language, and their fierce independence—kept to themselves, becoming a uniquely American phenomenon called the *Cajuns*.

World War II opened up a new world for these Cajuns. They discovered there was much more to life than their isolated swamps, marshes, and prairies, and many began a migration to the cities. Baton Rouge, as the seat of government with its oil and gas industry, booming post-war economy, and bustling stores and shops became home for many of these former trappers and fishermen.

Another migration had also begun after the war—this one born in the red clay hills of Mississippi. These sharecroppers, pulpwood haulers, mechanics, and store clerks fled their small towns where the wealth was inevitably controlled by one or two founding families with little or no opportunity for anyone else. Protestant and Anglo-Saxon, these *rednecks* were as different from the *Cajuns* as cactus is from seaweed.

Staunchly Catholic, Cajuns loved their fiery gumbos, sauce piquant, jambalayas—and "passing a good time." The Baptist and Methodist rednecks thrived on fried okra, black-eyed peas, pork chops, and corn bread. The hot-blooded tempers of the Cajuns were in direct contrast to the cold, tight-lipped rages of the rednecks. One group loved dancing—the other thought it merely a prelude to immorality.

Into this cultural, social, and religious amalgam, almost in the shadow of the giant Standard Oil of New Jersey plant with its seemingly endless steel towers, smokestacks, and buildings of all sizes, Lane Temple brought his family to live in the late summer of 1946.

★ ★ ★

Surprised, Catherine resisted at first, then let her arms circle Lane's waist as she returned his kiss. She soon felt that unmistakable tingling sensation down her spine and the warmth rising in her breast. Placing her hands on his chest, she pushed against him and stepped back. "My goodness!" she gasped. "What's wrong with us? It's broad daylight!"

"Aw, don't be such a stick in the mud." Lane took a deep breath, glancing around. "Nobody's up here."

Catherine brushed her hair back from her face, smoothing her dress down around her hips. "There just might be any minute, though."

"There's always tonight then, isn't there, sweetheart?" Lane grinned slyly. She smiled back, her eyes knowing.

"You know we still have that room Walker reserved for us at the Heidelberg," Lane winked. "I don't think the kids would mind if we stayed one more night."

Catherine's eyes softened. "I have to admit—it does have a lovely view of the river."

"Well, on to the more mundane. What do you think of our new home?" Lane stood with Catherine on the observation deck of the Louisiana State Capitol, Huey Long's 450-foot monument to himself. Wearing his khakis and starched white shirt, the mandatory dress for Mississippians going to town, Lane placed his palms flat on the low concrete wall, gazing out over the formal south gardens with their walkways angling in geometric patterns among the flower beds, crepe myrtles, and spreading live oaks. "Nice, isn't it?"

The wind from the river blew Catherine's hair about her face in a shimmering brightness. Wearing a new dress of pale green linen, she looked ten years younger than her thirty-one years. "It *is* pretty," Catherine agreed, her eyes straying from the gardens to the mile-wide span of the Mississippi River. Its tan surface glittered in the sunshine as though it had been recently varnished. Flowing in a graceful curve, it dis-

appeared off into the misty blue distance, on its way
to the Gulf of Mexico.

To the west, on the opposite side of the river, she
saw the little town of Port Allen, surrounded by the
deep green expanses of the sugarcane plantations.
Farther to the south and west were the watery beginnings of the great Atchafalaya River Basin, the largest
wetlands wilderness area in the country.

"That's the main business district," Lane continued, pointing due south. "And that's Third Street,
where most of the stores are located."

At the south end of the street Lane had just mentioned, Catherine could barely make out a large me-
dieval-looking structure through the huge oaks that
surrounded it. "What's that—way over there?"

Lane squinted in the bright afternoon sunshine.
"Oh, that's the Old State Capitol. Mark Twain said it
was the ugliest building on the Mississippi."

"Can't tell much about it from here."

"I kind of like it myself," Lane said absently as he
looked down at the Grand Staircase that led up the
front of the building. "Walker took me to see it when
I came down here last month. You see that statue?
That's Huey Long."

Catherine took Lane's arm with both hands. "I
heard he's buried under it. You think there's anything
to that?"

"Yep. That's his grave, all right." Lane began walking to the left along the low wall. "Walker told me his
daddy took him to the funeral back in '35. Said it
looked like half of Louisiana showed up for it."

On the eastern side of the observation tower, they
gazed down at the formal rose gardens that led up a
slope to the Old Arsenal, surrounded by a ten-foot-
high wall. "See that building down there behind the

brick walls? That's where the guns and ammunition were kept for a lot of different armies over the last hundred years or so. Somewhere around there, the only battle of the American Revolution outside the thirteen colonies was fought."

"You're beginning to sound like a tour guide," Catherine smiled, squeezing his arm.

Lane gave her a sheepish grin. "Walker gave me the whole history of the town, just about."

Catherine harbored a nagging fear of leaving the little town she had lived in for twenty-one years—and the only home her children had ever known. The only other place she had lived was a town the size of Sweetwater and the thought of moving to a city in another state unsettled her. *It's the only way we'll ever have any real money again though, and I'm certainly tired of four years of just barely getting by.* "You're really looking forward to moving down here, aren't you?"

Lane thought of the long days spent in his dull, dusty office back in Sweetwater, waiting for a client to call—any client. Yet he dreaded the end of those tedious days when he would have to go home to Catherine who could tell by his face that no one had needed a lawyer named Lane Temple. "Yeah—I certainly am. Anything's better than sitting there watching that little town just dry up." *And me right along with it.*

They continued walking along the observation tower past the Capitol Lake that bordered the grounds on the east and the north. Across it, on the northern shore, stood Our Lady of the Lake Hospital where Huey Long had died of an assassin's bullet. Lane pointed out the vast industrial complex and docks along the river and beyond them the iron superstructure of the Earl K. Long Bridge spanning the river over to the west bank.

"What's that?" Catherine asked, pointing to the white Antebellum home across the river and south of the bridge. From that distance it looked like a doll's house, standing in a clearing in the endless sweep of cane fields. Next to it was a miniature sugar mill, with rows of tiny cabins that had once housed slaves and were still homes to many of their descendants.

Lane put his arm around Catherine's shoulder, walking back to the south side where they had begun. "That's the Poplar Grove Plantation. It'll really get busy over there when grinding season starts in a couple of months."

"Grinding season?"

"That's what they call the sugarcane harvest down here." Lane made a sweeping gesture toward the south with his left hand. "Well, what do you think of your new home?"

"That's exactly what I'd like to see now," Catherine replied. "This grand tour is fun, but I want to see our house."

A hint of a frown appeared briefly on Lane's face. "Sure thing. We'll go right now." Lane put his arm around her waist as they headed toward the entrance.

"Is it out near the lakes by the university?" Catherine asked excitedly. "I simply love that area!"

"I expect everyone does," Lane replied in a resigned tone. "But only the ones with a lot of money can live there. I told Walker how much I could afford for a home and he found something for us. It's in the north part of town, not too far from the plants."

"Well, we'll have plenty of money after you're with Pelican Oil for a while." Catherine walked ahead of Lane into the tower gift shop and over to the elevator.

Lane pushed the button with the down arrow. "It may take longer than you think. I told Walker I couldn't go to work for his daddy's oil company."

Catherine turned to Lane with a surprised look. "B-but I thought it was all set."

"It was," Lane shrugged. "Something about the whole deal just didn't sit right with me, though. I really can't explain it."

The elevator doors slid open with a dull thud. "But how are you going to get a practice started in a strange town without some help?" Catherine stepped quickly inside.

"Walker wasn't mad when I turned him down. He even said *he'd* refer some business to me," Lane explained. "Don't worry about it. This isn't Sweetwater."

With a jerk and the grinding of cables, they began the long descent to the main floor.

"The whole idea was to move here so you'd have contacts." Catherine chewed at the nail of her right forefinger. "I thought we were lucky to be able to sell our house—now I'm not so sure. What's the purpose in coming here?"

"The purpose is that Baton Rouge has a lot of business and a lot of people." Lane tried to hide his own anxiety. "It's growing in a hurry—not drying up."

"Oh, I just *know* it's going to take *forever* for you to really make any money." Catherine folded her arms across her breast and stared at the elevator doors.

"Is it *that* important to you?" Lane sensed a feeling of desperation in his wife.

"No," she hesitated. "I guess not. I suppose I just wanted the children to have a little more." Catherine flushed slightly with embarrassment, having revealed more than she wanted to. Deep down she knew having money *was* that important to her.

★ ★ ★

"Well, here we are." Lane pulled his seven-year-old Ford over to the curb, parking in the shade of an ancient elm tree.

"Oh, it's lovely!" Catherine exclaimed, raising her left hand to her throat. She stared at the imposing two-story house with second-story gallery and scrolled iron railing. The wide porch was set off by white columns resting on heavy stone bases. It extended across the front, wrapping around to the west side where it was shaded by a huge live oak whose lower limbs bent down almost to the ground. She breathed deeply, smelling the crimson and yellow four-o'clocks, the roses, and the damp earth of the flower beds.

Lane got out of the car, walked around it, and opened Catherine's door. He took her hand, but could not hold her gaze as she got out of the car.

Catherine noticed the slight frown on his face. "What's wrong, darling?"

"Our place is around back," Lane confessed as he turned to look at her.

Catherine noticed the afternoon sunlight shining on the scar that ran from the corner of Lane's mouth to a point beneath his ear. It looked as though a sliver of ivory had been glued to the side of his tanned face. She thought of all the wives whose husbands didn't come home from the war and suddenly felt a sense of shame as she stared at Lane's apologetic expression. "Oh, darling, it'll be just fine wherever we live—as long as we're together." Taking his face in her hands, she kissed him warmly at the edge of his mouth where the scar began.

Lane grinned like a boy with a new puppy. "Well,

come on then! Let's go take a look!"

Holding hands, they walked down the hard-packed gravel drive that ran along the east side of the house to a double garage with an apartment above. One of the bays held a green Plymouth coupe. The other was empty.

The steps from the back porch of the house led down to a brick patio with a three-tiered fountain. The water flowing from level to level made a tinkling sound, almost like background music for the song-birds that flitted in the green-gold sunlight shining through the limbs of another ancient live oak. The warm air carried the fragrance of jasmine and ole-ander.

Catherine followed Lane to a screened-in patio built onto the end of the garage facing the backyard. As they entered into the dappled light of the patio, Catherine noticed two white wicker chairs and a small table resting on the brick floor.

They climbed an open wooden staircase up to the porch above. It was painted gray and bordered by a white wooden railing. Using his key, Lane opened the door to the garage apartment and they went inside.

"How do you like it?" Lane asked with a half smile. "Not too bad, huh?"

Catherine gazed around the single room that was both kitchen and living room. The kitchen had a small Frigidaire, a white enamel-topped table with four straight-backed wooden chairs, and a sink with a flowered cloth tacked along the edge of the cabinet and hanging down to the linoleum floor.

The other end of the room contained a brown sofa and matching chair with a coffee table and one end table. The lamp on the end table had a picture on the shade of Roy Rogers riding Trigger. Above the sofa hung a bad reproduction of Van Gogh's *The Potato Eaters*.

"What a depressing painting!" Catherine lifted it off the wall, placing it behind the couch. "I hope we aren't reduced to something like *that* family."

"Don't worry, Cath," Lane laughed, "even poor lawyers live better than that. Besides—the only way they eat potatoes down here is French fried."

Catherine walked into the tiny hall, then peered into the two identical bedrooms and the bath with its black-and-white checked tile.

"What do you think? Can we all live here?" Lane asked when she returned. He made a face at the living room. "We can get rid of some of this stuff—like that couch and those chairs—and bring down our own furniture. Our table won't fit, but we can use two of the beds." He stared hopefully at his wife. "Well?"

Catherine walked to the sink, glanced down at the dark water stains around the drain, then out the window onto the small part of the backyard between the garage and a red brick wall at the rear. In the enclosed area below her stood a fig tree and a weeping willow, its bows sweeping down toward the ground like shining green water, falling in the last rays of the sun. A serene smile came across Catherine's face. "I think we'll make it all right, darling."

★ ★ ★

"I hate that school!" Dalton sat at the kitchen table, staring sullenly at his mother.

"Oh, hush and eat your oatmeal!" Catherine scolded over her shoulder. The front of her cotton print housedress was damp from dishwater. "You've been there only *one* day."

"There's too many kids and none of 'em like me."

80

Dalton folded his arms across his chest and pouted. "Besides, they make fun of my overalls. Nobody wears overalls but country hicks! I look like I'm going out to pick cotton."

"Dalton—that's enough!"

Dumping three spoons of sugar into his bowl, Dalton began wolfing down the oatmeal.

Jessie stepped next to her mother, placing her bowl into the hot soapy water. "Want me to finish those for you, Mama?"

"No, sugar. You just make sure Sharon's ready. You know how slow she is."

"Okay, Mama."

Catherine surveyed her oldest child, noticing how the pink blouse brought out the rosy color of her cheeks. Her shoulder-length hair caught the early morning light in a pale gleaming. "You certainly look nice today, honey."

"Thank you, Mama," Jessie replied, fluffing up her hair and heading toward the bathroom. "C'mon now, Sharon. You've been in there long enough."

Catherine collected the dirty dishes from the table and dumped them into the sink. As she began washing them, she glanced down at her sun-spangled willow. Like a white flash, Cassidy's hair caught the sunlight as he hurried across the tiny yard. He reached for the nearest low limb on the fig tree and, using his feet on the trunk, began his climb.

"Cassidy Temple—you get down this minute!"

Cassidy continued his struggle to find a hold on the first limb as though he hadn't heard anything.

Catherine turned around from her dishwashing. "Dalton, go get your brother. He's in the tree again."

"Aw, Mama," Dalton protested, his mouth full of oatmeal. "I ain't finished yet."

"Dalton—now!"

Dalton scraped his chair back and ran for the door, his cheeks bursting from his last three spoonsful.

Catherine looked back down at Cassidy, who had managed to get one leg up on the limb. *What a child! Two more years until you're in school. How will I ever make it?*

Dalton ran across the yard, pulled his brother down under protest, and led him back across the yard. "You're gonna break your neck one day, Cass!"

"Won't either! I'm Tarzan."

Jessie came out of the bathroom with Sharon, who was carrying her booksack by its handle like a briefcase. Then she picked up her stack of books from the table next to the couch, tucked them under one arm, and took Sharon by the hand. "Let's get on downstairs now. We don't want to miss the bus."

"Wait for Dalton, Jessie," Catherine called over her shoulder. "And don't stand close to the street."

"Oh, Mama, I'm not a child anymore," Jessie protested. "I'm in the eighth grade now."

Dalton slammed through the door into the kitchen, pulling Cassidy by the arm. "I'm tired of chasing him down, Mama. Why don't you put a harness on him?"

"Don't talk that way about your brother, Dalton," Catherine chided gently. "You hurry and brush your teeth and get on down to the bus stop with your sisters."

"Okay, Mama." Dalton ran off to the bathroom, returning in a matter of seconds with his hair slicked down.

"Didn't you bring any books home last night, Dalton?" Catherine asked as he headed out the door.

"No, ma'am. We don't have homework yet."

Jessie and Sharon kissed their mother goodbye and followed after Dalton.

Catherine pulled up a chair and sat Cassidy down in it, squatting next to him. "Why are you always running off like that, Cass? Don't you know you can get hurt?"

"No I won't, Mama. I'm a big boy now."

"But you're not minding me."

Cassidy turned his bright blue eyes on his mother and grinned with perfect innocence. "I don't mean to be bad, Mama. I just like to play."

Catherine took his face in her hands, squeezing his cheeks. "Oh—you!" Then she pushed his chair up to the table and sat his oatmeal down in front of him. "Eat! And don't get up until that bowl's scraped clean."

As Catherine turned back to finish the dishes, her bedroom door opened and Lane walked into the kitchen, straightening his blue and gray striped tie over a crisp white shirt. He wore his dark blue suit, and his black shoes gleamed in the bright sunlight coming in the kitchen window. "Just a quick kiss for me today, Cath. I'll grab a cup of coffee after I get to the office."

"No. I want you to have something here before you leave." Catherine dried her hands on a dish towel that hung on a hook above the sink. "Don't you look sharp this morning!" She ran her fingers over his fresh shave.

"Got to try to meet some people," Lane grinned. "Let 'em know there's a new lawyer in town."

"Where do you plan to meet these people so early in the morning?"

Lane rubbed Cassidy's hair playfully. "I don't really know yet, but I've got to get out and let people know the office is open for business—get something started.

Yesterday was settling-in time—today I go to work." Lane tried to sound confident, but his last months in Sweetwater had left him with the taste of desolation in his mouth like an old copper coin. He was already agonizing about his quick decision not to go to work for Pelican Oil with the prospect of a steady paycheck.

"Sit down. I'll get your breakfast."

"I'm really not very hungry." Lane tried to smile as he bent to kiss Catherine on the cheek, but couldn't quite pull it off. "I'll catch a quick bite later."

"At least have some coffee." Catherine poured him a cup from the drip pot she had warming on the stove.

"Thanks." Lane sipped the coffee as he stood next to his wife, watching his son spoon down the oatmeal. "What do you and Cass have planned for today?"

"Just like back home, I guess," Catherine shrugged. "A little laundry, grocery shopping."

Lane finished his coffee and slipped the cup into the soapy water. Noticing the downcast expression on Catherine's face, he tilted her chin up with his forefinger. "It's going to be all right, Cath. I promise."

Catherine gazed into his deep brown eyes, rubbing the bridge of his nose where it bent slightly—legacy of the Japanese rifle butt. "I know, darling."

"After all, this is *only* our first week," Lane said, his face brightening. "You'll have to give me at least *two* weeks to make my first million."

Catherine smiled as he kissed her on the cheek and hurried out the door. She listened to the sound of his shoes thudding down the wooden stairs. Lifting the kettle from the stove, she ran water into it from the tap, turned on the gas burner, and set the kettle on the stove. When she returned to her dishwashing, she listened to the rumbling of the Ford's rusty muffler as Lane pulled away from the curb.

Steam began hissing out of the kettle spout as Catherine finished her dishes. She spooned tea leaves into the blue ceramic pot and poured in the boiling water while Cassidy began playing with a red dump truck on the kitchen floor. As she walked over to the living area and picked up his and Dalton's clothes from the floor, she kept a close eye on him. Taking the quilt from the couch where her sons had slept, she folded it and put it and the pillows away in the hall closet.

Catherine finished straightening up the living room, both bedrooms, and the bath after the hectic morning hour. "You having fun, baby?" she asked, returning to the kitchen.

"I'm not a baby, Mama," Cassidy pouted up at her before continuing his truck motor sounds as he pushed the truck around the floor. "I'm a big boy now."

"You sure are. Guess I just forgot." Catherine held a small metal strainer over her cup with the grapevine pattern bordering the rim. Someone had given them the set for a wedding present and there were only three left. She cherished each one, having never seen any others like them. Pouring the steaming, dark tea into the porcelain cup, she added sugar and cream and glanced down at Cassidy. "Want to go downstairs?"

"Yes, ma'am!" He sprang up from the linoleum floor with his truck, then followed his mother out onto the porch and down the stairs to the brick patio.

Catherine sat in one of the white wicker chairs, holding her teacup with both hands. She sipped the tea slowly, relishing the strong, sweet taste of it and the milky smoothness. With the palm of her left hand she wiped the thin sheen of perspiration from her brow. The air was oppressive and heavily laden with moisture, carrying the scent of jasmine, roses, and the damp, rich leaf mold of the flower beds.

Suddenly the sunlight angling across the backyard disappeared as a breeze stirred high in the crown of the live oak, then rustled the broad leaves of the banana plants that grew just beyond the screen at the end of the patio. Catherine smelled the rain and felt its refreshing coolness before it reached her. The first heavy drops clattered across the tin roof of the apartment and shook the rose petals out in the yard. Then the wind ceased and the rain settled into a steady drumming on the roof, splattering mud in the flower beds.

Catherine shivered slightly as the wind came once more, sweeping through the trees and across the backyard, blowing a fine, cool mist through the screen. Emotions swept through her like the sudden storm: fear and loneliness and a deep sense of regret at having come to this strange city and a life so different from the one she had known. She assigned that most intolerable of emotions—self-pity—to the darkest recesses of her mind, refusing to acknowledge its existence.

Lightning flickered like faulty wiring in the heavens. Thunder crashed nearby. Catherine noticed that Cassidy seemed energized by the storm. He picked up his truck, turning around and around as he held it out like an airplane.

"Come over here near the wall, Cass." She spoke loudly over the sound of the wind. "You'll get wet."

Cassidy smiled at his mother, continuing his circles.

Catherine picked him up and sat back down in the chair, holding him in her arms. She rocked her body back and forth with the wicker creaking in mild pro-test. Tears ran in hot channels through the cool spray on her cheeks as she held her son close. She wiped at them with the back of her hand, surprised that she had begun to cry.

Hearing his mother's soft sobs, Cassidy leaned back and looked into her eyes. "What's wrong, Mama?"

"I don't know, baby. I just don't know." Catherine continued her gentle rocking as the rain slackened. The leaves of the trees glistened with a pewter light. Somewhere in the distance, the harsh sound of a crow rang out in the sudden, breathless hush of the storm's ending.

# FIVE

# The Man in the Chair

★ ★ ★

Lane liked him from the first moment he saw him, but the second thing the man in the chair told Lane almost ended their friendship before it got started.

"Morning. My name's Coley Thibodeaux." The man's face was slightly hawklike with its thin nose, prominent bone structure, and clear gray eyes. He wore brown penny loafers, faded jeans, a pale blue shirt, and a lightweight herringbone jacket the color of his eyes. "Let's get some coffee."

"Lane Temple." He took the extended hand, finding it cool and hard—the grip amazingly strong for such a slim man. "Thanks, but I can't go right now. I've got work to do." He turned to go up the stairs.

"No, you don't."

Lane felt a sudden anger rise in his chest. The muscles knotted and moved beneath the skin along his jawline.

Coley smiled, his teeth bright in the dim light. The corners of his eyes crinkled beneath the dark hair combed straight back from his high forehead.

"I don't believe I heard you right," Lane said flatly through clenched teeth as he gripped the scarred wooden bannister, his knuckles whitening. He knew the remark shouldn't have caused his temper to spark like it did, but the subject of his work had become a decidedly sensitive spot with him.

"Don't get mad, no." Coley put on his most agreeable Cajun accent. "I jes' axe you to come have coffee wid' me and pass a good time, yeah."

"What?" Perplexed, Lane turned back around in the narrow hallway, trying to figure out what was going on.

Coley broke into soft melodic laughter. "I'm a lawyer myself. See?" He pointed to the door at the bottom of the stairs just inside the entrance to the narrow building.

Lane looked at the frosted glass of the door. *Coley J. Thibodeaux, Attorney-at-Law*.

"I tol' you, I'm a lawyer, me." Coley smiled again, then reverted to his more conventional English. "That's how I know you don't have any business yet. Not on the second day after you open your office, you don't. Not out here in Dixie where there's only two or three other lawyers."

"Dixie? We used to sing that at our pep rallies—high school *and* college."

"Dixie's what everybody calls this area of North Baton Rouge around the plants," Coley explained. "Mostly working-class Cajuns and rednecks, good people—most of 'em."

Lane knew instinctively that this man could be a big help to his fitting into these new surroundings and his new job. "Is that Cajun English you were talking?"

"Yep. It's the way we talked when we went to

town," Coley continued Lane's education. "At home all we spoke was French. Daddy wouldn't allow English."

"Where you from?" Lane took a pack of Camels from his inside jacket pocket, offering one to Coley.

He shook his head. "Bayou Ramah."

"Where's that?" Lane asked, flipping his lighter open and lighting his cigarette. Picking a bit of tobacco leaf from his lip with his thumb and forefinger, he stared down at Coley. He could tell from his years of leading men into combat that there was a tough core behind the placid-looking exterior this cheerful little man presented to the world.

"In the Atchafalaya Basin." Coley glanced at the slight dent in the bridge of Lane's nose and at the scar across the side of his face. Then he studied his eyes carefully. "Marines. *Got* to be. Where'd you start— 'The Canal'?"

Lane was caught off guard by being recognized as a marine as well as by Coley's calling Guadalcanal "The Canal." "How'd you know that?"

Coley's melodic laugh seemed to float in the stale air of the hallway. "You've got a piece of the 'Stare' left. Not much, but it's still with you."

"Now I know why you're in that chair." Lane felt an instant kinship with Coley. "Where'd you get hit?"

"Tarawa." Coley's gray eyes clouded over for just a moment, then became clear and bright again as he gazed up at Lane. "November 22, 1943."

"General J. C. Smith, 2nd Marine Division. Forty-eight hundred in that Jap garrison. All of 'em died except for seventeen prisoners—and they were all wounded." Lane sat down on the second to bottom step, placing his briefcase next to him. "*Everybody* heard about Tarawa."

Coley stared at the anemic light filtering through the dust and cobwebs of a high narrow window at the rear of the short hallway. "We didn't think it would be all that rough—at first. The Forts and Liberators bombed that island for days. Then the ships bombarded it. Those little yellow rascals took it all and lay there in their bunkers—waiting for us."

The smoke from Lane's cigarette drifted toward the dark air of the ceiling as he let Coley continue. He had the feeling that Coley needed to talk this out of his system.

"Biggest problem we had was getting hung up on those reefs in our landing craft. Didn't take long for their artillery to get the range."

Lane saw something flicker for an instant in Coley's eyes—something that he had seen in the eyes of so many men on those barren, war-blasted atolls in the South Pacific—the unalloyed terror of battle.

"We had to get out and wade to the beaches. That's when they caught us in the crossfire." Coley shivered slightly, ending his story abruptly. "But the corps gave me six months' rehabilitation and these new, round rubber legs"—he patted the tires of his wheelchair—"and here I am."

The tip of Lane's cigarette glowed brightly in the shadowed hallway as he drew the smoke deeply into his chest. "You still get night sweats?"

"Not so bad now. I only wake up two or three times a month." Coley recognized Lane as a part of the brotherhood of fighting men—men who have lived with fear so long they never fully return to what they were before the war found them. "I've been out of it three years though."

"They say it takes a while."

Coley gazed at the smoke curling from the tip of

Lane's cigarette. "Those dreams used to stay with me for days. I could almost hear that ungodly screaming they made in those Banzai charges—smell the cordite like I was still there."

"Well, we're home now, buddy," Lane smiled, dropping the cigarette butt into a battered trash can at the foot of the stairs. "Safe and sound."

"Praise *God* for that!" Coley remembered the time when he would have said *Not quite sound,* but now had an aversion to anything that resembled self-pity.

"Amen," Lane responded, thinking of his Sunday school days. *How long has it been since I've used that word?*

"I'm glad you didn't take that job with Pelican Oil."

Lane raised his eyebrows in surprise. "Is there anything about me you *don't* know?"

"I'm learning more every minute," Coley smiled wryly. "But I *already* know a lot about Walker Jones."

"How's that?" Lane found himself wondering how a small-time lawyer like Coley could know so much about a big-time business like Pelican Oil.

"He lobbies the legislature for Pelican Oil," Coley replied with a hint of distaste in his voice.

"You work for the state legislature?"

"No, I'm in it. I'm the state representative for this area. It takes in parts of three other parishes," Coley explained. "Some of them have potential oil reserves."

Lane gazed through the glass entrance door at the clouds of white smoke boiling out of the tall stacks of the Standard Oil Refinery across Senic Highway as he tried to assimilate his rapidly building file of information on Coley Thibodeaux. "You certainly get around for a man in a wheelchair."

"A man usually does what he wants to," Coley shrugged. "I think this *wheelchair's* what got me elected to the House of Representatives. Back in '44 people were looking for a hero and decided to make one out of me."

"I never paid much attention to politics," Lane admitted, becoming intrigued by Coley. "What's it take to qualify for the House?"

"Somebody held a mirror under my nose and it fogged up. They said that qualified me," Coley said with a straight face. "I figured I could do as good a job as the next fellow. Better than some I know of."

Lane liked Coley's dry sense of humor, but couldn't shake what he had said about Walker Jones. "What's the problem with Walker? He's always treated me square. Even got me the stuff I needed to study for the Louisiana Bar Exam. Found my house and this office too."

"Well, I haven't seen your house, but he certainly did a great job with the office space."

Lane glanced around at the tiny hall with Coley's office downstairs and his above. "What's so great about it?"

"It belongs to me." Coley spread his arms wide. "My Dixie empire. I've got a little apartment at the back of my office where I live. Makes it convenient."

"Not bad," Lane agreed. "But you still haven't told me what's wrong with Walker."

"Nothing I can talk about right now." Coley stared directly into Lane's eyes. "Let's just say you'll be a lot happier working for yourself. Especially with me downstairs."

"I'll accept that—for now." Lane was embarrassed to ask the next question, but figured Coley would be better than anyone else he could find. "That red neon sign on the big building across the street. The one with the 'A' in front of the bear. I hate to sound like an ignorant redneck, but what does it mean?"

" 'Ignorant redneck'—that's redundant, isn't it?" Coley said with a deadpan expression.

Lane fell into the game. "I guess you're right at that. Kind of like saying uncouth Cajun."

Coley laughed. "The man who owns the whole block is named Hebert, H-e-b-e-r-t, but it's pronounced A-bear."

Lane grinned at Coley, feeling, for some reason, better than he had in days. "Let's go get that coffee."

"And pass a good time, us," Coley smiled back, as he spun the wheelchair around and headed out the door.

Lane walked along next to him as they crossed the oil-stained concrete of the service station that adjoined the narrow frame building where they had their offices.

The early sunlight glinting on the windows of the Standard Oil Administrative Building across Senic Highway winked out as if someone had thrown a switch. On the horizon, dark purple rainclouds moved swiftly upward, tumbling toward them against the pale morning sky.

★ ★ ★

The coffee shop occupied one corner of the huge Hebert building that took up an entire block across Senic Highway from the Standard Oil Corporation. At seven-thirty on Monday morning it was packed. The booths along the plate glass windows fronting Senic and Weller Avenue, as well as the long counter with its red-cushioned stools, were filled with men wearing khakis, blue jeans, and heavy work shoes, or business suits, white shirts, and ties.

Many of them had just gotten off the "dog" shift at

the plants in the area. Others were just beginning their workdays in the stores and offices and on construction jobs. Plumbers and policemen, carpenters and delivery truck drivers found common ground with businessmen and accountants, bankers and lawyers in this round-the-clock gathering place.

Lane held the glass door open for Coley as he wheeled into the coffee shop. They found a two-man table nestled in the corner where the windows joined a massive support pillar made of hewn cypress.

Pulling the chrome and red-cushioned chair out of the way for Coley, Lane sat with his back to the cypress beam. "Can I ask you another question?"

Coley looked at the noisy horde of people about them, leaned forward in his wheelchair, and chuckled, "Sure, if you think you can hear me in this place."

Lane glanced at the double glass doors leading out of the coffee shop to the east along Weller Avenue and to the south along Senic Highway. "I've never seen anything like this—even up in Memphis. What in the world is this place?"

"I guess it is a little unusual," Coley agreed. "Hebert got the idea of a community-type shopping center where you could get just about anything you needed under one roof."

"Looks like it's working pretty well," Lane remarked, glancing at the bustling coffee shop as well as the people coming and going through the two sets of double doors.

"You should see it on Fridays and Saturdays." Coley pointed to the eastern doors. "Down that way's the barber shop and on the other side of it is the bar and then the liquor store."

Lane could see the Closed sign on the heavy glass door of the barbershop. Inside, a row of six chairs lined up as though for inspection in front of shelves and a gleaming mirror that covered the entire back wall.

"Over this way," Coley continued, "is the main part of the building with the grocery store, the dry-goods store, hardware, and drugstore."

"Does this Hebert own everything around here?"

"Not quite." Coley nodded out the window. "Standard Oil owns the service station and everything from here all the way over to the Mississippi River."

"What about that?" Lane pointed to a paintless clapboard building on the corner opposite the coffee shop. It fronted directly on Senic Highway across from the main gate of Standard Oil. At the rear was a gravel parking lot. Metal signs advertising Jax and Pabst beer as well as Camel and Lucky Strike cigarettes were tacked to the walls.

"Dad's Bar." Coley watched a short, stocky man in khaki work clothes park his bicycle along the sidewalk, walk around to the parking lot, and enter through the rear door. "When the 'dog' shift gets off, part of 'em come in here—some go in Dad's. Dad's customers usually stay a lot longer."

"De usual for you, Coley?" The waitress suddenly appearing next to them didn't quite manage to cover the missing eyetooth with her lip when she smiled. Her hair was as red as her fingernails, except for its dark roots. The black material of her uniform strained at the white buttons running down the front. She set two heavy white cups of steaming coffee before them.

"Mais, yeah, cher," Coley answered smoothly. "And the same ting for my fran' here. Sally, meet Lane Temple. Lane, this is Sally Benoit."

"Pleased to meet you, cher," Sally half smiled

again, scribbling on her pad with the stub of a yellow pencil. "Back in a minute wid' ya'll order."

Lane watched Sally head back toward the kitchen area. "B-E-N-W-A-H? Is that right?"

"B-E-N-O-I-T, Ben—wah," Coley explained, smiling at Lane's attempt at the spelling.

Lane shook his head slowly, glancing at the men coming in and out of the coffee shop and the waitresses in their black-and-white uniforms weaving in and out of the crowd. "I don't know if I'll ever get used to the names down here—or the people."

"Don't try so hard. It'll come to you."

"By the way . . . what's the usual?" Lane asked with some uncertainty. "I kind of like to know what I'm eating."

"Kush-kush. You'll love it. It's cornmeal browned in bacon grease."

Lane spooned sugar into his coffee, sipping it and watching the clear morning sky grow darker as the thunderstorm moved in. Out over the river the clouds were webbed with lightning when the first drops spattered against the windows. People on the sidewalks scurried for shelter.

Sally returned, placed the two bowls of kush-kush and a small pitcher of milk on the table, refilling their coffee cups from a stainless steel pitcher. "You got nice-looking friends," she beamed at Coley. Giving Lane a coy smile, she sashayed back to the swinging doors that led to the kitchen.

Lane tried to ignore the flirtation as well as Coley's smirk. "How do I eat this stuff?"

"With a spoon," Coley replied, sprinkling sugar on his kush-kush without looking up. "Y'all use them up in Mississippi?"

Lane watched Coley add milk, stir the mixture,

and dig in. "Hmm-boy! That's good!"

Following suit, Lane tasted a spoonful and was pleasantly surprised at the rich bacon-flavored, toasted-corn taste. "This stuff is fittin'."

"Fittin'?"

"For you backward Louisiana folk, that means tastes good," Lane smiled, then returned to his breakfast.

Coley finished his last bite and leaned back, sipping his coffee. "You gonna love the food down here— soon as your palate becomes civilized, that is. We got crawfish bisque, jambalaya, and about a dozen kinds of sauce picants—and that's just for starters."

Trying to imagine what all this exotic food would taste like, Lane watched a beefy man about six feet tall wearing scuffed brown work shoes, khakis, and a yellow baseball cap step unsteadily out the back door of Dad's Bar. He took a few deep breaths, seemed to regain his balance, and headed briskly across the street toward the side entrance of the coffee shop.

Coley continued to sing the praises of Cajun food as the man gained the small lobby that led to the barber shop and coffee shop. Turning in Lane's direction, he glanced around briefly, spotted Coley's back, and stalked toward him.

"You little sawed-off, crippled-up worm," the man said as he spun Coley's wheelchair around to face him. His red face acted as an anchor for a purple-veined bulbous nose. Glancing at Lane, he showed this slim man in the blue suit the same contempt he showed all men who wore coats and ties to work.

Lane slid his chair back a few inches, transferring part of his weight to the balls of his feet. He noticed an anchor with a snake twined around it tattoed on the man's bulging bicep beneath his rolled-up shirt-sleeve.

"Hello, Thurman. Nice to see you in such a good mood this early in the morning." Coley stared up calmly at his accuser. "What can I do for you?"

Thurman opened his mouth to speak. Nothing came out but unbridled rage in a spray of spittle. His eyes bulged as he drew back his knotty left fist, but something went wrong. It wouldn't move forward.

Lane had suddenly appeared standing next to Thurman, his left hand gripping the man's left wrist.

"Settle down, partner," Lane said evenly.

Never one to heed advice, Thurman had no intention of settling down. His right fist moved in a blur toward Lane's head, touching nothing but air. As Lane crouched beneath the sweeping right arm, the force of the blow carried Thurman on around with his back to his opponent. With a swift push of his foot in the seat of the big man's pants, Lane sent him sprawling across the floor.

Scrambling quickly to his feet, Thurman turned to face the slim man who seemed to have simply disappeared as he swung his big right fist at him. "I'm gonna *kill* you, pretty boy," Thurman snarled, doubling up both fists in front of him.

Adrenalin now pumped through Lane's body, the instinct for self-preservation paramount in him. At the sound of the word *kill*, his marine training and the years of combat took control. It was *the* word never taken lightly in the corps. Something seemed to snap in his mind and, in that terrible moment of time, his eyes changed.

It was well known around town that Thurman loved to fight. Folks said he loved it better than drinking and fishing and deer hunting. And he was exceptional at it. Seldom had he shown fear when facing another man, but as he saw the change take place in Lane's eyes—as if some dark film had been drawn over them—Thurman's face began to sag as though he could no longer control the muscles that held his scowl in place.

Thurman's gaze shifted to Lane's right hand. The fingers were already bending at the first joint, the thumb laid along the inside of the hand, forming a flat, hard wedge. It was obvious that this bothered him. As Thurman continued to stare, Lane turned slightly to the left, knees flexed, legs apart in perfect balance.

Through the plate glass, a blaze of lightning streaked the dark clouds gathering behind Lane as the rain began in earnest.

Now the cold sweat popped out on Thurman's body. Lane could see it trickling down the side of his face. Thurman was a well-known predator, but today he had become the prey. He seemed to visibly deflate, as if filled with the knowledge of his impending, inevitable defeat.

Thurman deliberately turned around as though not to disturb some delicate balance, and walked quickly out the diner's double doors.

Lane watched him run across the street in the rain and dart through the back door of the bar.

The coffee shop returned to normal, except for occasional glances at the man in the blue suit who had beaten Thurman without striking a blow.

Coley straightened his chair back to the table. "Well, that probably did more to get you some clients than an ad in the Yellow Pages."

Lane sat back down and sipped his coffee. He noticed his hands were trembling. "I don't understand."

"People out here in Dixie got more respect for a good fistfight than good courtroom demeanor any day. You didn't exactly fight Thurman—but then, you didn't have to."

"I lost it, Coley." Lane rubbed his eyes with his fingertips as though trying to get rid of the invisible film. "I could have killed him—or maybe gotten killed."

"Semper fi, Mac." Coley used the marine catch-all phrase of the South Pacific. In this instance it meant *But you didn't—so just forget about it.*

Lane found Coley hardly disturbed by the incident. He tried to picture himself in a wheelchair, virtually helpless before Thurman's assault, but couldn't. "Maybe it's none of my business, but what did this guy have against you?"

Coley grinned over his coffee cup. "Thurman's mad at the whole world. I just happen to occupy the part he's in right now."

"Must be more to it than that."

"A little," Coley admitted. "He beat up his wife one time too many and she not only called the cops but finally decided to divorce him."

"And you took the case."

"Yep. I usually don't handle divorces, but this was an exception." Coley glanced at the back door of Dad's Bar where he saw Thurman running out, carrying a bottle inside a crumpled brown bag. "He kept going back to her house, so I got a peace bond against him. Last night they put him in jail."

"And I thought it was probably just your abrasive personality," Lane said with a straight face.

"Maybe I should smile more. You think?"

Lane watched Thurman climb into a battered pickup and roar out of the gravel parking lot behind the bar. "You sure didn't let this bother you."

Coley watched Thurman glare at him through his truck window while he waited for the light to change. "After what the Japs did to this ol' body, I don't worry much about somebody like him." He smiled brightly back at Thurman's scowl through the rain-streaked window.

They sipped their coffee, watching the rain as it washed the dirt from the sidewalks and the streets.

As they were preparing to leave, a gray-haired man in his mid-fifties walked over to their table. He wore khakis and carried a black safety helmet with both hands. "Morning, Coley."

"Morning, Abner." Coley turned to Lane. "Lane, this is Abner Hollis. He's the brains behind Standard Oil, but nobody's supposed to know. He's disguised as a lab supervisor. Abner, Lane Temple. Watch out for him, Abner—he's a lawyer."

"So I've heard." Abner nodded to Lane, smiling behind his steel-rimmed glasses. "I got some legal business needs doing—a little property transfer," he shrugged, glancing at Lane. "I thought your friend here might handle it for me. I know how you're so busy with the legislature and all."

Coley gave Lane an I-told-you-so wink. "I think he probably could. How about it, Lane?"

"Sure thing." Lane turned to Abner. "Why don't we go on over to the office right now?"

# SIX

# THE LEGACY OF TONY LEJEUNE

★ ★ ★

"Cushions! Get your cushions right here!" Wearing jeans, hunting boots, and his heavy topcoat, Lane stood in the dimly lit, shadowy area beneath the stadium. It reminded him of stories he had read about the catacombs beneath Paris, except that here everything was rough concrete—the floor, the walls, and the massive square pillars that towered upward to support the sloping underside of the structure.

People were pouring through the gates in front of him, dressed as if they were on their way to church instead of a football game. Most wore coats and hats and scarves against the late October chill.

"Daddy, why can't we just go on in like everybody else?" Dalton sat on a stack of cushions lined up against a side wall. He wore a red wool jacket and his hunter's cap with the flaps pulled over his ears. A lock of brown hair fell across his forehead.

"You're missing out on all the fun just sitting there, son." Lane tucked the cushion he was holding up under his arm, stepping over to Dalton. "Besides, this way we get to make a little money and see the game for free."

"But, we'll miss the kick-off," Dalton complained. "I'm bored and I'm gettin' cold too."

Lane lifted his son off the cushions and squatted down beside him. "Let me show you how to fix both those problems. You take this cushion and stand right over there beside that big concrete pillar. Hold it up like this and say real loud, 'Get your cushions—for a warm, soft seat! Only twenty-five cents!' "

Dalton stared at the people rushing past. "I don't wanna," he whined, putting his head down.

"Just try it," Lane implored, tilting his son's head up, "for your ol' daddy."

Dalton forced a smile. "Okay." Taking the cushion he walked away, repeating his sales pitch.

Lane watched a woman in a rich, brown fur coat hurrying along, her hand tucked under her husband's arm. Seeing the little eight-year-old boy holding the cushion out, she asked her husband for a quarter and bent down next to Dalton. His face brightened as she spoke to him. Giving her the cushion, he took the quarter and raced back to Lane.

"Look, Daddy! I got a quarter." Dalton held out the shiny coin, his face beaming with pride.

"I told you it was fun," Lane smiled. "And you just made a nickel."

"I did?"

"Yep."

Dalton grabbed two cushions, holding them with both arms as he raced back toward his position.

"Dalton!"

He turned around, eager to be back on his way. "Yes, sir?"

"Are you still cold?"

"No, sir!"

Just as Dalton got back to his place next to one of the rough pillars, a young man in a black tuxedo, escorting a woman in evening dress and an ermine wrap, handed Dalton a dollar bill. Dalton handed him two cushions, glancing over at Lane. Lane held up two fingers. As Dalton reached into his pocket for the two quarters, the man walked off.

"Mister," Dalton called out, holding out the two coins. "You forgot your change."

"Keep it," the man smiled.

Lane stepped back into the flow of the crowd, renting the cushions and keeping his eye on his son. *What a time that boy's having! Hope he likes football. Maybe he'll get a scholarship. I'd like to see that.*

Suddenly a sound like rolling thunder crashed through the lofty concrete recesses of the stadium. Lane looked out across the crowd and saw the purple-and-gold-clad LSU band marching up one of the ramps to take their place in the stadium. Shortly afterward, a whistle blew sharply and the crowd roared to their feet with the kick-off.

"Let's go, son. We get to watch the game now."

"But what about the cushions?" Dalton asked in alarm, staring at the few stacks that were left.

"The men who pick them up after the game will take care of them."

"Do we have to go?" Dalton gazed at the few stragglers coming in through the gates.

"We'll come back next week. How's that?"

"Good," Dalton beamed up at his father, his cheeks flushed with the cold. "This is fun!"

Lane lifted his son onto his shoulders and walked

up the long ramp toward the opening that led out into the stadium.

★ ★ ★

The bright angel looked down on the tiny living room where Catherine sat with her children on the gleaming hardwood floor amid the foil and ribbon and glitter of present wrapping. Jessie and Sharon were helping her with a few last-minute presents, while the boys romped and tussled on and off the couch.

"I've always loved that angel, Mama," Jessie observed, staring at the top of the Christmas tree.

"Me too, honey." Catherine glanced at the white-robed, golden-haloed angel, then at the lights, bubbling with colors of red and green and white. "My daddy brought that home one Christmas Eve when I was just a little girl. I still remember it though. He was dirty and greasy from work, but when he showed it to Mama, she hugged him anyway."

Jessie had heard the story before. "I sure wish I could have known him. I know he must have been a good man, 'cause Gramma's still in love with him after all this time."

Catherine smiled at her oldest child. "Yes, she still is. I didn't know anyone but me could tell it, though."

"Mama, can we have a flambeau?" Sharon used the scissors to cut the bright paper to the size she wanted.

"A what?" Catherine never ceased to be amazed at the things her youngest daughter learned. "That's a mighty big word for such a little girl."

"It's like a torch. Our teacher said it lights the way for Pere Noel on Christmas Eve."

Catherine brushed Sharon's soft brown hair back

from her face. "And who is Pere Noel?"

"He's the Cajun Santa Claus, Mama," Sharon beamed up at her, obviously proud of her newfound knowledge. "Everybody in south Louisiana's supposed to know that."

"Well, I guess we'll just have to depend on you to teach us about all the important customs down here. Think you can handle that job?"

"Yes, ma'am." Sharon finished tying a bow on the package she had wrapped. "Look, Mama. I did it by myself." She held out the present with jolly Santa Claus faces on the paper that had been folded and taped by tiny loving hands.

"Oh, that's just lovely, Sharon." Catherine held the present up near the lights of the tree. "Your daddy will be so proud of it. Especially since you wrapped it yourself."

"It's a necktie, Mama. I picked it out over at Hebert's last week. Remember?" Sharon's dark blue eyes sparkled in the Christmas lights.

"Mine's purty too, Mama." Cassidy leaped off the couch, hit the waxed floor with his sock feet, and slid with a crash of falling boxes and the tinkling of breaking ornaments into the base of the Christmas tree. Grabbing his wrinkly present from the pile, he held it above his head. "See!"

"Look what you've done, you little monster!" Jessie cried out. "Get away from here!"

"Now, now, it isn't all that bad, Jess." Catherine tried to soothe her daughter, knowing she was still having a hard time adjusting to school even after four months. "He didn't mean to make a mess. After all, he's just a little boy." She straightened the presents and began cleaning up the shards of glass.

"I'm a *big* boy!" Cassidy protested, standing to his feet and pushing his chest out.

"All right, big boy," Catherine grinned, "go back and play with your brother while we finish with the presents."

Dalton turned around on the couch where he had been gazing out the window. "Let's go outside and look at the Christmas lights, Mama. I can see some from here."

"Can we, Mama?" Sharon joined in. "Can we, please!"

"But it's cold out there!" Catherine shivered. "Brrr—I can feel it already."

Cassidy chimed in. "Santa Claus! I wanna go see Santa Claus in the big window."

"But that's a long way, Cass." Catherine found herself weakening before the eager faces of her children. "And your daddy's got the car."

Jessie struck the final blow for the light-show excursion. "We'll bundle up real good, Mama."

"Well—all right then," Catherine relented, "but put your coats and hats on."

As the children rushed around, grabbing their clothes from closets and bedposts, Catherine put on her deep-red wool coat and tied a matching scarf over her head. Then she pulled Cassidy's cap on his head against fierce protests and buckled the straps of the earmuffs under his chin.

"Everybody ready?"

"Yes, ma'am!" all four chimed together.

Holding Cassidy's hand tightly, Catherine led them out to Evangeline Street and they began their walk west and then south on Longfellow toward Hebert's Department Store and the Christmas display.

The stars glittered with a cold, hard light against

the vast black dome of the sky. Lights glowed in the windows of every house they passed, the tinsel and colored balls and shiny ornaments gleaming on the trees in a merry celebration of the season. Catherine loved seeing the glow of excitement on the faces of her children, thinking of the time that seemed so very long ago when she had felt the very same way about Christmas.

"Look, Mama, it's baby Jesus!" Cassidy broke free from Catherine's hand and raced across the dry grass, glittering with frost. A nativity scene sat in the front yard under a gnarled old cedar tree, its limbs sheltering Mary and Joseph and the babe who lay in His manger.

"Cass, you come back here!" Catherine warned. "You can't go into someone's yard like that!"

"Why can't he?" A plump woman with a round face and short gray hair opened the front screen door and stepped out onto the tiny concrete porch of her stucco house. She clutched a black shawl about her shoulders and carried a small brown paper bag. "It's my yard and I say it's all right. Besides, little boys ought to be able to do whatever they want to on Christmas Eve."

Catherine couldn't help but smile as she walked over to the nativity scene to meet the woman. "Merry Christmas, then. I'm Catherine Temple and these are my children—Jessie, Dalton, Sharon, and the one holding the baby is Cassidy."

"Merry Christmas to you all," the woman smiled back, her dark eyes twinkling with good cheer. "I'm Mrs. Anthony LeJeune, but you can call me Marie. My Tony died seven months ago. We was hoping we'd have this one last Christmas together, but—we didn't. He loved to put up this little manger and the figures

111

and tell the children how Jesus was born."

"I know!" Cass beamed, holding the carved wooden figure of the baby. "In a stable in Beth-lee-him." He pronounced the word slowly and distinctly. "My gramma told me all about it."

Marie squatted down beside Cassidy. "That's the real miracle of Christmas, Cassidy. That Jesus, who is God's only Son, came down here born as a baby. And in a few years He grew up to be a little boy like you. He knows just what it feels like to be a little boy. Did you know that?"

Cassidy appeared spellbound by Marie's words. "No, ma'am. I didn't think about that part."

"I bet you're a smart little boy," Marie continued as Cassidy stared at the baby Jesus her husband had carved from a piece of cypress. He had collected cypress knees from the Atchafalaya swamps to use for his carvings. They cluttered the small storage shed in back of the house, and Marie could never bring herself to throw them out. "Can you tell me about Easter?"

"I get colored eggs and a lot of candy!"

"Is that all?"

Cassidy placed the baby carefully back in the manger. His eyes narrowed in thought as he glanced over at Marie. "I know! They killed Jesus, but He come back out of that ol' tomb jus' like He told them He would!"

Marie nodded her head in approval. "That's right. He died for all of us so that if we believe in Him we can all go to heaven." Her eyes glistened as she considered this exuberant little boy with the bright smile and the shiny hair spilling out beneath the bill of his cap.

"We'd better be going, kids!" Catherine spoke

softly as she would have in church. An inexplicable peace had settled over her as she knelt with her children, listening to the old, old story of Jesus' birth. She stared at the little nativity set, a work of love left behind by the man who had carved it. *I think I would have liked Tony LeJeune very much.*

"First a little Christmas treat," Marie smiled warmly. She took a sugar cookie out of the paper bag and handed it to Cassidy, then gave one to each of the others. "I made them myself as I do every year. I hope you like them."

Cassidy chewed the three quick bites he had already taken. "Ummm, good," he mumbled, crumbs dropping down the front of his blue plaid jacket.

All four children seemed reluctant to leave the little scene under the cedar tree, even when Catherine reminded them of the Santa Claus' toy shop and reindeer display in the store window just ahead.

"Thank you so much, Mrs. LeJeune," Catherine waved as they walked off down the sidewalk.

Catherine led her children along the sidewalks, past the houses with their dry winter lawns and leafless trees, their branches forming stark and elegant sculptures in the warm glow of the Christmas lights.

★ ★ ★

Lane closed the door quietly behind him, stepping into the tiny kitchen. He placed his briefcase and topcoat on the table. Catherine stirred sleepily on the couch, pulling her knees up and curling into a ball, her bare feet peeking out beneath the hem of her flannel nightgown.

Slipping his shoes off, Lane walked carefully across the linoleum toward the hallway.

"I'm awake, darling," Catherine mumbled, not opening her eyes.

"Sorry, I tried to be quiet." He set his shoes near the door and went into the living area.

"We took a walk and looked at the lights." Catherine kept her eyes closed. "All the way to Hebert's."

Sitting on the couch next to his wife, Lane gazed at her long lashes, casting their wispy shadows on the delicate skin beneath her eyes. In her curled-up position, with her pale hair tousled and gleaming in the lights from the tree, she looked more like a girl than the mother of four children. "I tried to get away, but I had to get that brief finished before the holidays."

"The children tried to wait up for you, but they just couldn't after the long walk." Catherine's eyes opened slightly, then closed again.

Lane took Catherine's left foot between his hands, rubbing it gently. "I think your feet would be cold on the equator in the middle of July."

"Ummm—that feels good," Catherine moaned, shifting her position slightly. "And when you finish, don't forget there's another one that needs attention."

As Lane rubbed the warmth back into Catherine's feet, he looked around the tiny, crowded apartment. He had hoped to have his family in a larger home before Christmas, but it had proved to be a long road back after his years away in the war had forced them to use all their savings.

"I'll get the presents." Lane closed both bedroom doors, then took a chair from the kitchen and placed it in the hall. Standing on it, he removed the square board that covered the entrance to the attic and took the presents down. After placing them under the tree, he sat back down next to Catherine. "I wish we could have gotten them more. Two presents each isn't much."

Catherine sat up on the couch and stretched. "Well, we'll just have to get more money—somehow."

"I'm doing the best I can, Cath." Lane could feel the same old complaints coming and tried to avoid the subject of finances on Christmas Eve. "The people out in this part of town are mostly just working folks and they can't pay much."

Staring at the bubbling lights on the tree, Catherine sighed. "I'm tired of living like this, Lane."

"Let's wait till after Christmas. I'm too tired to talk about it tonight." Lane took his jacket off, laying it on the arm of the couch, and stretched his legs out.

Catherine turned to look at him. "Why don't you take some of the business Walker Jones tries to send you—or maybe handle some of those people you think aren't good enough for you to take their cases?"

"It's a matter of ethics." Lane took a deep breath, letting it out slowly. "I don't think I'm better than anybody else. There's just some people that I'd rather not represent."

"Those with money, apparently," Catherine suggested with an edge to her voice.

"It'll just take time." Lane lay back, his head resting on a blue pillow with pale yellow butterflies embroidered on it. "Can't you have a little patience?"

Catherine had felt an inexplicable sense of peace and joy kneeling with her children and Marie in front of the little nativity scene carved out of cypress knees. But she had forgotten that now. "I'm tired of being patient—and being crowded into these three rooms. If you'd think of your family more and your pride less, maybe you *could* make some money."

Lane was too tired to respond. He stared at the

tree. The glow of the lights, the shining ornaments, and especially the sharp smell of cedar called him back to Christmases past when things seemed much simpler—and more peaceful. *If you think money is so important—I'll get plenty of money. I'm tired of fighting you.*

"After all, you're going to be thirty-four years old next year, Lane," Catherine continued, unaware that she had told him the same story so many times he no longer listened to what she was saying. "Time's slipping away from us."

"Hmmm," Lane mumbled from the front steps of sleep. He heard Catherine's voice merely as a distant droning sound.

"We need to have a place where we can entertain our friends. Maybe have some of your clients over for dinner." Catherine heard the soft plopping sound Lane's lips made as he expelled his breath past them in sleep. She stared at his limp form, head turned at an odd angle on the backrest.

Placing the pillow at the end of the couch, she eased him gently down, lifted his legs, and straightened them out. Then she went to the hall closet, took down a flower-patterned quilt, and covered him with it. *I'm sorry to complain so much, Lane. I really don't mean to. You're trying so hard for all of us. Guess it's just being alone here all day—me and Cassidy. And he's not much of a conversationalist.*

Being careful not to awaken him, Catherine sat on the edge of the couch next to her husband. Taking his hand in hers, she let her fingertips trail softly along the veins that ran from his wrist down to his knuckles and fingers. Stopping at the plain gold band, she rubbed its hard, smooth surface. Leaning over, she kissed him gently on the cheek and lips.

Catherine rose from the couch, walking barefoot into the bedroom where her girls were sleeping. She sat on the bed, brushing Sharon's brown hair back from her face. *My little bookworm. Never give your mama a minute's trouble, do you? Sometimes I wonder what's going on behind those big blue eyes of yours. You hardly ever talk about yourself. Maybe you're the smartest of us all—keeping your own counsel.*

Jessie turned over in her sleep so that she faced her mother. Catherine smiled at her eldest child. *Just look at my Jessie. With the face and voice of an angel. Wanting everyone you meet to like you. You just can't please everyone, baby. I hope you learn that before it gets you into trouble. There's no telling how far you can go with your talent.*

Catherine kissed her girls, tucked them in, and went into the other bedroom. As she sat down next to Dalton, she thought how much she depended on him for little things like running errands—and chasing down Cassidy. *You're not the best student in the world, but nobody works harder than you do. Your daddy's counting on you to follow in his footsteps and play football. He says he can tell already you've got the natural talent. Maybe you'll be a college quarterback like he was. What I hope is you'll grow up to be as good a man as he is.*

*Cassidy—sometimes I just don't know what to think of you. My most lovable and exasperating child. You're as quick—and as wild—as a deer. You make people love you without even trying. Whatever you do with your life—it won't be boring.*

After kissing her boys good-night, Catherine went back to the kitchen and made herself a cup of tea. She switched the knob on the cathedral-shaped radio, its amber dial glowing dimly where it sat on the counter next to the refrigerator. Turning the dial through the static of the stations gone off the air, she finally heard music. Frank Sinatra's version of "Have Yourself a Merry Little Christmas" floated softly through the small room.

Catherine took her tea into the living area and sat on the couch next to Lane. She thought of those wolf-lean years when he was away at war and of how her memory of him kept her going during the tough times when the money was scarce and she felt so alone and helpless without him. When he got back she just knew all the hard times were behind her and she would have all the things she had before the war—and more—but things hadn't worked out like that at all.

*I'm just selfish. I have four beautiful children and a fine husband. I should be as happy as anybody. What's wrong with me? Why am I so uneasy all the time? I have to remember to tell Lane how much I love him. Seems like I hardly ever do that anymore.*

The lights glowed with their soft colors on the children's presents beneath the tree. The song continued its bittersweet celebration of the season.

*. . . from now on our troubles will be miles away. . . .*

# SEVEN

# BEGINNING OF SORROWS

★ ★ ★

Sitting on the high-backed wooden pew, Lane stared at the dimly lit frescoes high above him on the curved ceiling of the St. Louis Cathedral. The guide, whose name was Lester and who wore a red coat and tie, which gave him the appearance of a little white-haired gnome, insisted that Lane take the five-minute tour while he waited for his "friend."

Lester extolled the church's past as they strolled along the wide aisle from the altar to the rear of the building, explaining that an Italian artist had come to New Orleans and painted the frescoes in 1850. St. Louis was the oldest active cathedral in the United States, built in 1794. Lane tried to look interested in the little man's litany of facts as he glanced about the hushed church for his client.

He came just as the guide was winding down his tour. And he was like no one Lane had ever known in Mississippi—or Baton Rouge, for that matter.

The man who preceded Lane's client into the

church looked as if someone had hit him across the forehead with an iron pipe. He stood well over six feet tall, having no neck to speak of. His chest and shoulders pulled at the seams of his charcoal gray suit coat. Beneath a shiny head fringed with dark, bristly hair, his predator's eyes took in the area at a glance. Lane never did find out what the big man's name was.

Ross Michelli, of medium height and build, looked as unassuming as a bank clerk in his black overcoat and fedora as he entered the church after getting the barest nod from the man in the gray suit. He smiled when he saw Lane, his teeth gleaming brightly against his olive skin. His heels clicked on the marble floor as he walked directly toward Lane, stopping beside him.

Glancing at him, Lane saw that the man's lips were as red as a young girl's, that his dark eyes were depthless and ancient looking.

"Glad to have you with us," Lester smiled at Michelli. "We're about done here though."

"Don't let me interrupt." Michelli took his hat off, holding it in front of him. His thick black hair, shot through with streaks of gray, looked freshly cut. "Go ahead with your talk."

Lane felt immediately uneasy in Michelli's presence and had to control a strong urge to run from the building. He knew now why Coley had warned him not to take this case.

"This is Joan of Arc." Lester pointed to a life-sized statue done in serene pastel colors. "She led the French army in defeating the British at Orleans, France, in 1429. For this reason she's also known as the Maid of Orleans. She was burned as a witch, but in 1920 she was declared a saint."

"I'm sure that made her feel much better." The hint of a smile crossed Michelli's face.

Lester cleared his throat and hurried through the rest of his prepared speech, ending the tour.

Lane dropped a dollar bill for the cathedral's up-keep into the proffered plate.

"I certainly enjoyed your talk about the witch-saint," Michelli remarked, reaching into his inside coat pocket. "How much do you think it's worth?"

Lester winced at Michelli's referral to Saint Joan. "Twenty dollars!" He seldom got that much all day long.

"I agree." Michelli dropped a twenty into the plate. Then he put his arm around Lane's shoulder, leading him down the aisle toward the altar at the far end. His heels rang with a hollow sound on the marble floor.

Lane stared at the dozens of votive candles to the right of the main altar, glowing warmly in their squat glass holders. A woman with frizzy gray hair escaping from beneath her black lace mantilla knelt at one of the pews. As they passed by her, she clutched her black glass beads tightly, murmuring the Rosary.

Michelli hadn't bothered with introductions when he walked over to Lane. There was no doubt in either man's mind who the other was. "I hear good things about you from my friends in Baton Rouge, Mr. Temple—that aside from an excellent knowledge of the law, you value discretion. And I need a lawyer from out of town since the judges down here seem to have lost respect for the ones who work for me."

"Did you hear about me from Walker Jones?"

"Names aren't necessary, Mr. Temple," Michelli admonished mildly. "I have many contacts—especially in the legislature, those august guardians of our morality." He glanced at Lane with a knowing smile, his teeth set like kernels of corn in his gums.

"You understand that this case has to be strictly on

the up-and-up," Lane explained, his voice cracking slightly.

"Is there any other way?" Michelli glanced back at the woman who still had her head bowed. "We have witnesses that my nephew was miles away when that redneck cowboy was beaten up outside the night-club."

They had come to the altar. Michelli bent down on the kneeler and rested his arms on the carved wood rail, the rows of candles like a garden of light flickering before him. He dropped some coins in a brass offering plate, lighting one of the candles.

In a few moments, Lane knelt beside him. "Why did you choose a church to do our business?"

"It's peaceful here." Michelli's expression was incredulous. "What you got against churches?"

Lane had no idea how to answer the question, so he merely glanced at Michelli and shrugged.

"Let's go then." Michelli took a last long look at the bank of candles and rose from the kneeler. "Some people—religion makes 'em nervous. Don't worry about it."

Lane followed Michelli out of the cathedral's massive front doors onto Chartes Street. They turned left, walking past two old men in ragged coats who sat together on a park bench. Their faces shone like ebony in the afternoon light. One played trombone while the other coaxed the blues out of his battered trumpet, his eyes squinted shut.

" 'Basin Street Blues,' " Michelli remarked, dropping a five-dollar bill into the cigar box. "I been to Memphis, New York, Chicago—all over the country. No place but New Orleans can you hear music like this."

Lane stood with his hands in the pockets of his tan

trench coat, the bright March sunlight holding no warmth as it cast Jackson Square into a dazzle of light and shadow.

Turning right on St. Anne, they ambled along the sidewalk next to the tall piked iron fence, the music fading away behind them. Strewn at random along their path, easels held oil and watercolor paintings, some still taking shape under the deft strokes of the artists. Lane stopped once to stare as a swamp scene full of ancient cypress, gray moss, and dark water came to life at the tip of an old man's brush.

"You see that?" Michelli pointed across the street to a two-story brick building with iron columns and wrought iron balustrades. It ran the length of St. Anne from the cathedral to the Cafe du Monde next to the Mississippi River. "The Pontalba Apartments—oldest in the country. The other one's on the opposite side of the square on St. Peter Street."

They crossed Decatur Street to the Cafe du Monde and took an open-air table at the rear near the levee. A white-jacketed Negro, who had been joking with another waiter, hurried into the building at a flick of Michelli's wrist. He reappeared in two minutes with a tray holding two thick white mugs of *cafe-au-lait* and two heavy saucers of *beignets*.

Lane watched Michelli spoon sugar into his mug, then sprinkle powdered sugar from a dull metal shaker onto the crispy brown *beignets*. "What *is* this?"

"The pride of the French Market," Michelli mumbled around the pastry he chewed with obvious pleasure. "Go ahead, try one and tell me if you've ever tasted anything this good."

Lane imitated Michelli, biting into one of the hot pastries. Surprised at the rich sweetness and the light, chewy-crispy texture, he ate all three of his, washing them down with the strong milk-whitened coffee and chicory. Neither spoke until they had finished and were sipping on refills that the waiter brought as soon as their cups were empty.

"Ahhhh," Michelli breathed in a long sigh. "What do you think of our little New Orleans delights?"

"Great," Lane said truthfully. "Sure beats the doughnuts I've been eating all these years."

"Well, enough polite conversation," Michelli shrugged. "Now to the real business. I want you to defend my nephew because you're smart, you've got an all-American face—and because you got no connections in Louisiana politics."

"I don't quite understand."

"I could use one of a dozen good lawyers from down here, but the judge his case is going before is a hard nose. He don't like me or any of my family. Using a hick like you, he's got to think everything's on the up-and-up—that my nephew is as clean as this morning's wash. You know what I mean?"

Lane flinched at the word *hick*, but let it pass. "Yeah. I think I know what you mean."

"Good. All you got to do is present the evidence— nothing but the facts. It'll all work out fine."

Lane took a deep breath. "I won't be a party to anything illegal—false witnesses, things like that."

Michelli's mouth smiled, but his eyes remained cold and remote. "You just present the evidence and the witnesses we give you. That's all you got to do. Understood?"

"Yeah." Lane glanced over at the man in the gray suit who sat at a corner table so he could see the entire patio area of the Cafe du Monde. He had followed them from the cathedral like a bulky gray cat at just the proper distance.

Michelli's eyes never left Lane's as Michelli reached inside his coat, took a brown, sealed envelope from the pocket, and tossed it on the table. It lay in a cold splash of sunlight amid the cups and spoons and spilled sugar.

Lane stared at the envelope for what seemed like a long, long time. He heard the palm fronds clattering softly above him in an errant breeze from the river. The air seemed to take on a sudden chill as he reached out and lifted the envelope from its pool of yellow light.

Michelli rose without a word and left the patio, followed by his gray shadow.

Lane felt the envelope grow heavy and burdensome in his hand. Taking out his pocketknife, he slit it open and counted out ten one-hundred-dollar bills. *That's almost as much money as I've made since I moved to Baton Rouge—and it's only the down payment for the trial.*

Stuffing the envelope into his jacket pocket, Lane dropped a dollar on the table, happened to see the expression on the waiter's face, and placed another beside it. He left the cafe and walked the narrow streets of the French Quarter, taking little notice of the two-hundred-year-old buildings with their second-story galleries and wrought iron railings or the neighborhood grocery stores with bins of plums and bananas set out on the sidewalks and ceiling fans humming softly behind screen doors.

★ ★ ★

A fluttering of wings jerked Lane from his reverie as he sat on a concrete and wood-slat park bench in the square, staring at the statue of Andrew Jackson astride his rearing stallion. He had lost track of time during his ramblings through the quarter and felt stiff and cold from his sojourn on the bench.

Leaving the park area through huge iron gates, he crossed Decatur Street, climbed the grassy levee next to the Cafe du Monde, and walked down the long slope to the river.

A huge piece of gnarled driftwood, worn smooth and white as old bone, rested against some rough chunks of concrete at the water's edge. Sitting down on the polished surface of the wood, Lane glanced up-river at the ferry churning through the muddy water toward Algiers on the far shore. Beyond the ferry, the windows of cars and trucks winked in the late after-noon sunlight as they crossed the Huey Long Bridge.

Lane remembered that first week in January when the man with the big, smelly cigar and the vested suit with solid gold watch bob and chain had come to his office. Charged with embezzling, he had given Lane two hundred dollars up front to defend him.

Lane had co-mingled the funds with his own ac-count to pay some outstanding bills. He had put the money back the next month, but somehow that black-and-white distinction between right and wrong he had believed in all his life had begun shading slightly to gray.

Thus began the timeless struggle in the heart of Lane Temple. *That wasn't so bad. After all, I did put the money back. And Michelli—nobody's ever convicted him of a crime. Besides, it's not my concern what he does outside the courtroom. All I can do is take the ev-idence and defend his nephew with what I've got.*

Sensing movement to his left downriver, Lane felt the old marine training instinctively come back on him, but quickly gained control of it before it trans-lated itself into action.

Walking along the water's edge, a thin black boy in faded overalls, a straw hat, and brogans that were at least two sizes too large for him carried a cane pole over his shoulder. About fifty feet from Lane he stopped, took a cricket from a tin can tied to his belt, and baited his hook. Then he sat down on the trunk of a tree that had been uprooted somewhere upriver and washed ashore, dropping his line into the muddy water.

In a few minutes Lane strolled over to him. "Are they biting today?"

The boy looked up at him and grinned, his teeth gleaming brightly and his dark face almost featureless in the shadow of the wide-brimmed hat. "No, suh."

Lane glanced downriver at a grain elevator that cast its shadow across the deep water where it loaded the ocean-going vessels. "Why don't you try down there? I'll bet there's a lot of fish where that grain falls into the water."

"I used to." The boy's eyes grew wide. "It was a lot easier to catch a mess of fish down there, but one time a big one took my line—almost pulled me in the river wid him. Dat thing act like he mad at me, trying to drag me down in that dark place where he live. Naw, suh, it a lot harder to fish over here, but I still catch a mess if I jes' be patient."

"I expect you're right about that." Lane stared at the deep water in the shadow of the grain elevator. Suddenly the dark surface swirled and a huge prehistoric-looking fish broke through. The sunlight caught its ponderous, scaly body with a malignant glint as it rolled over. Lane caught just a glimpse of its cloudy eyes, long snout, and the rows of razor-sharp teeth before it disappeared beneath the current.

Glancing downriver, the boy gave no indication

that he had seen the monster, but merely stared at his fishing line where it disappeard into the muddy water.

"What was that thing?" Lane had never seen anything that evil looking in his life.

The boy never looked up, as if to do so would be inviting disaster. "Dat what tried to pull me in de river!"

★   ★   ★

"Hey, Lane. Why don't you come in for a quick cup of coffee?" Coley sat in the narrow hallway in his usual jeans and rumpled sportcoat, leaning forward in the wheelchair to unlock his office door. "I made a pot before I went out to get the newspaper."

Lane stopped at the bottom of the stairs. "I got a lot of work to do down at the courthouse."

"Loosen up a little, boy. And you don't need to wear a coat and tie to search records, even if you are making a little money now." Coley swung the door inward and rolled into the office. "C'mon in. I hate to drink alone."

As Lane followed him in, he saw Coley stop at the crude little homemade table he had built from the weathered cypress boards taken from an old slave cabin. He took the white ceramic French-drip coffeepot from the single burner hotplate and poured two demitasse cups full of the dark coffee, adding sugar from a jelly jar that was crusty brown from a long succession of wet coffee spoons. The heady aroma of Community Dark Roast coffee filled the small, cluttered office.

Lane took one of the two straight-backed wooden chairs with deer-hide seats. They sat near the single window that looked out on the Standard Oil complex. He took the cup from Coley, sipping the hot coffee, savoring its rich strong flavor. "I believe you make the best coffee in Louisiana."

"I do," Coley agreed readily. "I used to be number two, but Mama died. She taught me how."

Lane stared at the hand-lettered sign hanging on the wall next to Coley's desk that sat across from the door near the other window. It read:

> "How much do you love me?" I asked Jesus.
> "This much," He replied.
> And He stretched out His arms,
> And He died.

"You look at that thing every time you come in here, Lane." Coley wheeled his chair over next to him. "But you never ask me about it."

"I'm asking."

"Well, since you insist," Coley grinned, "I'll tell you the story behind it."

"I've heard your stories before." Lane glanced down at his watch. "I can't afford to take the whole day off."

"Okay. You get the *Reader's Digest* version. A fellow in prison sent it to me."

Lane glanced out the window at the early morning traffic on Senic Highway, waiting for Coley to continue, but he didn't. "Well, is that it?"

"You wanted the short version." Coley knew he had him hooked now. "Oh, his name is Elton Landry."

"C'mon," Lane said impatiently. "You might as well tell me the whole thing."

"I thought you'd never ask." Coley took his cup in both hands, his thin brown fingers holding it with a surgeon's touch. Taking a swallow of the coffee, he began his story. "I grew up with that boy down in the basin," he nodded at the sign above his desk. "We fished and ran traps and hunted together since we were old enough to wear long pants. He was always wild—same as I used to be, I guess. Well, anyway, while I was in the service he knifed a man in a barroom brawl—over a woman. When I saw him in Angola, he'd been there four years."

"What were you doing at Angola?" Lane never knew where Coley's stories would lead. "I thought they brought the prisoners down to the courthouse at St. Francisville."

"I wasn't there on business," Coley explained, with a strange half smile on his face. "Not legal business anyway. I go there to minister to the prisoners sometimes—when I can get somebody to take me. It's a rough drive."

Lane's eyebrows lifted in surprise. "I didn't know you were a preacher."

Coley chuckled. "I'm not. But you don't have to be to tell people about Jesus."

Lane glanced at the sign again, shifting in his chair. He had been brought up in church, but somehow what he was hearing from Coley made him uneasy.

"Anyway, he gave his life to Jesus that same day I first saw him and made that little sign for me later on." Coley's gaze turned inward in thought. "The last time I saw him, he'd started a little Bible study group in the prison. Had a dozen or more men in it. Most of 'em he'd led to the Lord."

Lane felt obligated to say something. "It's uh—an interesting play on words—that verse."

"Yeah," Coley agreed. "It's also the truth."

Lane finished his coffee, placing the cup on the cypress table. "Well, I gotta be going."

Coley's eyes narrowed in thought. "Lane, I need to talk to you a minute."

"All right, but make it quick," Lane said impatiently, glancing down at his watch.

"I think you're headed down the wrong road." Coley's solemn tone caught Lane off guard.

Lane stood up. "You said you weren't a preacher, but I think I feel a sermon coming on."

Coley shook his head. "No, I'm not preaching to you, Lane. I'm just a friend who's concerned."

"About what?" Lane tried to pretend he didn't know what this was leading up to, but couldn't quite pull it off.

"I think you already know." Coley sat his coffee cup down, rested his chin on his clasped hands, and stared into Lane's eyes. "Michelli, for one thing."

Lane looked away from those clear, steady gray eyes. "Why? I'm just defending his nephew. We're not going to the prom together."

"The whole thing's a setup. They've got witnesses who weren't even at the scene that night." Coley's gaze never wavered. "Anybody with one eye and half-sense can see that."

"How would you know?" Lane felt like a witness under cross-examination. "This happened down in New Orleans."

"It's the way they always work. I've seen Michelli's men in the Capitol trying to influence legislation—labor laws, Port Authority regulations, things like that. Let's just say that diplomacy isn't their strong suit."

"I'm just handling the trial—not doing any follow-up investigation. It's not my responsibility where the evidence comes from."

"You're a good man, Lane." Coley took a deep breath and let it out slowly. "You don't need to get involved with people like Michelli."

"I've got a family to take care of," Lane said hotly. "A wife and four children, in case you've forgotten."

"I haven't," Coley replied evenly. "That's exactly why I'm concerned. That, and because you're a friend."

"This is all strictly within the code of ethics," Lane snapped. "I'm *not* doing anything illegal."

Coley stared calmly at him. "No—you're not, are you?"

Lane tried to ease the thick tension in the room. "C'mon, Coley. What's so bad about it? Some drunk gets beat up in a bar fight. Happens all the time."

"He *wasn't* a drunk." Coley stared at the morning sunlight streaming in the narrow window next to his overflowing desk. "He owned a hardware store and refused to pay Michelli so he could stay in business."

"How could you know something like that? I didn't—and it's my case." Lane began pacing back and forth on the waxed pine floor of the office.

"I've lived in south Louisiana all my life and I read the newspapers. That's how I know."

"Well, I'm not going to think about this anymore right now. I've got work to do."

"One more thing, Lane."

"All right," Lane shrugged. "What is it?"

" 'The love of money is the root of all evil.' " Coley's face was pained when he said it.

Lane stopped and stared at Coley. "What's wrong with money?"

"Nothing at all. But there is something wrong with the *love* of money."

"Aw, c'mon, it's not for *me*. I don't love *money*. I'm doing this for the children—and Catherine." Lane took the few steps to the office door and opened it.

Coley wheeled his chair around behind his desk. "Did Catherine love you when you got married?"

Lane looked puzzled. "Well—certainly." He could never quite follow the flow of Coley's conversation, feeling that he was always being caught off guard.

"How much money did you have then?"

"I've really got to go now, Coley." Lane thought about the thirty-nine dollars he and Catherine had gotten as wedding gifts, which was the sum total of their assets at the time. He also remembered how very happy they had been. "Thanks for the coffee. And don't worry, I'll be all right."

# EIGHT

# A FIGHT FOR LOVE AND GLORY

★ ★ ★

"Oh, Lane, it's beautiful!" Catherine stood in front of the triple mirror outside the fitting rooms. Holding the hem of the rose-colored evening dress out with one hand, she turned first one way, then the other, admiring how the smoothly flowing taffeta, which stopped a foot from the floor, accented the slim lines of her ankles. "Do you think we can afford it?"

Lane leaned against one of the fluted columns that supported the open balcony of the second floor. "Why not? It's why I'm putting in all these hours." *Seems like the only way I can make you happy anymore. Well, maybe I'm expecting too much from you, Catherine. I guess it's enough to have my work and take care of my family. Passion can't last forever.*

"I personally think it's stunning on you." Mrs. Muse, a handsome woman with gray hair and a trim figure who had worked in the ladies' department for twenty-five years, placed a forefinger to the side of her face and tilted her head slightly. "It's such a lovely contrast to your fair skin and blue eyes. Of course, we have it in pale blue, green, or cocoa if you prefer."

"Do you like it, dear?" Catherine put both hands on her slim waist and faced her husband.

"If you looked any better I couldn't stand it," Lane smiled. He had to admit that it made him happy to be able to buy expensive clothes for his wife. "You're prettier now than you were on our wedding day."

"I'm certainly glad that flat-hip look has gone out of style," Mrs. Muse injected. "All those squarish straight skirts and padded shoulders—made us *all* look like old maids. Small waists and round hips are back to stay, I hope."

"I'm with you, Mrs. Muse." Lane gave Catherine an admiring glance.

Catherine smiled at her husband, noting the beginnings of dark circles under his eyes. "You look tired, dear. Maybe you're working too hard. We hardly ever see you anymore."

"Speaking of which, I've got an appointment in twenty minutes." Lane gave Catherine a quick kiss on the lips and turned to leave, taking a few steps before he stopped.

"Please, Daddy, don't go," Jessie complained. "We were all going to have lunch together after we finish shopping."

Lane gazed at his oldest child, still unable to believe that she had become a young woman of fourteen. "I'd love to, baby, but this is something I can't miss."

"Are you sure you can't stay, Lane? We'll be finished in a few minutes." Catherine glanced away from the mirror.

"You'll be finished when the two of you buy out the ladies' department of Rosenfield's here," Lane smiled, making a sweeping gesture about the building with his hand. "Walker set up this meeting for me, though. It's a personal injury case, and he says I could make some big money on it."

Catherine turned from the mirror and walked over to Lane. She admired the way the beige summer suit hung on his lean frame. Gazing into his tanned face, she noticed for the first time the fine sprinkling of a few gray hairs at his temples. Stepping back, she held his deep brown eyes with her own. "I feel like it's me who's making you spend so much time away from all of us."

*Of course, it's you! All I heard for months was how poor we were.* "Don't be silly," Lane joked, feeling torn between his love for Catherine and the pressure he felt she was putting him under. "It just comes with the job. When I get better established, I won't have to put in all these hours. Then you'll get tired of seeing this ol' mug around the house."

"No, I won't," Catherine said solemnly.

Lane glanced at his gold watch, a present from Ross Michelli. "Well, I really have to get moving now. You ladies have fun and save enough money for groceries."

Catherine watched Lane hurry out of the store. *Maybe I did complain too much about the money. He's always in such a hurry now.*

"You'll be the envy of all the other wives at the governor's reception, Mama," Jessie bragged as she stared at Catherine's new dress. "You *are* going to buy it, aren't you?"

"You think it's worth what they're asking?" Catherine had felt a twinge of guilt when she first saw the price tag on the dress. "Hebert's had some cute dresses in their window."

"Oh, Mama!" Jessie said in an exasperated tone. "Hebert's is for those plant workers—not a lawyer's wife."

Jessie's words disturbed Catherine in a way that a shark might disturb the water in its passage—with just a tiny rippling of the surface, its huge bulk going unseen. Catherine felt only the slight ripples of Jessie's words. She didn't want to see what moved beneath them. "There's nothing wrong with working in a plant, Jessie. Your daddy grew up working on a farm and he's always been proud of that."

"I thought you wanted something better for us, that's all." Jessie shook her head slowly. "Sometimes I think you don't know what you really want, Mama."

"I just don't want you to think that you're better than anyone else, that's all."

"Can I have some new blouses and shorts for the summer, Mama? I saw some real cute ones advertised at Dalton's." In the manner of fourteen-year-olds, Jessie paid no attention to her mother's advice, but her mother was aware the girl had seen with her own eyes the pleasures that money could buy.

"I guess so." Catherine refused to let any cloud darken their day together. "Why don't you help me pick out some shoes and a bag to go with the dress first. Looks like Mrs. Muse had to go help another customer."

"I'd love to!" Jessie beamed. "This is such fun, Mama. I'm glad we're not poor anymore."

"We're not rich either."

"But we're going to be one day," Jessie beamed. "That's why Daddy's working so hard."

Catherine decided to drop the subject altogether. "Tell you what," she remarked as she headed back into the dressing room, followed closely by Jessie. "I'll call

Mrs. LeJeune and see if she can keep the children a little longer so we can go to a movie. Would you like that?"

"Oh yes!" Jessie unzipped the dress for her mother. "Can we see *The Postman Always Rings Twice*? Lana Turner's in it. It's supposed to be a good murder mystery."

Catherine slipped out of the evening dress and into her own. "I think you've got your mind on John Garfield, young lady—*not* Lana Turner."

Jessie blushed and looked away. "You have to admit, he *is* dreamy!"

"Why don't we see *Song of the South*?" Catherine suggested. "I've always loved Joel Chandler's stories."

"Uncle Remus!" Jessie pouted, following her mother out of the dressing room. "Brer Rabbit and Brer Fox? That's for kids like Cass and Dalton. I'll bet Sharon wouldn't even like it."

Catherine went into the shoe department and began browsing. "Well, I'm afraid that *The Postman Always Rings Twice* is a bit—steamy for you."

"Well, how about *The Best Years of Our Lives*, then?" Jessie glanced at the selection of shoes on their clear plastic shelves. "It's about men coming home from the war. Maybe you'd rather see that with Daddy, though."

"When does your daddy have time to go to the movies?" Catherine was surprised at the sound of her voice. It had a grating quality to it that she didn't recognize as her own. *How long have I been doing this?*

"I've got it—*The Big Sleep*. You always liked Humphrey Bogart and Lauren Bacall. And it's playing at the Paramount right across the street from the Piccadilly. I love to eat there. You can get anything you want."

"Well, I do like Bogart, and the food's good at the Piccadilly." Catherine picked up several shoes, turning them over in her hands and checking them for comfort.

"Mama, will you leave those ol' maid shoes alone and try on a pair of these?"

Catherine took the shoe Jessie handed her. "Spiked heels and these tiny straps. There's hardly anything to it—and just look at the price!"

"They emphasize the leg," Jessie grinned. "That's what the fashion magazines say."

"Well, maybe you're right," Catherine admitted. "They would look good with the dress. I'm glad the styles are getting more feminine now. I think a lot of women are glad the square-shouldered look is finally going out."

★ ★ ★

Catherine and Jessie sat on black-cushioned stools inside the Beanery, a tiny restaurant tucked up against the Fidelity Bank Building on Third Street. The entire menu consisted of nothing but New Orleans-style red beans and rice with an optional side order of smoked sausage.

Men in business suits or work clothes and women dressed for office work sat on the stools at the narrow counter or waited their turn standing along the plate glass window that looked out onto Third Street and the downtown business district. The clatter of the kitchen and the food being served along the counter mingled with a dozen conversations. Blue smoke curled from cigarettes and cigars, drifting upward in the dull glare from outside.

"I don't like this place. It's too little and too noisy." Jessie picked at her food with a bent fork. "Beans,

beans, and more beans. Who wants nothing but beans?"

Catherine frowned at her eldest child, wishing she would mend her increasingly fractious ways. "You know something, Jessie. It seems to me that the more you have—the more you complain."

"Well, I've got a right to complain," Jessie whined as if to substantiate her mother's comment. "This place is a dump. Why did we have to come here?"

"Because we didn't have time to wait in that long line at the Piccadilly and see the show too," Catherine answered between bites. "Besides, your daddy told me about this place. He says these are the best beans he's ever eaten, and I'm beginning to agree with him after only two bites. I wonder how they make them so rich and smooth tasting?"

"We cook 'em for six hours, that's how." A burly man in a white apron and cap leaned his hairy arm on the counter next to Catherine. The stub of a cigar protruded from between his crooked teeth, and a washtub belly poked at the apron from behind. "I get here at three in the morning, put 'em on at four, and the customers are gobblin' 'em down at ten. My name's Nick." He glanced around the tiny restaurant. "I own the joint. Me and the bank next door."

Startled at first, Catherine was soon reassured by the man's open, honest face and warm smile. She also noticed that he looked and smelled clean enough to perform surgery. "Well, I'd certainly like to know your secret. There must be something more to it than just cooking them for a long time."

"Oh, there is." Nick leaned forward with a conspiratorial smile, whispering, "You got to be born and raised in New Orleans. It's almost like a religion down there."

Appalled at her mother's conversation with the crude-looking stranger, Jessie slipped off her stool. "I'm going to play something on the jukebox, Mama."

"Okay, sugar," Catherine answered, handing her a dime from her purse, then turned back to Nick. "I'm afraid I don't qualify as a bean cooker, then." She took another bite of the beans and rice, nodding her approval.

"You don't even know how to eat 'em." Nick placed a slim bottle on the counter next to her plate. "Louisiana hot sauce. It's against the law down here to eat red beans and rice without it. Well, it oughta be anyway."

"I don't think my taste buds could handle it." Catherine tried to beg off. "I'm not used to hot seasonings."

"This isn't the hot kind—that's Tabasco," Nick explained patiently. "Here—let me start you off right." He unscrewed the cap, dashing a few drops of the red liquid on Catherine's food. "Now, tell me if it isn't better."

Catherine took a tentative bite, chewing it slowly. "Hmmm—it's much better. Really brings out the flavor."

"We'll make a Louisianian out of you yet," Nick declared, "and you'll be eternally grateful."

The sounds of Tex Beneke's orchestra blared from the jukebox, playing the novelty tune "Hey! Ba-Ba-Ba-Re-Bop."

"How do you know I'm not from here?" Catherine grimaced toward the blaring jukebox.

"You got to be kiddin', lady." Nick grinned as he turned toward the kitchen. "Enjoy your food. By the way, that's not such a bad song. Stupid . . . but it's got some life to it."

"Aren't you going to ask me to come back?"

"One plate of ol' Nick's beans and they all come back," he replied, pushing through the double metal doors that led to the kitchen.

"What an awful song," Catherine protested. "Don't they have anything decent on that jukebox?"

"You'll like the next one," Jessie said, climbing back onto her stool. "It's for old fogies."

Catherine placed her fork on her plate, wiping her face with a napkin, and turned to her daughter. "There's something I want to talk to you about, Jessie."

"This sounds serious." Jessie took a big bite of the beans and rice, then glanced around her. "Are you sure this is the right place?"

"No one's paying any attention to us," Catherine assured her. "It's about the hours you've been keeping. It was after eleven o'clock when you got in last night."

"Oh, Mama, I'm not a baby anymore. I'm fourteen years old," Jessie whined. "Besides, a bunch of us just went out together for a Coke."

"Well, I want to know exactly where you're going from now on, and I want you in by ten o'clock at the very latest." Catherine put her hand on Jessie's shoulder. "What would your daddy say? He thinks you're still his little baby girl."

"He wouldn't think *anything*," Jessie almost snapped. "He's never around enough to even know I'm alive."

"Jessie! That's a terrible thing to say about your daddy," Catherine chided. "He's working, putting in all those long hours so we can have nice things and a better place to live."

The wheel of records inside the jukebox spun in a silver blur as the record arm reached up, picked one off, and placed it on the turntable. The sound of Doris

Day's smooth rendition of "Sentimental Journey," backed by Les Brown's band, floated among the heady smells of foods that filled the little restaurant.

"I know it, Mama." Jessie poked at her food with her fork. "Sometimes I just wish things were like they used to be when he was home more."

*Gonna take a sentimental journey, to renew old memories. . . .*

"Well, I've got a big surprise for you that just might cheer you up." Catherine enjoyed the glow that brightened Jessie's face at the sound of her words.

"Don't torture me," she pleaded. "What is it?"

"We may be getting our own home. We won't have to be jammed up in those three little rooms anymore."

"Oh, Mama, that's wonderful!" Jessie almost shouted. "Will I have my own room?"

"You certainly will. The house has four bedrooms and lots of closet space."

"I can't wait! When are we moving?"

"Settle down now," Catherine said. "Nothing's final yet, but that's why your daddy's been working so hard—to get enough money together for the down payment."

"But—where is it?" For years Jessie had wanted to live in a two-story mansion with huge white columns. "Is it out on the lakes by LSU where you've always wanted to go?"

Catherine shook her head. "We don't have that much money, Jessie. Someday maybe, but not now."

"Well, where is it, then?"

"About fifty feet from where we live now."

"The Worthingtons' house?" Jessie's food remained untouched and forgotten. "They're leaving?"

"Uh-huh. He's retiring and they're moving back to

New Jersey. They never liked the South much anyway."

"When are we gonna move?" Jessie's eyes were
bright with excitement. "Will it be before school starts
next year? Can I have new curtains in my room?"

"We don't know yet. Oh, maybe I shouldn't have
told you," Catherine sighed. "It may not even happen."

"But there's a good chance?"

"Yes, there is, and we'll probably know something
in a couple of months."

"Oh, I just can't wait. I'll be able to have friends
over for the night."

"Eat your lunch, Jessie."

"Okay, Mama." Jessie took a big mouthful of the
beans and rice. "Hey, these are good. Why don't you
learn to cook like this?"

"It's a secret recipe."

"Just ask ol' Nick back there," Jessie grinned. "I bet
he'll tell you. I saw him making eyes at you."

★ ★ ★

The trees near the terrace and scattered about the
green, manicured gardens and lawn behind the Governor's Mansion were strung with Japanese lanterns
that would be lighted at dusk. The soft summer air
carried the scent of gardenias and roses and jasmine
as well as honeysuckle blossoms that the governor
himself had ordered brought in from the countryside
north of town. They always reminded him of his
sharecropper's home in the hills of Jackson Parish.

The governor's country music band, minus their
lead singer who had traded his cowboy hat for the
mantle of diplomacy, played a toned-down instru-
mental version of "Nobody's Darling But Mine."

Lane and Catherine stood with Walker Jones and his wife, Aline, in the long reception line that wound along a curving brick path. At its head, beneath a blossoming magnolia tree, Governor Jimmie Davis greeted his guests with his old-fashioned southern hospitality and his newly acquired Hollywood smile.

Aline Jones was short and dumpy with a round, pretty face and short dark hair. In her bright yellow dress she resembled a pansy with thyroid trouble. "Isn't it wonderful that they've made a movie of the governor's life?"

"I think it's great," Walker Jones agreed with a wink at Lane. "He's out in Hollywood so much it doesn't give him time to mess things up in Louisiana like the other governors have."

"Oh, you should be ashamed of yourself, Walker," Catherine chimed in. "I think he's as nice as can be. I certainly never heard anything bad about him."

Jones stared at the governor greeting his line of guests as though he were at a big family reunion. "And you're not likely to either. He's just a good ol' boy who made it big with 'You Are My Sunshine' and used it to ride right on into the Governor's Mansion—and then on out to Hollywood."

"Did he write that song?" Catherine stared with rapt fascination at the governor and the lesser emissaries gathered around him, thrilled at the trappings of power and the glamour of show business.

"He and Charles Mitchell did," Jones continued, reveling in his knowledge of the governor. He considered himself an expert at cocktail party repartee. "Jimmie goes way back in the music business. He sang a lot of blues songs back in the thirties when hardly anyone but Negro artists were doing that."

"Lane's always liked his music," Catherine re-

marked, taking Lane by the arm. "Even before we decided to move to Louisiana. Haven't you, honey?"

Lane felt awkward and out of place, knowing that
he wouldn't have been on the guest list if Jones hadn't
wrangled an invitation for him. "Always have—especially his gospel music. I think that's what he does
best."

Jones had come abreast of the governor and was
shaking his hand. "Governor, you remember my wife,
Aline. And this is Lane Temple and his wife, Catherine."

The governor greeted them warmly, then turned to
Jones. "I hear you and the Pelican Oil Company are
going to make our state rich, Walker."

"We're certainly going to try, Governor," Jones
grinned. "We might just make a few dollars ourselves
too."

"Somehow, I don't doubt that a bit." The governor
glanced at Lane as their party passed by, making way
for other guests, and spoke to him in a tone that
seemed only half in jest. "You're traveling in fast company with Walker there, son. See that you keep your
head about you."

"I will, sir." Lane had been impressed not by the
governor's renown in politics and show business, but
by the fact that he seemed genuine and relatively unaffected by his fame. "I certainly will."

White-jacketed Negro waiters made their way
among the throng. Balancing silver trays laden with
champagne glasses, their skin glistened in the angled
light. Others stood at blue-and-white-striped kiosks
slicing huge baked hams and sides of roast beef for
the guests.

Jones stopped one of the waiters and handed everyone a glass of the pale, bubbly liquid. "Let me propose a quick toast."

"Be sure it *is* quick, darling." Aline glanced at Lane and Catherine. "Sometimes Walker is as long-winded as a Baptist deacon saying grace."

Jones frowned at his wife, then lifted his glass. "Here's to good friends—and the money we're all going to make with the Pelican Oil Company."

Lane and Catherine stared at each other with surprised expressions.

Noticing their faces, Jones explained, "Oh, we're gonna cut you in on some of it, Lane. Daddy believes in rewarding veterans for service to their country. Besides, you're a good lawyer—dependable and discreet."

Lane was grateful for the business Jones had thrown his way, but had never taken seriously his talk of cutting Lane in on the big money deals. He quickly dismissed the statement as political grandstanding. "This monkey suit is choking me to death," he complained to Catherine, tugging at the stiff collar of the rented tuxedo. "And people say *women* are slaves to fashion!"

"I think you look very handsome," Catherine encouraged, knowing how Lane hated formal occasions. "And leave that collar alone. People are beginning to stare."

"Let 'em stare," Lane protested. "I'm gonna loosen this bow tie before I turn blue."

"You go right ahead and do that, Lane," Aline encouraged. "We've already had our time with the governor. It's all downhill from now on anyway."

"Well, what did you think of him?" Catherine helped Lane loosen his collar while trying to keep his tie looking neat.

"Who?"

"The governor, of course."

Lane looked across the grounds at the still-lengthy file of guests in the reception line. "He reminds me of *half* the men I know in Mississippi."

"How many people do you know who sell thousands of their records or have a movie made about their life?"

"I mean, he talks and acts like them," Lane explained. "He's just a country boy who worked hard and made the best of his talent."

Catherine gazed about her at the decision makers and power brokers of Baton Rouge—and the state of Louisiana. "What a lovely party! I'm so glad we came. Aren't you, darling?"

At that moment Jones interrupted their conversation. "Well, look who's coming to see us." He stepped next to Lane, whispering conspiratorially, "Senator Andre Catelon. The governor is the only man in the state with more political power than this guy."

Lane glanced to his right, but the senator never registered in his vision. He saw only the woman walking toward him with an earthy elegance. Her green eyes were like fire and ice in her oval-shaped face. The dark, shoulder-length hair glistened in the pale gold light through the trees, moving softly with the flow of her body—toward him.

"Hello, Senator." Jones greeted the stocky man like an emissary from a new republic. His black hair, flecked with gray, was combed straight back from his low forehead. "Nice to see you again this soon. You too, Bonnie. I'd like ya'll to meet some friends of mine."

Introductions were made all around. When Lane shook hands with Bonnie Catelon, she seemed to let her touch linger for a second too long. He forced himself not to stare at her long eyelashes and full red lips. She in turn let her eyes linger on his rugged, tanned features and lean, athletic body.

Catherine moved closer to Lane, locking her arm inside the crook of his elbow, staring hard at Bonnie Catelon.

Bonnie held her gaze steady, her expression that of a mildly amused house cat.

After a few minutes of small talk, Andre Catelon glanced at his daughter. Catelon had long ago lost control over Bonnie and no longer made any attempt at redirecting her, except when it came to something that would damage his image. Turning to Lane, he said in his best Senate chamber voice, "Walker tells me you're a competent lawyer, Mr. Temple."

"Walker says a lot of things," Lane grinned, finding himself growing warm in the glow of Bonnie Catelon's green eyes. "A few of them he even *thinks* about before he says them. And I wish you'd call me Lane, Senator."

"Okay, Lane." Catelon's face was a swarthy mask full of bright teeth as he smiled only with his mouth. His obsidian eyes remained as remote as Antares at eventide. "Walker and I have a few private enterprises going that may require a good lawyer. Think about doing some work for us, will you? I guarantee the rewards will be worth it."

Lane glanced at Catherine, who had still been watching Bonnie closely until Catelon's last words diverted her attention. Her face brightened as she shifted her gaze to Catelon. "We'll both think about it, Senator."

"Good for you, Mrs. Temple." His expression acknowledged her blond good looks. "I can see your wife has a real instinct for business, Lane. I have this theory that women make all the important decisions anyway."

Lane gazed at his wife as she smiled up at him, her flaxen hair blowing about her face and neck in the afternoon breeze. Beyond her and slightly out of focus, he could see the dark beauty of Bonnie Catelon like a negative image of Catherine. "I suspect you're right about that, Senator."

"Well, we have to be going." Catelon's voice sounded as rich as honey. "Nice meeting you folks."

With one last glance at Lane, Bonnie walked off beside her father, the hem of her black silk dress moving lazily in time with her hips.

The afternoon faded into evening about the rear grounds of the mansion with the tinkling of wine glasses and the drone of a hundred polite conversations. The Japanese lanterns were lighted, spreading a festive glow beneath the trees.

Catherine and Lane found themselves seated at a white wrought iron table in a secluded little nook next to an ivy-covered brick wall. The scent of the gardenia blossoms next to them was intoxicating. Catherine sipped her champagne, content to sit with her husband and watch the privileged and the moneyed few at their leisure.

The country band had been replaced by a four-piece ensemble dressed in formal wear. The vocalist, a slim black man of twenty-five, stepped to the microphone and began to sing "As Time Goes By" in a smooth baritone.

Catherine took a long swallow of champagne. "I saw how that woman looked at you this afternoon, Lane."

Lane remembered the sway of Bonnie Catelon's black silk dress as she moved away in the sun-dappled shade of the giant oaks. "What woman?"

"You know what woman."

"Oh, her." Lane tried to sound flippant but found his voice go husky. "She's nothing compared to you, sweetheart. A mere child."

"She's twenty-two years old and she looks nothing like a child." Catherine found her own voice growing strident and deliberately tried to soften it.

"How in the world did you find out how old she is? You just met her two hours ago." Lane felt that he would never be able to fathom the almost uncanny way Catherine could accomplish things when she put her mind to it.

"Aline told me," Catherine declared. "She also told me the *child* is divorced."

*. . . the fundamental things apply as time goes by. . . .*

Lane took a swallow from his crystal goblet and set it down on the table harder than he had intended. "Catherine, don't make something out of nothing. It's been too good a day. Let's not spoil it now."

"You're right," Catherine smiled, reaching across the table for Lane's hand.

"This is what we've been working so hard for, isn't it?" Lane made a sweeping gesture with his hand. "All this glamour and glitter and—fun."

Catherine thought Lane's voice had a weary, almost hollow quality to it. "You don't sound as if it's what you really want. I thought every man wanted to be a success."

"Every man does, I suppose," Lane admitted, the weariness still in his voice. "What really matters is how he defines success—and what he does to get it."

"Do you think we made a mistake coming down here?" Catherine somehow felt that the happiness of the day was being slowly siphoned away by her husband's words. The balmy June evening suddenly seemed oppressive.

"No. It's not that." Lane stared out into the infinite darkness beyond the trees. "We didn't have much of a future in Sweetwater. But—hey, let's forget about all this nonsense and enjoy the little shindig. How many times are we going to get invited to the Governor's Mansion?"

Catherine's happiness returned at the sound of Lane's voice, cheerful and full of life. "You really think Bonnie Catelon's nothing compared to me?"

Lane squeezed her hand. "That's what I said. You're like Easter morning and she's Halloween."

# PART THREE

# WINTER OF DISCONTENT

# NINE

# GLORY DAYS

★ ★ ★

The smells of wax from the hardwood floor in the corridor and chalk dust from the classrooms; the musty scent of old books that had been left out in the rain by students whose minds were occupied more with the opposite sex than the three *R*'s; the clanging of locker doors and the clamor in the hallway—all these took Catherine back to her own school days. Only her reason for coming to the school spoiled the nostalgia.

Glancing through an open door, Catherine passed a home economics class and saw some of the girls already busily preparing their meals on tiny white enameled gas stoves set into the counters. She remembered when her own high school class had prepared a meal for the football team. Lane had missed the game the following day with a stomach ailment from eating her half-cooked pork chops. *It's a wonder he ever married me after that!*

As Catherine walked on past the orange jack-o-lanterns and the black witches on their broomsticks decorating the walls, she noticed the *Office* sign lettered in black on the frosted glass door and headed for it. The bell rang just as she reached it and, as if by magic, the stragglers in the hallway disappeared into their classrooms. She opened the door, stepped into the office, and walked over to a high counter.

"Yes, ma'am, may I help you?" A girl of about fifteen with shiny blond hair and a starched white blouse walked over from a long table where she had been sorting report cards.

"I have an appointment with Mr. Garrett." Catherine introduced herself, glancing at the varnished oak doors at either end of the long counter. The one to the left was marked *Assistant Principal.* "Would you tell him I'm here, please?"

"Certainly." The girl walked through the door without knocking and came back almost immediately. "He'll see you now, Mrs. Temple."

Catherine clicked across the gray tiled floor in her black pumps, but before she reached the doorway Garrett stepped through to greet her.

"Good morning, Mrs. Temple. Charlie Garrett." Garrett, lean and athletic, stood three inches above six feet tall. His dark brown tweed jacket matched the color of his neatly combed wavy hair. "I'm glad you could come."

Catherine took his extended hand. "Thank you. It's nice of you to take the time."

Garrett motioned her to one of two overstuffed chairs near the left wall of his office. As she sat down, he called out the door, "Cindy, would you bring us some coffee, please?"

While Garrett took his seat, Catherine was staring at the dozen or so football trophies lined up on the window ledge behind his desk. They gleamed in the morning light like a bright reflection of the glory days of their owner. "Looks as if you've had quite a career." As she turned back toward him, he flashed her his best all-American smile, but behind it she thought she saw a wolfish gleam in his brown eyes.

"I was just lucky, I guess," Garrett said, lowering his head momentarily. "I played end at LSU. Made All-American my senior year."

Cindy entered the office without knocking and set the coffee service on the small wooden table between Catherine and Garrett. With a quick smile at Garrett, which he ignored, she left, leaving the door open behind her.

Garrett got up and closed the door, returning to his chair with a slight frown etched on his clean features. "That girl must have been raised in a barn. Sugar or cream?"

"Both, please." Catherine was glad she hadn't asked for tea as she watched Garrett spoon the sugar and pour the cream into the rich dark coffee. The aroma filled the office as he handed her the gold-rimmed cup. It tinkled musically on its saucer as his big hand trembled slightly.

Even though Jessie was stunning with her brown eyes and bright blond hair, Garrett had expected a somewhat dowdy appearing Mississippi hill-wife as her mother and was caught completely off guard by Catherine's fragile beauty. He took in the soft curves of her lavender sweater and the swell of her hips beneath the gray skirt. Noticing that she was becoming uncomfortable under his stare, he cleared his throat and said in his most professional assistant-principal voice, "I think we're going to have a real problem with

Jessie if something isn't done soon. That's why I asked you here."

It was Catherine's turn to be caught off guard. "I— I didn't know it was that serious."

Garrett seemed to realize something all at once. "I thought your husband was coming—"

"He had a jury trial in New Orleans. A very important client," Catherine replied defensively. "He wanted very badly to be here, but you know how judges are. The trial has been postponed once already and he wouldn't tolerate another delay. Lane could have been found in contempt and put in jail if he didn't showed up there today."

Garrett had never heard of an attorney being put in jail for contempt, and postponement was the name of the game for most of them. He had also noticed the new Chrysler when Catherine had driven into the parking lot outside his window. "Your husband makes a lot of money, Mrs. Temple?"

"I don't see where that has anything to do with Jessie's behavior!" Catherine responded, her face flushing slightly under Garrett's steady gaze.

Pinching the bridge of his nose with thumb and forefinger, Garrett stared at Catherine with narrowed eyes. "No—I guess it doesn't."

Catherine was beginning to feel uncomfortable. She shifted in her chair, crossing her legs and smoothing her skirt down over her knees.

Garrett made no effort to hide his interest in the movement as he admired her sheer stockings—the flowing curve of her calf down to her ankle as smooth as water over stone. He stood up to break the distraction, walking over to the window where he stared out at the regal-looking black Chrysler. "Is your husband away from home a lot, Mrs. Temple?"

Catherine was becoming more uneasy. She shifted around in her chair to look back at Garrett. "I thought we came here to talk about Jessie—not my husband."

"That's precisely who I am talking about." Garrett turned around and leaned back against the windowsill, his hands braced on either side of him. His face was shadowed by the light streaming in behind him. "I've been in charge of discipline here at Istrouma for five years, Mrs. Temple. I've never seen a child with behavior problems at school where there wasn't something wrong in the home."

"I can assure you, Mr. Garrett, there's nothing wrong in *our* home!" Catherine's voice was shaky. She took a deep breath, letting it out slowly. "On the contrary, we're doing better now than we ever have. All my children are well provided for."

Garrett pushed off the windowsill, walked over to a picture frame and straightened it. It held a black-and-white print of him catching a pass for the winning touchdown against Ole Miss. "I didn't ask you here to criticize you or your husband, Mrs. Temple. I'm only trying to find out what's bothering Jessie."

"What's she been getting into?"

"Getting *out of* is more like it, I'm afraid. She's cutting classes." With a glance at Catherine's trim ankles, Garrett returned to his chair, sat down, and crossed one long leg over the other. He clasped his hands together in front of his chest, squeezing them together as though he were cracking walnuts.

"How long has she been doing this?"

Taking a pack of Lucky Strikes out of his inside jacket pocket, Garrett tapped one out of the pack and stuck it between his lips. "Mind if I smoke?"

"No."

He lifted a silver lighter from the left front pocket

of the jacket, flipped the lid open, and flicked the lighter into flame. Squinting into the smoke as the tip of the cigarette began to glow red, he put the cigarettes and lighter away and let smoke flow out through both nostrils. "We had a few problems with Jess—Jessie at the end of last year. Nothing serious, so I talked with her a couple of times and thought nothing more about it. Sometimes things like that happen when it gets close to the end of the term."

"But now things are worse?"

"I'm afraid so." Garrett breathed smoke deeply into his lungs and placed the cigarette on the side of a heavy glass ashtray on the table. "She's not only cutting classes, but her grades aren't nearly what she's capable of making."

Catherine sipped the hot, dark coffee, feeling it burn all the way down. "They were all right for the first six weeks."

"Yes, I know. The first month she did fine and that held them up for the first report card. But during this last month they've taken a real nose dive."

"Well, Lane and I will just have to have a little talk with her. I'm sure we can straighten her out."

Garrett leaned over and took a final draw on the cigarette, stubbing it out in the ashtray. "I haven't told you everything yet, Mrs. Temple."

Catherine's blue eyes darkened with concern. She felt as though Garrett were talking about someone else's child and she was only an observer.

Garrett smiled faintly with the corners of his mouth. "Don't look so gloomy, Mrs. Temple. It isn't as bad as all *that*." He waited until Catherine returned his gaze and continued. "Jessie's starting to hang out with Gene Duhon."

Composing herself, Catherine looked above Garrett's head as though someone were standing behind him. "I've never heard her mention him before."

"I didn't think she would," Garrett remarked, "since he's a senior and she's only fourteen years old. But even if he were her age, you wouldn't want her running with him."

"Why not?"

Garrett cleared his throat. "Well, for starters his ol' man's in Angola for armed robbery."

"I thought you said it wasn't all that bad?"

"I did. Gene's not in prison. His daddy is. He's just not the type you'd want your daughter to bring home for supper."

Catherine felt her face becoming flushed with embarrassment. Jessie had always been such a good student before this. "Is he causing Jessie to skip school?"

"He's not exactly twisting her arm. She did it last year before she even knew him. I think she's drawn to him because he's the exact opposite of what I imagine your husband to be—the negative image, you might say, of the kind of boy you'd want Jessie to be friends with."

"Lane will put a quick end to this relationship. You can be sure of that."

"Maybe we should have Jessie come in so the three of us can discuss this," Garrett suggested.

"We can handle our *own* family problems, Mr. Garrett!" Catherine said fervently. "Thank you for bringing this to my attention, though."

"Maybe when your husband has the time, the three of us could get together with Jessie and work these problems out before they get serious."

Catherine placed her coffee cup on the table and rose from the chair. "I really don't think that'll be necessary, Mr. Garrett, but I'll tell Lane of your suggestion."

Garrett felt confused and disappointed at the way the meeting had gone. And he was angry at himself for letting his weakness for attractive women distract him from doing his job. *Well, it's not entirely my fault. She is a real looker!*

Catherine walked past Garrett and out into the lobby of the school office.

Garrett followed after her. Feeling that he had made no progress at all toward helping Jessie get back on the right path, he tried once more. "I'd be more than happy to drop by your home one evening if that would be more convenient for you and your husband, Mrs. Temple."

"That won't be necessary, Mr. Garrett. Nice of you to offer though." Catherine realized that there had been little point to the meeting with Garrett. In fact, their discussion of Jessie had seemed almost academic with no real plan for remedying the problems she had been having at school.

As though he had read Catherine's mind, Garrett remarked, "Well, I guess we didn't do a whole lot for Jessie's situation today, did we? I'll keep working with her though."

Turning around to face Garrett, Catherine noticed Cindy scowling at her from behind the counter. "We appreciate your involvement, Mr. Garrett. But don't concern yourself too much. I'm sure things will work out just fine." She held out her hand to Garrett.

Garrett took Catherine's slim hand in his hard brown one. The touch of her fingertips against his palm caused a constriction to begin in his throat. "Thanks for coming by, anyway, Mrs. Temple," he said, a slight rasp in his voice. "It was real nice meeting you." Garrett gave her his best smile, the one where the corners of his eyes crinkled with boyish charm.

Slightly embarrassed, Catherine pulled her hand away from Garrett's. With no further social amenities, she turned and walked out of the office under the hard stare of the blond girl behind the counter.

★ ★ ★

Jessie sat on the front seat next to Catherine as she left the front of the school, driving down Huron Street past the towering spire of Istrouma Baptist Church to Senic Highway, where she turned right. They passed Granberry's Restaurant and Ben Peabody's Esso Service Station. She read the street signs as she continued north—Ozark, Calumet, Navajo, Wyandotte. *This place should be called The Reservation instead of Istrouma.*

Jessie gazed out the window with a bored expression on her face. She wore a red plaid skirt and a white blouse with a Peter Pan collar. The October light danced in her softly swirling blond hair as she turned to her mother. "Why aren't we going home? Where are the kids?"

Catherine glanced over at her daughter. Her mind had been on the meeting with Charlie Garrett, and in truth more on Charlie Garrett himself. *Oh, every woman likes the attention of an attractive man. There's nothing wrong with that!* "Mrs. LeJeune has the children and we need to have a little talk, young lady!"

Jessie took a deep breath and sighed. She knew that somehow her mother had found out. "I should have known you weren't taking me somewhere just so we could be together. So I cut a few classes. Big deal."

"Yes, it is a *big* deal." Catherine felt anger rising in

her breast and pushed it down. "We're going to discuss this in a civil fashion, Jessie. So none of your smart remarks."

"Yes, ma'am," Jessie muttered to the window.

"I know what!" Catherine brightened. "We'll go to Hopper's and get a malt. Would you like that?"

Jessie turned around as if someone had slammed a door. "No! I—I mean I'm not in the mood for a malt."

Catherine was surprised at her daughter's response. "Well, that's the first time I've ever known you to turn down a Hopper's malt."

Jessie turned and stared out the window.

"Well, *I'd* like one. You can get a Coke or just watch me drink mine."

"I really don't feel like going anywhere, Mama," Jessie almost whined.

"Oh, don't be silly," Catherine scolded. She felt Jessie would be more comfortable in the relaxed atmosphere of the drive-in than in Lane's study, the usual place for disciplining the children. "It'll be a nice place to talk."

Jessie frowned over at her mother as she made a U-turn in the light traffic and headed back to the favorite hangout of most of the local teenagers.

Catherine pulled into Hopper's, stopping the car in front of the plate glass window that fronted on the parking lot. Inside, a dozen or so kids from the high school were seated in booths or along the counter eating hamburgers and french fries, drinking Cokes and malts, and engaging in animated conversations.

In a few seconds, a carhop hurried out a side door toward them. He wore faded jeans and a long-sleeved white shirt, along with a white paper hat that had *Hopper's* lettered in blue along the side. It sat at a rakish angle. A swirl of dark hair, slick with Brilliantine,

166

curled across his forehead. Of medium height and build, he had the exaggerated walk of the male adolescent who believes that other people are as preoccupied with his appearance as he.

"Nice car," the boy said, taking an order pad from his back pocket and a yellow pencil from behind his ear.

Catherine smiled up at him. "I'll have a chocolate malt. Jessie, you sure you don't want one?"

At the sound of Jessie's name, the boy leaned on the door with his elbow and stared into the car, glancing around at the plush leather interior. "Jess! I didn't know your family had *this* kind of money!"

"You know my daughter?" Catherine felt a sinking sensation in the pit of her stomach.

Looking over at her mother, Jessie mumbled, "Mama, this is Gene Duhon."

"Pleased to meet you, ma'am." Duhon stuck his hand through the window, flashing Catherine a smile that reminded her of Charlie Garrett's.

Catherine took Duhon's hand as though she were dropping a dead rodent into a trash can. "Thank you," she said, noncommittally, frowning over at Jessie.

"You didn't tell me you had such a good-looking mama either, Jess," Duhon smirked, winking at Catherine.

"Are you ordering or not, Jessie?" Catherine almost snapped as Jessie stared out the window.

Duhon began scribbling on his note pad. "I'll just bring you the usual, Jess." He glanced again at Catherine. "I sure wish your daughter liked me as much as she does our cherry Cokes. Drinks 'em like the Coca-Cola people was goin' out of business first thing tomorrow morning."

"Is that what you want, Jessie?" Catherine was becoming incensed at the familiar way Duhon was treating them.

Jessie nodded her head slowly.

"I'll put it in a ice cream soda glass for you," Duhon offered. "The way you like 'em." He slipped his pad into his back pocket and swaggered back into the side door of the drive-in.

"So that's the Prince Charming Ch—Mr. Garrett was telling me about," Catherine said huffily.

Jessie stared wide-eyed at her mother. "You talked to Mr. Garrett about Gene?"

"I most certainly did!"

"When?"

"This morning."

"How could you do that?" Jessie's voice was beginning to break. "It's none of your business who my friends are!"

Catherine felt her face grow suddenly warm. Her vision blurred. Before she could stop herself, she slapped Jessie a stinging blow across the face.

Jessie gasped, putting her hand to the red splotch on the her cheek. She stared at Catherine with a look of disbelief. Her blue eyes grew suddenly bright with tears. From the corner of her right eye, a single teardrop slid down her smooth cheek, shining like a clear pearl in the pale afternoon light.

Catherine took Jessie's hand in both of her own. "Oh, Jessie, I'm so sorry."

Jessie looked away from her mother. Through the windshield, she saw Duhon strutting out the side door toward their car. She quickly wiped her eyes and flicked on the radio, turning the dial through static until she found a station. The announcer praised the sponsor in his smooth voice. "Remember, more doctors smoke Camels than any other cigarette."

"Would you roll your window up a little bit, Mrs. Temple?" Duhon stood next to the car, holding a tray with the malt and Coke glasses balanced precariously on its smooth metal surface. The car window slid up two inches. He hooked the tray to the side of the glass, folding out a rubber-tipped brace and adjusting it against the side of the car.

Catherine reached into her purse, took out a dollar bill, and dropped it on the tray. "Keep the change."

"Gee, thanks," Duhon beamed, the grown-up act lost in his little-boy excitement.

Jessie continued to play with the knob on the radio until she heard music. Al Jolsen sang "April Showers" in his grating baritone. "I wish they'd play something decent once in a while—like Frank Sinatra."

"Here, Jessie." Catherine handed Jessie the cherry Coke, taking her malt off the tray at the same time. She kept her gaze on the glass, avoiding the pain she had seen in Jessie's eyes.

Jessie took the heavy glass and held it on the seat next to her stack of textbooks.

Catherine glanced up at Duhon, who was still grinning down at them. "That'll be all, thank you."

"Yes, ma'am. Thanks for the tip. Sometimes I don't make this much the whole shift." He hurried off toward a yellow Ford convertible that was pulling into the front parking lot. It was packed with squealing teenage girls.

Wrapping a napkin around the heavy malt glass that was tall and cold and beaded with moisture, Catherine sipped the rich, thick ice cream mixture. It felt smooth and chocolaty-sweet as it slid down her throat. "I used to think the Sweetwater Drugstore made good malts, but they don't even compare with these. You can have part of mine if you want it, Jessie."

Jessie stared into her Coke glass, then lifted it and took a small sip.

Catherine set the malt back on the tray and turned to her daughter. She had never touched Jessie in anger, except for a few spankings when she was a child, and felt a deep sense of shame and regret for her action. "Jessie," she said softly, "I'm so sorry. I've been kind of—nervous lately."

"It's okay," Jessie mumbled into the Coke glass. The redness of her cheek where Catherine's hand had struck her had begun to fade. "I shouldn't have talked to you like that."

Reaching across the seat, Catherine laid her hand gently on Jessie's. "I was so upset when Mr. Garrett told me about your cutting those classes. And your studies—he said your grades are getting worse, too."

Jessie glanced over at her mother. "I'll do better. You won't tell Daddy about this, will you?"

"I'll have to. He's your father." Catherine was somewhat puzzled at Jessie's fear of Lane finding out as he had seldom had to be very strict with her. "He's got a right to know if you're having problems at school."

"Why? He couldn't care less."

Catherine was caught off guard again. "Jessie! That's a terrible thing to say. Your father loves you dearly."

"How would I know? He's never around." Jessie stared at the ice melting in the Coke.

"It's because he works so hard to make a living for us, honey." Catherine's voice was gentle and calm. "That's his responsibility and he's doing the very best he can. You should be happy to have a father like him."

Jessie's eyes were focused on something beyond the windshield.

Catherine decided to press ahead. "Your daddy's hard work is why we were able to buy the Worthington house. You should be happy now that you've got your own room, plenty of nice clothes—even a record player."

Jessie listened to the muted conversation of the girls in the yellow convertible a few yards away. Interspersed with bursts of laughter, it sounded hollow and pointless, grating on her nerves. The cars were whizzing by out on Senic Highway as the swing shifts headed in to the refinery and the chemical plants, while the day shifts made their way home to wives and children and evening newspapers.

Catherine took a deep breath to steady herself. "Jessie, I don't like this Duhon boy very much. Is he causing you to get into this trouble?"

"There's nothing wrong with Gene!" Jessie's eyes sparked with anger. She glanced out the window where Duhon was carrying a tray heavily laden with glasses over to the yellow convertible. "You know why he's working? He has to help support his mother and his little sister."

"I guess so," Catherine said without thinking. "Since his father's in prison."

Jessie scowled at her mother. "His father's a crook. That doesn't mean Gene is!"

"How does he get out of school?"

"He's a D.E. student."

"What's that?" Phrases like *Dumb and Embittered* flashed through Catherine's mind.

"Distributive Education. He goes to class in the

mornings and works from one to six here at Hopper's."

Catherine realized that the more she spoke harshly of Gene, the harder Jessie would defend him and the closer the bond between the two of them would become. "I guess you're right. He can't help what his father's done."

The words seemed to have a calming effect on Jessie for the moment, and she settled back against the seat, sipping her cherry Coke contentedly.

Catherine took her malt from the tray and drank some. The noise level from the convertible was increasing. As she began to roll up her window to drown it out, the sound of the metal tray chinking on the glass stopped her. Letting her breath out in a sigh, she spoke over the noise. "Jessie, we really need to get together with your father so the three of us can talk about these problems you're having."

"No, Mama! I promise I won't cut any more classes." Jessie turned in the seat, her eyes pleading with Catherine. "I only came over here a few times to see Gene when he took his break. We just sat in a booth and talked. That's all there was to it."

A sense of disloyalty and deception began to work its way around in Catherine's mind, but she pushed it aside. "Well—all right then. But if your grades don't improve or Mr. Garrett has to call me again—you'll be in real trouble."

"Thank you, Mama."

"One more thing." Catherine glanced over at Duhon as he hurried out the side door. "I don't want you seeing that boy again. If nothing else, he's too old for you."

"But—"

"You heard what I said, young lady! It's either this way or I tell your father."

"Can I at least talk to him at school? We only have a few minutes between classes and at recess."

"Well—I guess that's all right." Catherine found herself relenting against her better judgment. "But you need other interests at school, honey. You're much too young to be so interested in this one boy."

"Okay, Mama." Jessie's straw made a slurping sound in the bottom of her glass.

"You ready to go?"

"Yes, ma'am."

Catherine set her unfinished malt back on the tray and blinked the headlights to signal that they were ready to leave.

# TEN

# LAIR OF THE TIGER

★ ★ ★

The Bengal tiger paced ceaselessly back and forth, the muscles in its powerful shoulders and hindquarters rippling smoothly beneath the brownish orange and black-striped coat. As it passed from shadow into light it seemed to blaze with a cold fire. From time to time a deep rumbling growl would begin in its massive chest as it lifted its head, the open mouth white with teeth. Then as if it were no longer worth the effort, the tiger, well fed and pampered and groomed, merely yawned.

"I'll bet you'd rather be sinking your fangs into the neck of a water buffalo than that corn-fed cow meat they give you." On a stone bench in the shadow of a crepe myrtle, Lane sat talking to the tiger.

The restless beast stopped its pacing long enough to stare at Lane with intense yellow eyes, then as though dismissing him as inconsequential, it resumed its tireless patroling of concrete and iron bars.

Lane wore a maroon Ole Miss sweat shirt with the

Ole Miss mascot, Colonel Reb, a caricature of the typical white-moustached Southern Colonel, on the front. White gym shorts, white socks, and the spiked track shoes he was lacing up completed his outfit. "It's a tough world, Mike. Sometimes I feel a lot like I imagine you do. Except instead of iron bars it's courtrooms and legal briefs and monthly bills keeping me trapped."

The great cat, occupied with his own feline fantasies, no longer paid any attention to Lane.

"Well, if this isn't a coincidence!" Bonnie Catelon called out. Dressed in an orange sweat shirt, black shorts, and white tennis shoes, she walked up the sidewalk across from north stadium. "I never expected to see you here!"

Startled by the sudden intrusion in the early morning stillness, Lane glanced in the direction of the voice. Bonnie's long dark hair caught the early light as it moved in time to the rhythm of her gait. Lane felt his breathing become more labored as though he had just finished a warm-up lap around the track. He found himself staring at the pale glow of her skin. Forcing himself to look away, he bent to finish tying his shoe. When Bonnie had reached the bench and stood next to him, he looked up. "Good morning."

"Well, you don't act very happy to see me!" She stood with her hands on her hips and her head tilted to one side. The expression on her face was that of a six-year-old being told to stay out of the cookie jar.

Lane leaned his forearms on his thighs, his hands clasped together. "Just a little surprised, I guess. I didn't take you for the type to run around a track at six o'clock in the morning."

"You never can tell *what* people will do, I always say." Bonnie sat down next to Lane, then turned, placing her feet on the bench and drawing her knees up under her chin.

Lane glanced at her. "That's some outfit. You always wear colors like that to run in?"

"Today's Halloween." Bonnie said it like she was happily looking forward to trick-or-treat that evening.

"So it is," Lane agreed, remembering the children's costumes in the Hebert shopping bags lying on the dining room table when he had left home that morning. "Funny I've never seen you out here before." In the slanting light, he noticed tiny charcoal-colored flecks in Bonnie's green eyes.

"Oh, I've been doing this *ever* so long," Bonnie smiled mischievously. "How about you? Do you drive all the way across town just to run here?"

Lane glanced at her, then gazed studiously through the iron bars. "How do you know where I live?"

Lane saw it was Bonnie's turn to be caught off guard. "Someone told me, I guess. Probably Walker."

"Well, to answer your question, I come out here to run whenever I have business at the courthouse downtown—which is usually two or three days a week." Lane found himself distracted by the scent of Bonnie's perfume and the steady gaze of her green eyes. He momentarily forgot what he was talking about.

After a few moments' pause, Bonnie asked, "Are you all right, Lane?"

"Huh? Oh—yeah." He cleared his throat. "I—uh, know the coach here at LSU. He remembered me from the times we played them in football. Well, anyway he lets me use a locker and the showers here in the north stadium so I can clean up and put my grown-up costume on before I go to court."

"Put on your what?"

"My suit and tie," Lane grinned. "Always reminded me of some kind of costume men wear. Why on earth would men wear a skinny piece of cloth dangling around their necks? And people say *women* are slaves to fashion!"

"I don't think we're slaves to fashion," Bonnie remarked off-handedly. "But I do think we're slaves to men. After a fashion, of course."

"Slaves?"

"Oh, I mean it in the best possible way." She swung her legs off the bench, stretched her arms out with a sigh, and placed her hands on her knees. "I just think a woman is incomplete without a man. Like a station waiting for a train that never comes."

Lane smiled, glancing at her clean profile against the shadows of the crepe myrtles. "That's an interesting analogy. You should have been a poet."

"I was reading a copy of *Modern Woman* the other day," Bonnie explained. "The writer said that we have to realize we're dependent on men to accept ourselves fully as women. She also said that *independent woman* is a contradiction in terms."

"You really believe that?"

Bonnie shrugged and stood up. "Why don't we get some exercise?"

They jogged across the dew-wet grass to the track. After the first lap and a half, Bonnie was gasping for breath even though Lane had deliberately kept their speed down to a snail's pace. Although she was so obviously out of shape, he noticed there was something about the controlled grace of her movement that reminded him of the pacing of the tiger—something that suggested the pent-up energy of a caged predator.

"I'm afraid I've had it!" Bonnie stopped in front of

178

the bleachers, bending from the waist, hands resting on her thighs. "I'll wait here for you while you finish."

Running in place, Lane replied, "There's no need for you to do that. I'm going to finish my two miles. You'll just get bored sitting here."

"No." Bonnie straightened up, gazing coolly into Lane's eyes. "I *certainly* won't be bored."

Lane noticed she was still breathing heavily. "I thought you said you ran a lot?"

Holding his eyes with her own, Bonnie gave him a languid smile. "I lied." She walked off the cinder track and took a seat on the front row of the bleachers.

Feeling almost cramped with the slow pace he had held to with Bonnie, Lane now sped off down the track, hitting his stride in a flowing blend of speed, coordination, and relaxed breathing. He enjoyed the cool morning air against his face, heard the metronomic beating of his track shoes against the cinders, and felt the blood coursing through his veins. Somehow it all brought to mind the matchless precision of the human body—as well as his own achingly clear mortality.

As Lane finished the eighth lap next to the tiger cage, he glanced back over his shoulder where Bonnie sat in the distant stands. Beyond her, west of the Mississippi, dark purple and gray rain clouds were building on the horizon. He almost turned off on the little path that led through the grove of myrtles, but the orange fire of Bonnie's sweat shirt in the morning sunlight seemed to pull him back along the track like a strong current.

As Lane finished his run in front of Bonnie, she came out to greet him like a warrior home from battle. "That was beautiful. I'm sure glad I didn't leave."

"What are you talking about?" Lane breathed

heavily as he walked back and forth, cooling down.

"The way you run," Bonnie replied, her left hand placed gracefully across the base of her throat. "You move like something wild—a deer maybe."

Lane began crossing the infield of the track toward the myrtle grove and the stadium beyond. "Something *wild*, huh? I thought I left all that back in the Corps."

"The Corps?"

"Marines."

"Did you see a lot of action?"

"Some."

"You must have done a lot of running in your time," she said, smoothly changing the subject. She hurried to catch up with him.

"I ran the hundred-yard-dash and the four-forty-relay in college, but only because the coach made me," Lane remarked absently. "I hate running. It's pure pain when you're *out* of shape and boring when you're *in* shape."

"Why do it then?"

"Makes me feel healthier."

When they came to the stone bench, Lane stopped and turned to Bonnie. "Well, I enjoyed your company. Maybe I'll see you again sometime."

"Where are you going now?" Bonnie had a half smile on her face as she gazed up at Lane. Her eyes looked almost luminous in the deep shade.

"I thought I might go down to the Toddle House for a little breakfast after I clean up."

"I've got a better idea."

Lane took a deep breath and sat down on the bench. He had to steel himself before he spoke. "We need to get something straight, Bonnie. You didn't show up here by accident and I'm a married man. If I'm wrong about this, forgive me, but I'd like to know why you're—you're flirting with me."

Bonnie sat down on the bench, staring at her slim ankles. "You're right. I—I just *liked* you for some reason when I met you at the governor's reception that day. I don't understand it, but I just wanted to see you again."

Lane glanced over at her. Something deep inside him said to get up and leave, but his legs suddenly felt heavy, as if they wouldn't support his weight.

"Most of the guys I meet make a pass at me the very first thing." Bonnie now gazed at the tiger as she spoke. It suddenly stopped pacing, its yellow eyes holding hers almost as if he recognized her. Bonnie returned the tiger's stare until it resumed its appointed rounds. "I guess they all think a divorced woman is an easy mark. Anyway, you seemed like someone I'd like to get to know—just as a friend."

"There's nothing wrong with that I suppose." Lane felt the emptiness of the words as he spoke them.

"Good! Then I've got a surprise for you." Bonnie stood up quickly. "I know you'll like it."

Lane relented without any further struggle against that small voice inside of him. *What's the harm?*

★ ★ ★

Built in the 1920s at the southern boundary of the city limits, the Baton Rouge Municipal Dock had been equipped to handle freight from oceangoing vessels, riverboats, and barges. It also dispersed the cargoes between the vessels themselves. The burgeoning river traffic of the country's farthest inland deepwater port brought about by the wartime industrial expansion soon made the docks obsolete. New ones were built and the old one, abandoned to the elements and the lush growth along the riverbank, lapsed into rusty, weathering disrepair.

Lane sat in the passenger seat next to Bonnie as they clattered along the wooden twenty-foot-wide runway in her red MG convertible. The plank-floored runway led from the levee out to the old municipal dock at the river's edge. Tin-roofed with wooden walls, the runway resembled a covered bridge. Windows lined the walls, their glass panes shattered by stones and decorated by the neat round holes of .22 rifle bullets.

"Don't you think it's a little cool for swimming?" Lane still wore his running clothes, Bonnie having promised him she would have him back in time to shower and get downtown.

Bonnie glanced over at him. "What's the matter? Don't you trust my driving?"

Lane found himself fascinated by the patterns of light flashing on Bonnie's hair, swirling about her face and shoulders, as they zipped past the open windows. "I think it's this old building I don't trust."

"Don't worry," Bonnie smiled, "the end will be worth the perils of the journey."

"*Peril* is the word, all right."

Ahead of them the long tunnel brightened as they approached the wide expanse of the dock itself. Suddenly the river appeared just beyond it. Bonnie hit the brakes hard as they sped off the floor of the runway onto the heavy timbers of the dock. The little car skidded across the slick surface with the muted cry of rubber against wood, thumping against a weathered eight-by-twelve that had been bolted to the floor at the very edge of the dock.

"There now—isn't this beautiful?" Bonnie opened her arms as though embracing the scene before them.

Lane stepped quickly and gladly out of the car. His knees felt weak as he stared down at the muddy, roiling water forty feet below the bumper of the MG. "How long have you had this death wish, Bonnie?"

Bonnie clasped the steering wheel with both hands, laughing softly. "It's fun to live out here on the edge, Lane. You ought to try it sometime."

Lane remembered the machine-gun bullets whining around him like angry hornets as he leaped from the landing craft of some nameless South Pacific island and charged through the chest-high surf toward the safety of the palm groves; the final heart-stopping scream of the old sergeant running next to him as he caught a round in the gut and disappeared beneath the waves; the eyes of the young Japanese soldier at the moment the blade of the Samurai sword passed through his neck. With an effort he blocked the memories out. "On the edge, huh?"

"Sure," Bonnie replied, opening the door. "It really gives you an appetite."

"My appetite's fine, thank you."

Bonnie took a wicker basket and a Thermos bottle from behind the seat, walked over to where Lane still stood gazing down at the river, and sat on the smooth surface of the timber. Opening the basket, she spread a red-and-white checkered cloth next to her, placed four sausage biscuits wrapped in wax paper on the cloth, and poured the red plastic Thermos top full of steaming coffee. "This is my favorite spot for breakfast."

Lane nodded in appreciation of the view and sat down across the spread cloth from Bonnie. Below them, wisps of night mist still drifted above the surface of the river. Tugs and barges and deepwater vessels plied the tan current and swung at anchor from the docks. Along the muddy banks, willows moved gently in the morning breeze, their slender leaves flashing green-gold in the morning light. Across the river, dark clouds continued to climb against a pale blue sky as the rain and the cold moved inexorably toward them from the northwest.

"You're not talking?"

Lane took his eyes from the river. "Sorry, I guess I got lost in the view."

Bonnie unwrapped a biscuit, placing it in front of Lane. "I only have the one cup. Hope you don't mind sharing."

"Sharing usually makes things better." Lane picked up the biscuit, taking a bite and chewing it contentedly. "This is good eatin'. Where'd you buy them?"

"I *made* these biscuits from scratch," Bonnie pouted playfully. "What makes you think I had to *buy* them?"

Washing down his food with the hot coffee, Lane spoke between mouthfuls. "You just don't seem like the domestic type—that's all."

After they had finished breakfast, Lane sipped his coffee and watched the river traffic. "Guess I'd better be heading on back. If I don't watch it I'll end up sitting here all day." He screwed the top back on the Thermos bottle and stood up.

Bonnie began cleaning up and placing the breakfast items back in the basket. "How's your law practice going?"

"Can't complain."

Placing the basket behind her seat, she remarked casually, "You do any work for Walker?"

"Not much. Why do you ask?"

"Oh, just curious I guess." Bonnie walked around

the car, leaning back against it, her hands resting on the fender above the front wheel well. "He and daddy are working on a big oil deal. State leases in the Atchafalaya Basin, I believe."

"Sounds like the stakes are too high for me."

Bonnie pushed off the fender and stood close to Lane, letting the back of her hand brush fleetingly against his leg. "Not necessarily."

Lane felt a watery sensation in his knees as his pulse quickened. Gazing down into her upturned face, he saw her full lips part slightly. Suddenly he felt the warmth of her body pressing against him, her arms around his waist. He let his fingertips trail along the silky skin of her cheek as he bent down to her.

Bonnie stood on tiptoe, closing her eyes. Lane's lips touched her own, gentle at first, then demanding as he pulled her even closer. She returned the passion and power of his kiss. Finally she drew away, her face flushed, her breath hoarse in her throat.

Lane released her, turning quickly and walking over to the edge of the dock where he stared down at the eddies next to the willows. "I'm sorry, Bonnie. I've never done that before—not ever since I got married."

"No—the whole thing was my fault." He heard her take a deep breath, letting it out slowly. "Can we still be friends? I like you so much, Lane."

A cottonmouth, drawn by the warmth of the mild autumn morning, slithered along the bank below toward a frog perched motionless on a sun-bleached piece of driftwood. As it moved silently behind its victim, the snake lifted its spade-shaped head above the coiled body. Its strike was a blur of motion far too quick for the eye to follow. The frog seemed to simply disappear from the smooth pale surface of the driftwood.

Watching the snake down through the willow limbs, Lane felt a chill at the back of his neck. "I don't know, Bonnie. I don't think we *can* be just friends."

Lane barely heard the brush of Bonnie's shoes against the wooden floor of the dock as she moved up behind him—felt a sudden warmth on his waist as she slipped her hands beneath his damp sweat shirt.

"Maybe you're right, Lane." Bonnie whispered, her voice soft as the last pale mist blowing across the water. "Maybe we can't be—just friends."

★ ★ ★

Catherine loved the musical sound her backyard fountain made as the water flowed down from one sculptured tier to the other. A warbler sang high above her in the crown of the giant live oak where the sunlight seemed to drift like pale yellow smoke as it shattered against the leaves. She smelled the fragrance of jasmine and the sweet olive tree she planted while they still lived in the garage apartment. Halloween morning, bright and mild and filled with music, seemed to her a presage of better days ahead for her and her family.

Setting the wicker clothes basket on the grass, Catherine began hanging out the clothes. She took wooden clothespins from the apron tied around her waist, held them between her teeth while she shook out the clothes and draped them on the line, then pinned them in place.

When Catherine was halfway finished with the clothes, she glanced toward the west, noticing the solid wall of clouds moving in on the city. *Oh, darn! Another front coming! Well, I'll just have to take them all down and hang them in the garage. If they can make*

*washing machines, it seems like somebody would make
a clothes dryer for the home.*

After she had hung the clothes in the garage, Catherine carried her basket along the brick walkway that led from the fountain to the wide back gallery. The first heavy raindrop struck her on the cheek just below the left eye. Then a sudden burst of rain clattered across the roof of the gallery like a shower of small stones, stopping as quickly as it had begun.

Climbing the wooden steps, Catherine placed the basket inside the utility room where the washing machine still churned away and went over to the back door that led into the kitchen. The doorknob resisted her attempts to turn it. Peering through the half-glass door, she saw Cassidy dragging a heavy chrome chair from the kitchen table across the linoleum floor.

"Cassidy!"

Cassidy glanced over his shoulder at his mother, but continued on with the chair.

"Cassidy! Cassidy—you come over here this instant and open this door!"

In the shadowy kitchen, Cassidy positioned the chair directly in front of the white enameled stove. Reaching up, he turned on the two burners on the left, then walked around the chair and turned on the other two. The blue circles of flame seemed to excite him. He clapped his hands as he stared at them.

"Cassidy! Leave that stove alone!" Catherine felt herself rushing toward panic.

Hearing his mother's voice, Cassidy turned around and stared at Catherine as though he were seeing her for the first time. He slowly shook his head.

Catherine watched in horror as Cassidy climbed up on the chair, stood for a moment, getting his balance, and crawled onto the center portion of the stove. Between the four circles of fire, he turned around, sitting with his legs crossed.

Struggling briefly with the door again, Catherine leaped down the back steps and ran around the side of the house to the front porch. The rain had begun in earnest now, making a hissing sound in the leaves of the trees. She ignored the front steps, jumping onto the side of the porch and running over to the front door. The locked door seemed to hold her out of the house like a living thing as she twisted frantically at the knob.

Retracing her steps, Catherine ran inside the utility room, grabbed a claw hammer hanging from a nail on the wall, and rushed over to the kitchen door. Just as she drew the the hammer back to break the glass, the door swung slowly open. Cassidy stepped out onto the porch, the teddy bears on his flannel pajamas smiling brightly. Wide-eyed, Cassidy appeared to be thorougly enjoying the whole episode.

Catherine dropped the hammer. It banged against the pine floor of the porch, one claw chipping out a piece of gray enamel paint as it hit. "Oh, Cassidy! Thank God you're safe!" Catherine lifted him in her arms, hugging him tightly to her.

"It's all right, Mama," Cassidy reassurred her in a calm voice. "I was just playing fireman."

Holding Cassidy in her arms, Catherine walked over to the swing suspended from the high ceiling at the end of the porch. She sat down just as her strength seemed to leave her. Slowly she began to swing back and forth. The sound of the rain pelting on an over-turned flowerpot beneath the overhang began to lull Catherine into a dreamlike state.

"What's wrong, Mama?" Cassidy squirmed in Catherine's arms, trying to see her face.

Making no reply, Catherine held her son close. She felt him relax and lay his head against her shoulder. Soon he was motionless but for the rise and fall of his chest, his breath soft against her neck as he fell into the easy sleep of the very young.

# ELEVEN

# I HEAR HER CRYING

★ ★ ★

"I'm so glad you could come, Mama." Catherine
sat with her mother in the living room of the Temples'
new home on Evangeline Street. The two women occupied the big tapestry-patterned Queen Anne chairs
next to the space heater. It hissed with blue and yellow
flames as it fought against the January chill seeping
into the room. Through the diaphanous curtains, the
azalea bushes lining the front walk trembled in the
blustery wind. Catherine pulled her rose-colored
cashmere sweater closer about her shoulders. "I just
didn't know what else to do so I picked up the phone
and called. I don't mean to bother you. "

Kate Taylor, dressed in her dark brown skirt and
jacket, looked as though she were on her way to teach
her English class. Her hair was almost entirely gray
now with only a few scattered flaxen streaks remain-
ing. She sipped her tea from one of the porcelain cups
that Catherine had treasured dearly over the years.

"Nonsense! You're my daughter. You could never be a bother to me."

Catherine smiled, letting her breath out slowly. She felt so much better now that her mother was with her. She thought of the times she would awaken so frightened in the night after her daddy had died and Kate would appear almost as if by magic at her bedside. This feeling was almost as she felt back then.

"That business about Cassidy and the kitchen stove disturbs me, though." Kate clinked her cup into the saucer next to her on a round wooden table. "I know the boy's rambunctious, but I never thought he'd do something like that."

"That's not all." Catherine balanced her cup and saucer carefully in her lap. "Not long after that we found him down at Mrs. LeJeune's at one o'clock in the morning."

"How in the world did that happen?"

Catherine shook her head slowly. "He just got up and left the house after we were all asleep. Mrs. LeJeune heard him knocking on the door and telephoned us after she let him in."

Kate remembered Cassidy as an infant, radiant as a cherub lying in his crib when she and Catherine brought him home from the hospital. Anxiety about her favorite grandchild's behavior began to toy with her like a cat with a wounded bird. "How did he manage to get out of the house?"

"It's amazing what he can do when he sets his mind to it, Mama." Catherine listened to the wind moaning outside the window. "He almost always finds the key no matter how hard we try to hide it from him. It's gotten to the point where I can't go to sleep until I make sure he has."

"I don't understand why he would go down to Mrs. LeJeune's in the first place."

Her eyes narrowed in thought, Catherine spoke with hesitation, as though she was choosing every word carefully. "Well, he likes her a lot and she just loves him to death. Maybe he thought she'd play with him or something."

"Is this the lady who baby-sits for him?" Kate felt she was beginning to understand the source of some of her daughter's problems already.

"Yes. She's a real jewel." Catherine stood up, placed her tea on the table, and walked over to the bank of tall windows that looked out on the front yard. "I don't know what I'd have done without Mrs. LeJeune."

Rising from her chair, Kate picked up her cup and saucer and walked across the thick burgundy-colored Persian rug covering the center of the floor. "Why don't we go in the kitchen? I think it's a little warmer in there."

Catherine left the living room, following her mother down the long dim hall that led to the kitchen. Gray light filtering through the tall windows behind her gleamed dully on the oak floors. The sound of her heels against the hard wood sounded hollow and lonely. It reminded her of the feeling that had come to her for weeks now when she awakened alone in her bed with no one to talk to in those stale hours before dawn.

Kate took a potholder from a rack next to the stove and opened the oven, pulling out the metal shelf. "Hmmm, that's surely going to taste good tonight," she remarked, admiring the brown flaky crust of the blackberry pie. She shoved it back into the oven and closed the door. "Ten more minutes and it'll be perfect."

Catherine set her cup on the kitchen table. "Maybe I'd better check on Cass." Walking back down the hall, she climbed the stairs, returning in a few seconds.

"How's my baby?"

"Fine," Catherine smiled weakly. "He looks like such an angel when he's asleep."

Kate sat down at the table, gazing about her at the spacious high-ceilinged kitchen. "You've really got a beautiful home here, Cath. You're a fortunate woman."

"Yes, I realize that." Catherine sat down across from her mother.

"Well—do you want to tell me about Jessie?"

"Might as well."

Kate was surprised at the leaden quality of Catherine's voice. "Surely you're not having any *serious* problems with Jess. She was always such a *good* girl. My, what a *sweet* voice that child has! I could listen to her for hours."

"Mrs. Price, the sponsor of the Glee Club at school, says Jessie's got more talent than anyone she's ever worked with before." Catherine glanced up at Kate, then quickly back down at her cup of tea. "If she doesn't pull her grades up though, she's not going to be able to stay in."

Kate was shocked at the news as she had always known Jessie to be an above-average student. She decided that she had asked enough questions though, and would let Catherine speak whatever was on her mind.

"Jessie's started seeing a boy named Gene Duhon. He's a senior and works half a day through a school program." Catherine got up and took her cup and saucer over to the sink. "She's cutting classes in the afternoon to go see him. The assistant principal's trying to help with her, but he's not having much luck. She was hardly ever home during the Christmas holidays. I don't even know where she was half the time."

Kate went over and stood by her daughter, putting her arm around her shoulder. "What's happening to your family, Catherine? You didn't have much money in Sweetwater, but you never had these kinds of problems."

"Oh, Mama, I don't know!" Catherine had felt almost helpless these past few months to do anything about Jessie's and Cassidy's behavior. Each time she tried it seemed things only got worse. Looming even darker in her life was her deteriorating relationship with Lane. He was becoming more and more remote—spending more and more time away from home. She couldn't bring herself to tell her mother about this, even though it was like carrying a stone around in the pit of her stomach.

The months of daytime frustration and the lonely endless nights worked their toll on her. "I just don't know what to do anymore. I just don't know." Suddenly her eyes filled with tears that flowed down her cheeks as she broke into an uncontrollable sobbing.

"There, there." Kate put her arms gently around her daughter, holding her close as Catherine sobbed out her grief against her mother's breast. "You just go ahead and have a good cry. It's going to be all right though. Just wait and see."

Kate held Catherine in her arms for a very long time, rubbing her back gently, stroking her hair, and speaking softly to her as if she were a child. She thought of the times Catherine had skinned her knees or had a fight with a playmate and had come running to her in tears. Then she could always ease her pain with a little peroxide and a Band-Aid, a few encouraging words, or some cookies and milk. *If things were only that simple now. We'll get you through it somehow, Catherine. I promise.*

★ ★ ★

"Come on down. It's time to eat." Kate stood near the foot of the stairs calling up to her grandchildren.

A door slammed. The rapid thudding of small feet on the upstairs hallway ended as Cassidy scampered around the railing at the top of the stairwell and stared down at his grandmother. He wore his Gene Autry cowboy shirt with fringe across the chest and along the sleeves. "I'm first!" he yelled, leaping onto the stairs without holding to the rail. Halfway down he stumbled, bounced on a carpeted step, and tumbled to the bottom.

"Oh, my goodness!" Kate rushed over to Cassidy, kneeling down beside him. "Are you hurt, baby?"

Cassidy rolled over and sat up, grinning at her. "I bumped my booty."

"You little rascal." Kate brushed the fine blond locks back from his forehead, taking his face in both hands. "You nearly scared me to death."

"I don't hardly ever get hurted, Gramma." Cass sprang to his feet. "I'm hungry. Did you make a pie?"

"I most certainly did!" Kate answered, happy that she could make Cassidy's face light up with joy. "And it's you and your daddy's favorite kind too."

"Blackberry!" Cassidy sped off down the hall without another word.

Dalton came down next in his jeans and high-topped black P.F. Flyer tennis shoes.

"Did you wash your hands, honey?" Kate never

failed to notice how much Dalton favored Lane.

"Yes, ma'am."

"Well, take off that football helmet before you sit down at the table."

"Yes, ma'am."

Kate watched her youngest granddaughter feel her way down the stairs with one hand trailing along the banister. "Sharon, you'll fall and hurt yourself if you don't get your head out of that book. I declare I don't believe I've ever seen a second grader read as much as you do."

Sharon smiled over her copy of *Treasure Island*. "I wish *everything* was like it is in books."

*Introspective*. The word always came to mind when Kate first saw Sharon peering through her small gold-rimmed glasses behind the cover of a book, lost in the wonders of literature. "Do you understand that book, sweetheart?"

Her blue eyes wide behind her glasses, Sharon nodded her head. "Well, most of it—I think."

Kate kissed her on the forehead. "You stay with your books, precious. You'll be the smartest one of us all."

"Jessie! Oh, Jess!" Kate had heard no sound of her oldest grandchild moving about upstairs. "It's time to come down for supper."

"Sometimes she's like that, Mama." Catherine appeared in the doorway at the opposite end of the hall. "Just leave her alone. I'll take something up to her later."

Kate hesitated for a moment, then started up the stairs. "No, y'all go ahead and start. We'll be down directly."

Kate stopped outside Jessie's door, tapping softly on it with her open hand. "Jessie—it's Gramma. We've got a nice supper waiting downstairs."

"I'm not hungry, Gramma."

"May I come in for a minute."

After a few moments of silence, the voice from behind the door held a tone of resignation. "Well—okay."

Kate entered the room, seeing Jessie sprawled on her bed, several copies of *Photoplay* and *Modern Romance* magazines scattered around her. She wore jeans, white socks, and what looked like one of Lane's old white dress shirts with the long tails hanging out. The shirt was wrinkled as if it had been slept in for several nights. Even without being brushed after she had washed it, her thick blond hair, hanging in a pleasant disarray about her shoulders, gleamed in the light filtering though a frilly pink lampshade.

Pinned on the wall above Jessie's white scrolled headboard were color photographs of movie stars torn from her assortment of magazines: Clark Gable, Elizabeth Taylor, Gregory Peck, and Betty Grable, as well as others smiled and pouted and preened for their unseen and unknown fans. Soft music drifted from the little white plastic radio on the night table.

With Jessie studying her magazine, Kate sat down next to the bed in a chair with a pink satin cover and a heart-shaped back. "Are you feeling all right, Jess?"

"Sure."

"Jessie, why don't you put your magazine away for a little while?"

Closing the magazine, Jessie sighed and turned over on her back, staring at the ceiling.

"I love you very much, Jessie," Kate said maternally. "Do you know that?"

Jessie remained silent for a few seconds. A single tear ran down the side of her face, making a damp spot on the white pillowcase where it fell. "Yes, ma'am. I know you do."

Kate placed her hand palm up on the chenille bedspread. "I know you've been upset lately and I just thought you might want somebody to talk to."

"I don't know what to say, Gramma. I just seem so mixed up about everything."

"Well, I wouldn't worry about it too much." Kate felt Jessie take her hand and grip it firmly. "We all get mixed up at one time or another, baby—even old people like me."

Jessie sat up, facing Kate, and crossed her legs. "You're not old, Gramma. And you're as pretty as anybody I know."

Kate smiled, happy to see that Jessie's heart was still as tender as it had always been. "Sometimes if we talk about things that bother us—it helps."

Jessie, her brown eyes filled with bewilderment, stared directly at Kate. "Something's happened to our family. We're just not like we used to be before we moved down here."

Kate nodded her head as if saying that she understood and for Jessie to continue.

"Mama and Daddy are so busy all the time and— it just looks like everybody's going off in a different direction. Mama's always out shopping or eating lunch with one of her friends or just riding around town in her big car. I usually stay here with Dalton, but I think Cassidy spends more time with Mrs. Le-Jeune than his own family."

Jessie bowed her head, rubbing the back of her neck with her right hand. As she looked up, her face seemed to darken. "Daddy's hardly ever home anymore, and when he is, it seems like he's usually sleeping. Mama says he's working all the time, but I don't think that's it. Sometimes late at night I hear her crying."

"Daddies have to put in long hours sometimes to take care of their families, honey. Maybe it's as hard on Lane as it is you and your mama."

For a moment Jessie's eyes flashed with a cold anger. "I don't think what he's doing is a *bit* hard on him."

Kate sensed that the conversation was leading toward something that she could never discuss with Jessie. "Do y'all still go to church, Jess?"

Jessie shook her head, her lips pressed together in a thin, pale line. "Not anymore. We did when we first moved here; then it was less and less until we just quit going. Mama dropped us off at Sunday school for a while, but we finally stopped that too. None of us wanted to be there when everybody else had their mamas and daddies with them."

Trying to cheer Jessie up, Kate asked with a note of enthusiasm in her voice, "I hear you've got a boyfriend. Is he good-looking?"

"Mama told you," Jessie frowned.

Kate determined that she would not sit in judgment on Jessie. She felt that there were others who were already spending inordinate amounts of their time filling that role. "Oh, you just wipe that frown off your face this minute," she went on good-naturedly. "Girls have been having boyfriends ever since Eve made her first swimsuit out of fig leaves."

Jessie smiled, then broke into soft laughter. "I bet she didn't go in the water with it on."

"She probably didn't," Kate agreed.

"Gene's a nice boy, Gramma." For the first time in a long, long while Jessie felt she could relax and talk to someone about the things that were important to her. "He's had a pretty hard life with his daddy in prison and everything, but he works every day after school and on weekends to help his mama pay the rent and buy food and clothes for him and his little brother. And he's got the cutest smile; and when he combs his hair just right, he looks a little bit like Robert Mitchum. *I* think he does anyway."

*A rose must remain. . . .*

As the song began on the radio Jessie recognized "To Each His Own" with the first few words that were sung. "Oh, listen—that's our song. Isn't it beautiful?"

"It sure is, honey."

Jessie paused long enough in her youthful infatuation to catch her breath. "I know I shouldn't skip class to go see him, but it's the only time we can get together, and all we do when I get there is sit in a booth and drink a cherry Coke when he gets a fifteen-minute break."

From her bedside chair, Kate smiled and nodded and listened while Jessie poured out the things that had been pent up inside her for such a long time.

★  ★  ★

With a sharp blast from its whistle, the ferry shuddered away from its dock on the Baton Rouge side of the river. Across the mile-wide expanse of muddy water, the little town of Port Allen nestled behind the grassy rise of the levee.

Catherine grabbed the iron rail to keep her balance as the ferry jerked forward. "I sure wish you didn't have to go *back* in the morning, Mama."

"Well, I reckon I'm getting old and set in my ways," Kate smiled, squinting into the bright January morning. "When you get to be my age you like to sleep in your own bed."

"Fifty-four's not old. Besides, you look ten years younger than your age."

"It's nice out here. I'm glad you suggested this little ferry ride." Kate held on to the rail of the upstairs deck, gazing out over the river toward the towering superstructure of the bridge four miles upriver. "I've certainly enjoyed seeing you and the children, Catherine."

"They all love you so much." Catherine glanced over at her mother as if seeing a part of her for the first time. "I guess I had forgotten just *how* much till they were apart from you for these past few months."

"I'm still kind of worried about Jessie. She seems so—so *restless* all the time."

"Fourteen's just a hard age to be," Catherine remarked. "I can remember some bad days myself."

"I'm afraid it goes deeper than that."

"You've really been good for her, though," Catherine assured Kate. "I can see the change in her already."

During her brief visit, it had become obvious to Kate that Catherine wasn't spending enough time with her children, but she had always made it a point not to interfere in her daughter's life since she got married and had her own family. She agonized over what she should do, knowing that she couldn't just leave things the way they were without at least trying to help. It was also readily apparent that Catherine's sense of values had been drastically undermined and that she needed some kind of guidance to get her back on the right path.

Kate glanced over at Catherine, who was staring upriver at the tall brick smokestack of the Poplar Grove sugar mill, cold and lifeless now that grinding season was over. She wore the brown leather jacket

Lane had given her that first Christmas after he came home from the war.

Kate thought how much Catherine still looked like the child she had been at twelve or fifteen, even though she was now almost thirty-three years old. *Sometimes I think she's still that age emotionally. Maybe I indulged her too much after her daddy died.* Pulling her navy topcoat about her, she shivered slightly and said, "Let's go inside and get some coffee. This wind's getting a little chilly."

They walked across the open deck, entering the little glassed-in coffee shop. Kate sat down at a small round table with a black formica top while Catherine brought them two cups of stale coffee in paper cups. The steady droning of the huge diesels acted as background for the tinny-sounding radio on a shelf welded to the gray metal bulkhead.

As she sat down, Catherine saw the owner of the snack bar peering at them through his dark glasses. He wore khakis and a green plaid shirt with a string tie. His dress and weathered face gave him the appearance of an aging cowboy. When he smiled at her, she looked away and he returned to browsing through the *Morning Advocate* while he sang along with Jimmie Davis on the radio. "And promise me that you will never be nobody's darling but mine."

Mother and daughter lapsed into an uneasy silence. Kate knew that Catherine and Lane were having serious problems, although it was never mentioned. She also realized that Catherine was at a loss as to what to do about it and could almost feel the burden her daughter carried. As sometimes happens when two people are close emotionally, Kate found that she didn't have to broach the subject herself.

"I—I'm sorry," Catherine hesitated, "that Lane

wasn't home more. I know that the two of you have always enjoyed your long conversations." She sipped the coffee and made a face, shoving it away from her.

"He didn't even come home two nights." Kate regretted the words, spoken from what had been at the back of her mind since the first night Lane didn't show up at all.

"Uh—a friend of his has a great law library in his office downtown near the courthouse." Catherine felt the hollow ring of the words as she spoke them. "Sometimes if he doesn't finish until late, he just stays over. There's a little sleeping area with a half bath and a cot."

"People change." Kate couldn't conceal the disappointment in her voice. "Lane always put his family ahead of everything—even his work. He seems so much different now than I've ever known him—almost like another person."

Catherine quickly wiped at the corner of her eye.

Kate reached across the table, placing her hand on top of Catherine's. "You know I've never interfered in your life, Cath, but there's something I feel I just have to talk to you about. I hope you won't get angry with me."

Catherine shook her head slowly and almost whispered, "I won't."

"You're putting too much stock in *things*—a fine home, expensive clothes, a big shiny car." Kate took a deep breath and continued. "There's nothing wrong with having nice things, but they won't satisfy you by themselves."

Catherine glanced at the man behind the counter, as though making sure he wasn't listening.

Kate continued, the drone of the diesels steady behind her voice. "When I was a little girl, my granddaddy told me something that I've never forgotten. We were sitting out on the back porch on a fine summer evening with fireflies dancing out in the woods. He said, 'Katie, God made us in a very special way. Our souls are so big only He can fill them up.'"

Suddenly Catherine's eyes sparked. She snatched her hand away. "I don't need to be *preached* to, Mama."

Kate's blue eyes softened as she almost felt the agony in her daughter's own soul. "I know that, darling. I just want so much for you to be happy."

At the sound of her mother's soft reply, Catherine's anger began to fade.

"I blame myself for what you're going through. I spent so much of *my* time making a living for us that I neglected the most important responsibility a parent has—the spiritual life of their children. I guess I thought taking you to church and Sunday school was enough." Kate felt an aching inside that caught at her breath. "I left your soul in the hands of other people. I never should have done that."

"You were the best mother any girl could ask for." Catherine's voice broke slightly as she spoke.

Looking steadily into Catherine's eyes, Kate asked somberly, "Is your life right with God, Catherine?"

"Mama, let's not talk religion."

"I'm not talking religion," Kate continued. "What I'm talking about is knowing the peace of God that only comes through His Son. All these *things* you have won't make you happy."

"Isn't that kind of old-fashioned, Mama? I've met a lot of educated people down here." Catherine felt the emptiness of her words, but continued as though compelled to do so. "They go to church sometimes, but they don't think it's important to believe *every-thing* that's in the Bible."

Kate felt a deep anger kindling in her breast, but fought against it for Catherine's sake. She spoke deliberately in a steady, even voice. "The apostle Paul was one of the most intelligent and well-educated men of his time. Would you like to know what *he* had to say about this 'old-fashioned' belief?"

Catherine stared at the table.

"He said, 'For I determined not to know any thing among you, save Jesus Christ, and him crucified.'" Kate had regained her composure by now. "He said that he wasn't sent to preach the gospel with man's wisdom because it would make the cross of Christ 'of none effect.'"

"I never heard you talk like this before, Mama. When did you learn so much about the Bible?"

"Since y'all moved down here, I've had a lot of free time." Kate's eyes were shining with a light Catherine had never seen before. "I started reading the Bible and discovered a miraculous truth."

"What truth?"

"That *every* single word in it is true. That the *only* answer to all our troubles—to everything that *any* human being ever needs rests in what Jesus did for us on Calvary." Kate closed her eyes for a moment, her face radiant in the shadowy coffee shop. "I always believed what was in the Bible, but now it's so—real. Sometimes I think it's more real than this ol' world I'm living in. Jesus is the best friend you could have, Catherine—including your mother."

The man in the dark glasses took them off and stared at Kate across the top of his newspaper. "Are you one of them lady preachers?"

Kate turned her head slowly toward the man, her

eyes leveled directly at his. "No! But I *am* a lady—and I'm *not* in the habit of talking to *strange* men."

A look of chagrin on his face, the man put his glasses back on and returned to his newspaper.

Catherine smiled with the corners of her mouth, remembering other times when her mother had set men straight. She never remembered her being intimidated by anyone.

Kate patted Catherine's hand gently. "I want nothing but the best for you, Cath. Maybe I'm just foolish—a meddling old woman—but you and my grandbabies—and Lane too—mean more to me than *anything* in this world."

"I know that, Mama." Catherine squeezed her mother's hand. "I'm sorry I got so upset."

Kate held her hand, letting her talk.

"It's just that—" Catherine glanced at the man behind the counter again, seeing that he was buried in the newspaper, and went on. "That Lane and I . . ."

"I understand." Kate thought of the hours she would be kneeling by the side of her bed in prayer for Catherine and Lane—and for her grandchildren who were caught up in their parents' problems. "All married couples go through these hard times. It took me a long time to realize that Jesus is the only thing that works. Don't make that mistake with your life."

The ferry jarred into the dock on the west bank of the river. Catherine and Kate left the little coffee shop to stand on the upper deck, watching the cars below clatter across the ferry's lowered ramp onto the dusty oyster-shell drive that led over the river to Port Allen.

Another line of cars, their drivers at the wheels, led along the right side of the drive waiting to board. After they were all loaded, the big diesels drummed with power, sending a shudder through the ferry as it pulled away from the landing.

Churning back across the Mississippi to Baton Rouge, Catherine and Kate talked of old times when Catherine's father was alive. She remembered when the three of them had gone to the state fair in Jackson and the vivid image of the view from the top of the ferris wheel.

As they approached the landing Catherine glanced to the left. Parked in the lot outside the Pentagon Barracks was a '39 Ford that was a dead ringer for Lane's. At first she was puzzled that his car would be there at this time of the morning with the legislature not in session.

Catherine's thoughts followed the pattern of the past three years. *Maybe he's got some important politician for a client. That sure would be good for us.*

"You see something interesting?" Kate squinted in the direction Catherine was looking.

"I think it's Lane's car. At least I hope it is. Could mean he's got an important client. Maybe things are starting to get better for us."

# TWELVE

# Silk

★ ★ ★

Built in 1822, the Pentagon Barracks over the years have housed such figures as Generals Lee, Grant, and Custer, as well as Jefferson Davis, the president of the Confederacy.

This sturdy yet elegant group of four brick buildings with Doric columns and upper and lower galleries is arranged as a pentagon with the fifth side open to the river. Initially they were used as U.S. Army barracks, but from 1886 until 1925 they served as dormitories for LSU cadets. Located in the shadow of the Capitol building, they were later remodeled as apartments for out-of-town legislators.

"Want some coffee?"

Lane heard the question from beneath the pillow.

"Wake up and get some of this inside you, sleepyhead." Bonnie smiled at Lane as he lifted his head to stare at her. "It'll put hair on your chest."

"I'm not sure I want any hair on my chest," Lane muttered, turning over and raising up on one elbow.

His hair was sleep-rumpled, the side of his face creased from the wrinkled bedclothes. "That's a sign of puberty and I'm a little old for pimples and a voice that cracks every ten minutes."

"That didn't make a bit of sense." Bonnie handed him the coffee. "Here, drink some of this. It might get your heart pumping some blood up to your brain."

Lane smiled, lifting the cup to his lips. "Hmmm, you sure make good coffee. If you weren't so ugly, I might consider taking you out in public sometime."

"I hope you don't think I'd actually consent to go." Bonnie tossed her head haughtily, her hair moving like a soft dark cloud about her face. "Not with a semi-literate, white-trash redneck like you. What would my friends think?"

"That a wallflower like you was lucky to have a date at all," Lane deadpanned, savoring the coffee.

Bonnie laughed softly. "What did I ever do with myself before you forced your way into my life?"

"Beats me. Played solitaire—ate bon-bons and listened to soap operas on the radio?" Lane knew she liked their verbal jousting matches.

"Do you have to wear that ugly green monstrosity?" She frowned at Lane's marine issue undershirt. "It looks like something you dug out of a Salvation Army box."

"How'd you guess?" Lane replied with a straight face. "I always like to get there early—be first in line. The best things go so fast, you know."

Lane finished his coffee, swinging his legs over the side of the bed. He rested his elbows on both knees, bent forward, and rubbed his face with both hands. *Listen to me talk, will you? I make about as much sense as Donald Duck. All this stupid talk to try to cover up how bad I feel every time I do this. But not bad enough to quit, huh, Lane? I've got to stop now. Bonnie's a nice girl, and a married man with four kids is the last thing she needs in her life. This is it! The very last time.*

As though she could read Lane's thoughts, Bonnie slid off the bed next to him. "By the time you get cleaned up, I'll have breakfast ready." She leaned over, taking his face in both hands, and kissed him on the mouth. With a flirtatious glance over her shoulder she disappeared through the bedroom door.

Twenty minutes later Lane sat on a blue-cushioned stool at the breakfast bar in the kitchenette eating fried eggs, smoked sausage, and buttered toast. He wore brown loafers and tan dress slacks and still had on his marine undershirt. After two and a half years it was becoming threadbare.

"Have you thought any more about going in on that oil deal with Daddy and Walker Jones?"

Lane chewed thoughtfully on a final bite of sausage, sipped his coffee, and set the cup on the counter. "Yeah, I've thought about it. But it's precious little I know about mineral law, especially in Louisiana."

"Oh, it's simple. Daddy told me so."

"Why doesn't he do it himself, then? He's a state senator *and* a lawyer." Lane sensed there was something shady about the deal, like an arthritic senses in his joints an approaching storm before he sees it. But this worrisome harbinger remained buried beneath his long hours at work and the addiction that had been building in him for the company of Bonnie Catelon.

"I don't know all the legal ins-and-outs of it, but for some reason they need a third party."

"He's president of the Mineral Board. Seems to me that ought to do it."

"I told you it's some kind of legal technicality—

about the bidding laws, I believe."

Lane hoped she would forget about the whole thing, but she continued to bring it up when they were together. "Why me, then? A chicken knows more about algebra than I know about oil and gas leases and the bidding laws."

"Because I told Daddy I'd like to see you make some *real* money, for one thing." Bonnie pinched a piece of dry brown toast off, tossing it into the congealing yellow of her half-eaten egg. "And because you have integrity."

Lane gave her a wry smile. "You mean like what I'm doing right now. *That's* integrity?"

A cloud crossed Bonnie's pale face. "Oh, you know what I mean. There's no *scandal* connected with your name. The news hounds won't be able to indulge themselves in yellow journalism. You know how they love to attack politicians—even the honest ones like Daddy. As far as the political and legal professions are concerned, you're as pure as the driven snow."

"I can think of a lot more appropriate phrases than that one to describe me, Bonnie."

"Oh, don't be so hard on yourself!" Bonnie said disdainfully. "We're not *hurting* anybody."

He stared at her incredulously. "That's the whole point. If Catherine ever found about this—I don't know *what* it would do to her. And my children. I can't even think about that."

"Maybe you *should* think about them." Bonnie punched holes in the white of the egg with her fork. "A hundred thousand dollars would surely put all of them through college and set them up after they finish."

"A hundred thousand dollars?" Lane found his thought processes muddled by the prospect of riches

and the enigma wrapped in flesh that was Bonnie Catelon.

"That's for starters. It could be a lot more, depend-
ing on how much land is involved and what it leases
for."

"I don't know, Bonnie. It just seems too easy." Lane
pinched the bridge of his nose with thumb and forefinger. "I—I really think we'd better call these little . . .
assignations off before someone gets hurt."

"No!"

Lane gave her a puzzled stare, surprised at the in-
tensity of her reaction.

"I—I mean, you can't *do* that, Lane." Two fine lines
creased Bonnie's smooth brow like fleeting portents of
her old age. "You just can't!"

Slipping off his stool, Lane turned and placed his
cup and plate into the small sink. "I don't know that
we really have any choice about it, Bonnie."

"Yes, we do! No one will find out." Bonnie's voice
was edged with desperation. "Please, Lane! I don't
think I could stand it if I couldn't see you."

Lane placed both hands on the counter, staring
into the sink, torn between his sense of honor and his
desire for Bonnie. He had always been faithful to
Catherine until now—even during the entire time he
was away from her during the war. He felt he still
loved her as much as he ever did.

But Bonnie had touched something deep inside
him that he never knew existed before—some kind of
primal passion that had proved irresistible, yet at the
same time filled him with a sense of darkness and
dread.

"Please, Lane." Bonnie's voice sounded almost like
the whisper of her silk nightgown.

"We can't. There's too much at stake."

"Just one more time. We'll go to Mardi Gras," Bonnie pleaded softly. "We'll use Daddy's apartment on Bourbon Street when no one else is there."

Lane gazed down at her. "I don't know."

Bonnie's clear green eyes slowly changed, as though smoke were drifting up into them from a fire smoldering somewhere far down below. Backing away from Lane, she turned and disappeared into the bedroom.

★ ★ ★

"Be careful, Gene! If we fall over I'll break a leg." Jessie sat on Gene's Western Flyer bicycle between the handlebars and the seat, holding on to his arms for balance. She wore a tan raincoat over her red sweater and jeans.

"Don't be such a big baby." Gene steered the bicycle down the Third Street sidewalk that was almost free of shoppers at that hour on Saturday morning. "You think I can't even handle a bicycle. I'm seventeen years old. My uncle let me drive his Chevrolet pickup three or four times already."

Jessie hoped her mother wouldn't find out that she had been with Gene again even though forbidden to do so. She had told Catherine she was going to the library to do research for a history report, but had met him instead at Ben Peabody's Esso Station on Senic Highway, near his house. "I'm hungry. Let's go to Sitman's and get a hamburger and a Coke."

"Hungry? It isn't even ten o'clock in the morning yet." Gene was mentally counting the money he carried in the right front pocket of his jeans.

"I don't care," Jessie whined. "I had to leave so early to meet you I didn't get any breakfast."

"All right—all right. You don't have to make a federal case out of it." Gene glanced up at the leaden February sky. *Watch it start raining at five o'clock today just when my shift starts.* "But let's go to the Toddle House. The food's a lot better than that drugstore and it's on this end of the street."

"Fine with me, just as long as you feed me."

Gene pulled over into the little alcove in front of the City Pawn Shop. He held the bicycle steady while they looked in the show window. "How'd you like to have that radio?"

"I already have one a lot better than that," Jessie bragged. "If you want to really impress me, let's go down to Esnard's and I'll let you buy me a diamond ring."

"You're a spoiled brat. You know that?" Gene guided the bicycle around, peddling down to the Toddle House on the next corner. He leaned the bike against the tiled wall beneath the plate glass window and took Jessie inside.

They sat at the long, low counter on brown imitation leather stools. A man in his late twenties with thinning sandy hair stood with his back to them, scraping the grease off the grill with a long spatula. He wore a long white apron and a genuine smile when he turned around to greet them.

"Morning, Gene. What are y'all having today?"

"Charles, I want you to meet a friend of mine, Jessie Temple. Jessie, this is Charles Hays."

"Pleased to meet you, Jessie."

Jessie smiled and nodded. "You too."

"Charles is like me," Gene explained. "Works and goes to school too. He's trying to get on with National Cash Register. Says he could get me a decent job if he does."

"That's right, Gene." Charles wiped his hands on

215

the white apron that hung over his shoulders and tied in back. "You gotta hit the books though."

After Charles had served them Cokes and hamburgers, he heard a delivery truck pulling into the lot behind the restaurant. "Got to go help unload. Keep an eye on things for me in here, will you, Gene?"

"Sure thing."

"I have to admit you're right about the food," Jessie mumbled through a mouthful of hamburger. "This is the best hamburger in town."

"I can't believe it," Gene replied, raising his hands to the ceiling in supplication. "I actually did something to please Queen Jessie of Evangeline."

Jessie swallowed and took the straw in her mouth, taking a long sip of the Coke. "That's not funny. Why don't you do something useful and play the jukebox."

Gene thought again of his dwindling supply of coins. "Sure. What's your favorite song this week?"

Jessie stared at her half-eaten hamburger as though expecting it to speak. "I know—play 'It's Magic' by Doris Day. That's the most beautiful song I've ever heard."

"I think that makes about ten most beautiful songs you've ever heard."

"Oh, hush and play the record!"

Gene walked to the jukebox just inside the door, dropped two nickels in, and studied the listing of songs. Punching two selections, he returned to his stool.

"What else did you play?"

"You don't want me to spoil the surprise, do you? It's a good one though."

"I'll bet."

*. . . you speak and I hear violins. . . .*

"Listen to that!" Jessie stopped the hamburger

halfway to her mouth. "Doris Day sings so pretty." She turned and gazed into Gene's eyes. "Do you hear violins when I speak, Gene?"

Gene set his Coke down and looked at the door behind the counter that Charles had disappeared through. "Here lately you sound more like a parrot squawking."

"Oh, you!" Jessie threw the hamburger onto her plate. "There isn't a romantic bone in your whole body. You can just take me home right now."

Gene regretted his words even as he spoke them. He thought about Jessie every minute he was away from her; pictured her cornflower blue eyes and blond hair every night as he fell asleep; thought continually of the soft warmth of her lips the three times she had kissed him.

For the last few weeks, though, she had proven almost impossible to get along with. He felt that the only thing she wanted was for him to spend all his money on her. "I'm sorry, Jessie. C'mon, finish your hamburger and we'll go look at the jewelry down at Esnard's."

"No," Jessie pouted. "You're not nice to me anymore. I want to go home."

"C'mon, Jessie. I was just kiddin'."

From the jukebox, Eddy Arnold sang "Bouquet of Roses."

"Ugh! Did you play *that*?" Jessie made a face at the jukebox. "I can't stand that hillbilly stuff. Reminds me of my daddy. That's what he likes."

"He does?" Gene had always associated professional people like lawyers with opera or the symphony. "He must be a pretty good guy then."

Jessie frowned. "He likes Jimmie Davis even better. 'You Are My Sunshine'—double ugh!"

Jessie finished her hamburger in near silence, replying only in monotones when Gene spoke to her. Gene knew he would have to take her home unless he came up with something to hold her interest.

"How about a movie?" Gene could feel the thin weight of the quarter and nickel in his pocket. Just enough for the price of two tickets for the first matinee. "*Red River* is playing at the Hart. John Wayne and Montgomery Clift are in it."

Jessie relented with mild theatrics. "All right then, but I want to go to the Paramount."

"Not *Key Largo*," Gene complained. "Lauren Bacall's pretty, but that Humphrey Bogart gives me a pain."

"You're just jealous 'cause he's a real man."

"He's a skinny old man with a harelip. Why should I be jealous?"

Jessie glowered at Gene, then crossed her arms and spun around on her stool.

"All right, all right—have it your way."

★   ★   ★

"I just love this place!" Jessie sat in the first balcony of the Paramount Theater where it curved around from the main part, running along the walls in a slim outcropping with room for only two seats and a narrow aisle. Behind and above her the second balcony, open only for the evening showings and special performances, loomed dark and inaccessible, while far below the dimly lighted main floor held only a few patrons for this first showing. "Look at that gorgeous ceiling."

Gene glanced about him at the curved spatial forms of the rococo-style architecture and the murals on the lofty ceiling. He thought the best part of the theater was the deep, plush burgundy-colored seats and the thrill of sitting out on a narrow precipice high above the main floor. "Yeah."

The heavy velvet curtains slowly opened and the house lights dimmed even more, signaling the start of the feature. After a few minutes Gene settled back against the soft cushion, easing his arm around the back of Jessie's chair and letting his hand casually come to rest on her shoulder.

"Oh no, you don't!" Jessie pushed his arm away. "You wouldn't even buy me a box of popcorn."

"I told you I didn't have any more money!"

"That's your problem." Jessie stared at the larger-than-life images filling the screen. "You know I don't enjoy movies without popcorn."

After the feature was over, Jessie and Gene stood on the sidewalk in front of the theater watching the flow of traffic down Third Street as the Saturday shoppers hit full stride. Above the bustling streets, dark gray clouds covered the sky from horizon to horizon.

Gene glanced up at the vertical neon Paramount sign towering above the marquee. "Looks like it might rain. Why don't we go down to the Ogden Park Record Shop and listen to a few tunes before we go home?"

Jessie shrugged and let Gene help her onto his bicycle. He smelled the faint fragrance of her shampoo as he leaned into his peddling.

"It's embarrassing riding on this bicycle," Jessie grunted as they bumped into a curb. "Why don't you try to borrow a car or at least your uncle's pickup?"

Gene listened in silence to the steady drone of complaints for six blocks until they pulled over in front of the record shop. *If you weren't so pretty . . .*

"I hope there's a booth open," Jessie remarked, hurrying inside ahead of Gene.

"Don't bother to wait for me, Jessie. I'll be all right out here." Gene smiled as he held the door open for two elderly women who were leaving.

Inside, customers were browsing through the narrow aisles among the bins and stacks of records. Posters on the walls enticed them to buy "I'm Looking Over a Four-Leaf Clover" by Art Moonie, or Ray Bolger's latest hit, "Once in Love With Amy."

"Oh, look! There's a booth open in the back," Jessie said excitedly. "You go hold it and I'll pick out some records."

Gene walked back to the glassed-in booth in the far corner, went inside, and sat down on one of the two straight-backed wooden chairs. Jessie soon entered with a stack of 78s enclosed in their paper sleeves.

"Look—I've got 'There I've Said It Again' by Vaughn Monroe and 'Put Your Dreams Away' by Frank Sinatra—and a bunch more." Jessie brimmed with delight as she dumped the records on the counter next to the turntable.

"Sinatra!" Gene picked up the record, making a face at it. "That little draft-dodging runt. You read in the newspapers about how tough he acts, but he wouldn't even fight for his country when he had the chance."

"Who cares," Jessie replied, refusing to let Gene dampen her enthusiasm for the music. "Start the turntable while I pick out the records."

After playing all the records, Jessie was listening to "It's Magic" for the third time. Gene had long since lost what little interest he had had in her music, as she hadn't selected one country music record for him to listen to.

Jessie finally took the record off the turntable, slipped it carefully into the paper sleeve, and held it to her breast with both hands. "Buy this for me."

"Do you ever listen to *one* word I say?" Gene gazed out the half-glass wall of the record booth. "I told you I didn't have any more money."

"It's only twenty-five cents."

"Only?" Gene shook his head slowly, frowning at Jessie. "Do you realize that's what I make an hour?"

"I want this record."

Gene turned the pockets of his jeans inside out. "Look. Are you satisfied now?"

Jessie tossed her head and began collecting the scattered records into a stack. "Well, I'll just bet I can find another boy to get it for me."

Gene glanced out into the store. With a deep sigh, he grabbed the record, knelt quickly, and slipped it down inside the back of his pants. Adjusting his leather jacket so that it covered the record, he stared coldly at Jessie. "Are you satisfied now?"

Jessie smiled triumphantly, picked up the stack of records, and left the booth.

# PART FOUR

★ ★ ★

# ASH WEDNESDAY

# THIRTEEN

# SNAKE OIL

★ ★ ★

Lane stood at the foot of the Grand Staircase gazing up at the 450-foot-tall Art Deco Capitol building. As he ascended the staircase to the fifty-foot-high main entrance, he read the names of each state in the union, beginning with Vermont (1791) and ending with Arizona (1912). At the top, he noticed the words chiseled in stone: *The instruments which we have just signed will cause no tears to be shed. They prepare ages of happiness for innumerable generations of human creatures.*

"A masterpiece of irony," Lane smiled almost bitterly, walking inside the main entrance. In Memorial Hall he stared at the large bronze relief map of Louisiana encircled by the names of the sixty-four parishes. Resting in the exact center of the gleaming parquet floor was the State Seal, guarded by a brass rail. Glancing around at the stone, bronze, and wood decor beneath the towering ceiling, Lane walked straight ahead to the bank of elevators.

After punching a button, Lane studied the bronze relief of Huey Long above the elevator doors. In a few seconds, as though acting out a ritual, he turned and walked across to the opposite wall. He placed his finger in turn into each of the three bullet holes in the solid marble, feeling their cold, smooth interiors. They marked the spot where Long was assassinated on September 8, 1935. Having done this on each of his previous visits to the Capitol, he was still unable to figure out why he was drawn to this tragic and lonely memorial.

Five minutes later, Lane was ushered into Senator Andre Catelon's plush office. Carpeted in Prussian blue with smoke-gray leather chairs studded in bronze, it was located in the southeast corner of the building. To the south it provided views of the formal gardens and the downtown business district beyond them. The other tall windows looked out on the rose gardens, Old Arsenal, and Capitol Lake to the east.

Behind a massive desk of walnut and Australian laurel wood, Andre Catelon reclined in his custom-made leather chair, a thin cigar clenched between his teeth. His pinstriped suit was tailored to make his stout body look slimmer. "Welcome to the halls of power, Lane. Nice to see you again."

Lane noticed from his standing position that Catelon's legs didn't touch the floor. He fought to keep a grin from breaking out on his face. "Thank you, sir."

"Sit down, my boy. Sit down," Catelon smiled like everybody's favorite uncle. "We don't stand on formalities here."

Lane sat in one of the five chairs in front of Catelon's desk, noticing the dozens of black-and-white prints on the walls, commemorating the landmarks of his political life. The largest one showed him shaking hands with Harry Truman.

"Would you like some refreshment—coffee, Coke, a little Scotch maybe?"

"No thanks."

"Bonnie tells me she's very fond of you." Catelon squinted at Lane through the blue smoke rising from his cigar. "Ran into you at the LSU track, I believe."

"That's right, sir."

"Bonnie's never been very athletic. I'm glad she's getting some exercise—good for the body and the mind, I always say," Catelon declared as if he were the first person in recorded history to think of such a clever thing.

Lane nodded.

Catelon grew expansive. "I've tried to be father *and* mother to her since my wife died—Bonnie was only ten at the time. All in all, I think I did a pretty good job."

"Yes, sir."

"She tells me you're a fine man," Catelon continued. "Kind of like the older brother she never had."

"We get along pretty well."

"Well, you're not here just because my daughter's fond of you. Rest assured of that." Catelon gave Lane a look as though they were collaborators in a minor conspiracy instead of a major one. "Although I have to admit, her persuasive powers are part of the reason."

Lane knew by now that Catelon had already written the script for their meeting and that any suggestion he might add to it would be ignored, graciously ignored to be sure, but taken without merit just the same.

"Now that Earl Long's governor, I feel it's incumbent upon those of us who have the state's best interests at heart to use its vast natural resources to the greatest advantage." Catelon took a quick puff on his cigar. "You do know what Long has in mind for this state, don't you?"

Lane started to say he only knew what some of Long's campaign promises were, but was interrupted by Catelon before he could speak.

"He's going to turn Louisiana into a welfare state." Catelon's dark eyes held an almost fanatical light now. "The man's insane! He's already expanding welfare programs and adding new ones of his own. More charity hospitals, free hot lunches in the schools, more free ambulance and dental services. In four years the state will be flat broke."

Lane started to comment, but Catelon continued to rattle off a list of Long's transgressions.

"Long's not only going to increase taxes, he's going to give away most of the money from the oil and gas leases in the Atchafalaya Basin." Catelon spoke as though Long planned to use money from Catelon's own personal bank account rather than from state lands in the Basin.

Letting his eyes follow the trail of smoke from Catelon's cigar, Lane watched it rise in wavering blue strands, disappearing into the gloom of the lofty ceiling.

"You know Dudley LeBlanc?"

Surprised that he had been included in the conversation, Lane replied, "I've heard of him."

"Now that's the kind of man Louisiana needs." Catelon stood up, leaning on his desk with both hands, the cigar still clenched in his teeth. "He made money the old-fashioned way—work. Came up with a patent medicine he named *Hadacol*. Got Bob Hope and Hank

Williams to promote it for him. It swept the whole country and made him a millionaire."

Catelon took a breath, dumped his cigar into a marble ashtray, and walked to the window. "New ideas and hard work. That's what we need. Not somebody like Earl Long who wants to give all our state money to a bunch of shiftless bums and nere-do-wells who wouldn't know a job from a boll weevil."

Turning away from the window, Catelon looked at Lane for the first time since he had begun his soliloquy on the evils of the "Pea Patch" governor. "Well, enough of my political philosophy. Hope I haven't bored you."

Lane suppressed a yawn. "No, sir." He was still trying to grasp the fact that, in Catelon's mind, the personification of the American Dream was a snake oil peddler.

Catelon walked over and stood next to Lane's chair. "I understand you're going to work with us on this oil and gas business."

Lane put both hands on the armrests of his chair as if steadying himself to speak. "Well, I really haven't made up my mind yet."

Catelon sat down next to Lane, an incredulous look on his face. "You must be joking, son. A deal like this comes along once in fifty years—and you're in on it! Walker told me you'd already signed the contract to handle the bidding for Pelican Oil."

"That's right, but he said that he'd void it if I decided against doing it. I said I'd talk to you and let him know."

"Well, it's settled then. Any sane man's not going to turn down a hundred thousand dollars with more to come over the next few years. We've got plans to sublease the land out to the big boys like Esso and Shell."

"I don't want to get involved in anything illegal." Lane's words came out dry and affected.

"Don't worry, we'll see that the state gets its fair share of the profits." Catelon smiled coldly. "You're a grown man, Temple. Fought a war, married a woman, had kids—don't act like you don't know what's going on here."

Lane got up and walked over to the east windows, pulled the heavy blue drape aside, and peered out. Below him, two boys around ten peddled their bicycles along the paths between the flower beds and the crepe myrtles, heading toward the Old Arsenal on its grassy, landscaped mound of earth.

Catelon appeared next to him. The smile had returned to his face. "Nothing wrong with a man earning a little money for his family."

Lane turned and gazed beyond Catelon's glowing smile and into his dark eyes. They looked as flat and cold as a shark's. He thought of Catherine and his children. *Well, this ought to be enough money to satisfy even her—and the kids will be taken care of if something happens to me.*

Something flickered deep inside of Lane, a small steady light that shined on the truth—that Catherine and his children had nothing at all to do with the decision he would make today in this room.

"Well, would you rather see Long give *all* our money away to a bunch of deadbeats?"

"No—I guess not."

★ ★ ★

Lane peered across the top of his newspaper as Coley wheeled through the door of the White House Restaurant and over to his table. "I've been meaning to ask you something for a long time now. I've known you more than two years and those clothes are the only ones I've ever seen you wear to work. Don't you *ever* change clothes?"

Coley grinned, glancing down at his jeans, blue button-down-collar shirt, and gray herringbone sport coat. "Every day—and when the legislature's in session I even wear a tie."

"What do you mean, 'every day'? You always wear the *same* thing every day and the cleaners aren't open at night." It was a mystery Lane was determined to solve as Coley's clothes were always clean. He couldn't figure out how he managed to keep them that way.

"Are you familiar with $E=mc^2$?" Coley dragged the chair opposite Lane away from the table and wheeled his chair into position.

"Can't you ever answer a question like a sane person?" Lane knew he would have to play the game or not get an answer to his question.

"Well?"

"Energy equals mass times the speed of light squared—quantum physics—Einstein's theory of relativity. Satisfied?"

"Amazing! An educated redneck." Coley picked up the menu, propped between the chrome napkin holder and a ketchup bottle, and began browsing through it.

"Answer the question!" Lane spoke louder than he had intended to, and several of the lunchtime crowd glanced in his direction.

Coley peeked over his menu, a mildly amused expression on his face. "That's right. You did ask a question. I have five outfits just alike."

Lane merely stared at the slim little man, his face hidden behind the menu.

"I believe I'll have the special." Coley replaced the

menu, folding his arms on the table. "Got the idea from Einstein. That way there's no distraction about what to wear every day, having to match colors, that sort of thing. Clothes in the cleaners—clothes to wear. Works perfect."

"You're a strange man, Coley."

"I prefer to think of myself as creatively eccentric."

Ten minutes later the waitress, whose rounded paunch testified to her enthusiastic participation in the "Free Meals for Employees" policy at the White House, set two large white plates of crawfish etouffee on the table.

Lane immediately dashed red Tabasco sauce on the burnt-orange colored mixture spread over a bed of white rice. He happily chewed a mouthful of the succulent peeled crawfish tails in their spicy sauce, then gulped a swallow of sweetened ice tea from a tall, moisture-beaded glass.

"I believe you took to Cajun food quicker than anybody I've ever seen," Coley observed. "You don't do half bad for somebody who used to say he'd just as soon put a live toad in his mouth as a cooked crawfish."

"Live and learn," Lane mumbled around another bite of the etouffee. "How do they fix this stuff anyway?"

Coley picked at his food, savoring the morsels he was able to eat since he had left part of his stomach in a South Pacific jungle. "Make a roux. That's the way you start about ninety percent of Cajun dishes. Then the usual onions, garlic, bell pepper, shallots—everybody has his own secret method."

Lane and Coley finished the meal with little conversation as the chink and rattle of glasses and dishes along with the talk of the other diners provided the background music. Topping the meal off with bread pudding drowned in a liberal portion of rum sauce, they sipped their coffee contentedly.

Lane broke the silence. "You know what I read in the newspaper?"

"No, but I think I'm about to find out."

"Some guy in California franchised a string of restaurants that sells nothing but hamburgers." Lane picked up his newspaper, pointing the article out to Coley.

"What'll they think of next," Coley remarked, scanning the article. "McDonald's—looks like they could have come up with a better name than that. How can they expect to stay in business selling nothing but ten-cent hamburgers? This is 1948—people are more sophisticated than that."

"You never know," Lane mused, folding his newspaper, "it just might catch on."

Coley greeted an elderly woman with gray hair and a black shawl draped over her shoulders. After a brief explanation of upcoming legislation that might affect her welfare check, she seemed satisfied, thanked him, and left.

"You see the article on the Palestine partition plan?" Coley picked at the almost full portion of bread pudding left in his dessert bowl.

"No. I don't keep up with the Middle East much," Lane replied, holding his hand over his cup as the waitress started to refill it. "Sand, rocks, and war—that's all I can tell you about it."

Coley's face held a solemn expression. "I think the UN's gonna recognize Israel as a separate state before too long. After almost two thousand years the Jews will have a country again."

"Sounds biblical."

"Fulfillment of prophecy," Coley continued somberly. "The Jews coming home again—for the last time."

"You ready to go?"

"I'm ready, me."

"I hardly ever hear you talking with that Cajun accent anymore," Lane smiled. "Why's that?"

"I bet you t'ink I forgot how, me." Coley whirled his chair around, speaking back over his shoulder. "You jes' follow behind wid me. We pass us a good time, yeah."

★ ★ ★

As happened almost every time he entered Coley's office, Lane's eyes were drawn to the handmade sign above the perpetually cluttered desk.

Noticing Lane gazing at the sign, Coley wheeled around, facing him. "That's a real message, isn't it? Yes, sir—I'll bet ol' Elton Landry never had any idea how many lives he'd touch when he gave *that* to me. I couldn't tell you how many people have told me what a blessing it's been to them."

"Is he still in prison?"

"Who, Elton?"

"No, Coley, Jesus. Who do you think I mean?" Lane glanced back at the sign, thinking of Jesus' arms stretched out against the rough-hewn wood of the cross.

Coley grinned, staring intently at the sign as though seeing something new in it. "Yep, still in Angola. And the strange thing is he feels more freedom behind those big wire fences than he ever did outside of them. Told me so himself the last time I went to visit him."

Lane had taken one of the chairs with the deer-

hide seats that sat next to the narrow window facing
Senic Highway. "I can tell you got something you just
can't wait to tell me, Coley. So let's get on with it. I've
got a lot of correspondence to dictate."

"Okay." Coley wheeled over next to Lane and
poured a cup of coffee from the little drip pot that had
been warming on the hot plate since early that morning. He offered it to Lane.

"No thanks. I'm about coffeed out." Lane held his
hand palm outward. "By the way, is Mrs. Clark coming in tomorrow morning? This stuff needs to get in
Monday morning's mail."

"Said she was," Coley replied, shuddering slightly
as he took the first swallow of coffee. "I don't know
how she does it—a woman her age. Works all week for
the Mineral Board and Saturdays and some nights for
us."

"C'mon, let me have your epistle for the day so I
can get to work."

Coley frowned at his coffee cup, setting it on the
table. "I've been hearing lately about some strange go-
ings-on in the 'House that Huey Built.'"

"The Capitol?"

"I don't mean that sharecropper's shack he lived in
up in Winn Parish."

Lane began to feel uncomfortable under the glare
of Coley's intense eyes. "Strange things are the norm
for that place. What's so special about these?"

"I heard your name being bantered about in certain closed circles." As he spoke, Coley's intense stare
never left Lane's face. "The 'high rollers only' kind of
crowd."

Lane shifted in his chair and glanced out the window, unable to meet Coley's eyes.

"More specifically, I heard the names of Andre Catelon and the Pelican Oil Company, Walker Jones, Esq.—president, now that his daddy's retired." Coley could tell by Lane's reaction that he knew something about the deal and that he was not proud of his part in it—if Lane had in fact committed himself to it. "Rumor has it that they want to tie up some very big tracts of state land in the Basin for oil and gas leases."

"Why are you telling *me* about this?"

"I think you're involved or you're considering going in on it." Coley heard the mounting anger in his own voice and spoke more deliberately. "Catelon would sell his mother to an Arab slave trader if he thought he could make a buck out of it, Lane. How could you even consider joining up with the likes of him?"

"I hardly know the man, Coley." Lane's words felt dry and brittle in his mouth as he spoke them.

Coley's voice seemed freighted with sadness as he continued. "If I'm not mistaken, you're on a little more intimate terms with his daughter."

Lane spun around in his chair. "What are you talking about? I love my wife."

"I don't think that's the issue here."

Lane's indignation wilted under the implacable truth of Coley's words. He glanced at the office door as if planning his escape route.

"Let's just stop the indignant husband routine, Lane. You're a friend and I don't want to see you lose everything."

Staring at the sign above Coley's desk, Lane spoke in a voice that was little more than a whisper. "How did you find out about Bonnie?"

"It's *not* a very big town. And the political crowd with its assortment of sycophants, toadies, yes-men, and various other hangers-on is *much* smaller. Hardly anything goes on that *somebody* doesn't find out about."

"I hate what happened between Bonnie and me." Lane thought of Catherine's fragile beauty, her blue eyes and pale hair—then the dark, sultry image of Bonnie Catelon overshadowed her. "And I'm going to put an *end* to it."

"When?"

"Soon." Lane evaded the question and rushed ahead. "But this oil and gas leasing business with the senator is as straight as *anything* gets in state government as far as I can tell. And Walker's an old marine buddy who's just letting me in on a good thing."

Coley propped his left elbow on the armrest of his wheelchair, his chin resting on his fist. The afternoon glare through the window cast the left side of his face into shadow, highlighting the prominent cheekbones of his thin face. His eyes seemed to darken with an almost palpable sadness. "I'm through talking, Lane. You're gonna do what you want to."

"I'll get it all straightened out, ol' buddy." Lane gave him a halfhearted smile.

Coley didn't respond to the smile, merely keeping his dark eyes directed at Lane's.

Crossing his leg nervously, Lane picked at a piece of lint on his sock. He felt Coley's gaze almost as though it were burning him. "I really *will* take care of things, Coley."

"Uh-huh."

"I *mean* it!" Lane cleared his throat, glancing up at Coley. "I don't want to lose my family. They mean more to me than anything in this *world*."

Outside, walking next to the curb along Senic Highway, a man wearing stained and ragged overalls, scuffed work shoes, and a tattered felt hat stopped

237

and gazed through the window of Coley's office. From the angle where he stood, he could see Lane in his tan business suit, his necktie like a blue strip of the sky against the white shirt.

A half sigh, half groan rose in the man's chest when he remembered wearing clothes identical to the ones Lane had on—those days when he would kiss his wife and children in the morning, leaving for work and always return to them afterward. He could still see the soft evening light through the trees lying in amber pools across his yard.

Taking a pint bottle, still inside its crumpled paper bag, from his back pocket, the man took a quick swallow, glanced around him and took another. With a shudder, he returned the bottle and shambled off down the highway.

Back inside the office, the cloud seemed to lift from Coley's face. He realized that for now he had reached the point in their conversation where anything else he said would only drive a wedge between him and Lane. "You know what you need?"

Puzzled at the sudden change in his friend, Lane replied uncertainly, "Yeah, a public flogging."

"Nah! That might help lift the *conviction* you're under," Coley replied quickly. "And you need to carry that around with you for a while longer."

"Would you try to make some sense for once in your life?" Lane was still trying to adjust to the sudden change in Coley's attitude.

Clasping his hands together and leaning back in his wheelchair, Coley announced, "What you really need is a trip down in the Basin—forget about work for a while—get your head clear."

Lane felt an unreasonable fear at the thought of being alone with Coley out in the swamps. Knowing how Coley felt about his involvement with Bonnie *and* her father, he pictured relentless hours of sermons about fidelity and business ethics. "With all I've got to do—are you crazy?"

"Probably. I picked you for a friend, didn't I?" Coley knew that Lane would be going with him or he would have gotten up and left by now.

"I don't have the time to spare."

Coley noticed the slightly hollow look in Lane's eyes. It reminded him of the "Stare"—only to a lesser degree. "You're going to come apart at the seams if you don't slow down a little, Lane. We'll leave early Monday morning and come back Tuesday night. It'll make a new man out of you."

"Sorry, Coley, I just can't do it."

# FOURTEEN

# SERENITY

★ ★ ★

Lane picked Coley up at five A.M. at his office-apartment, took Senic Highway up to Highway 190, and on across the Mississippi River bridge, turning south on Highway 1. All along the highway they passed by huge expanses of sugarcane fields, stark and blackened under the February sky where they had been burned after the grinding season was over.

South of the little river town of Plaquemine, they turned west toward the Atchafalaya Basin, coming to the point where Bayou Grosse Tete joined with Grand River. Heading south along the banks of Grand River, they stopped north of Bayou Sorrel.

Lane pulled his '39 Ford coupe off the road, parking underneath a chinaberry tree next to the camp that belonged to Coley's neighbor. The small board-and-batten shack with its tin roof and sagging gallery facing the water stood on a twenty-foot-wide strip of land between the pier and the narrow shell road. At the far end of the gallery, a lofty Tupelo gum lifted its stark, leafless limbs toward the pale morning sky.

Coley had pulled his chair off the back floorboard and wheeled down the pier before Lane could get their gear out of the trunk. Carrying a tackle box, two rods and reels, and a duffel bag over one shoulder, Lane stopped on the bank, staring nervously at the end of the pier.

Coley had stopped and spun his chair around. "C'mon, let's get moving. The fish get up early down here. We don't want to keep 'em waitin'."

"I hope you don't think I'm setting foot in *that* thing!" Wearing his khakis, a red flannel shirt, and a denim jacket, Lane walked out onto the rickety pier made of creosote poles driven into the muddy bottom of Grand River. Silvery-gray, two-by-eight cypress planks provided the decking.

Standing along the water's edge, half a dozen cypress gave the appearance of benign, gray-bearded sentinels. Long strands of Spanish moss trailing from their limbs moved languidly, touched by the vagrant breeze.

Coley had already strong-armed his way down from his wheelchair when Lane stopped next to him. Sitting on the pier with his thin, dead legs hanging over the edge, he had on jeans, a khaki shirt with flap pockets, and his marine field jacket. High-top black tennis shoes with soles as unmarked as the day he bought them dangled at the ends of his legs. "I don't see why not," Coley observed soberly. "With me paddling you're as safe as a baby in his mother's womb."

Lane stared down at the fragile craft, floating high on the surface of the dark water. Barely ten feet long, it had a flat bottom, a narrow beam, and low gunwales that curved gently upward from the center to the pointed ends. Like everything else in the bayou country, or so it seemed to him, it was made of weathered cypress. "What's it called again?"

"A pirogue. Now let's get a move on." Coley glanced at the orange glow spreading above the trees on the eastern horizon. "It's almost six-thirty."

Lane folded the wheelchair, placing it carefully in the center of the pirogue. Then he laid Coley's marine duffel bag on top of it. "What do I do now?"

"Wait 'til I get in." Coley scooted over to the side of the pirogue, lifted his legs over the side with both hands, and placed one hand on the opposite gun-wale—the other on the pier. Then he eased into the pirogue as it rocked gently from side to side.

With Coley holding the pier to steady the boat, Lane stepped onto the flat bottom, his hands gripping both gunwales. Then he knelt with his feet underneath his body.

"Now you relax and let me handle the balance." Coley pushed away from the pier with his light, slim paddle. "I think you better sit flat on the bottom."

Lane complied, the boat rocking dangerously as he repositioned himself. "You sure you can handle this thing?"

"Too late to worry about that now," Coley grinned. With long, smooth strokes, he headed them up Grand River.

The sun flared with a pale gold radiance along the tops of the distant trees at the far reaches of their vision as they headed north. The flat hull swished across the smooth, dark surface of the water, Coley driving his paddle in with the instinctive movements born of years of repetition.

"I have to admit this is beautiful country." Lane watched the long-legged snowy egrets stalking minnows in the shallows along the shoreline, their heads darting in the shadows. Directly above them, a red-crested pileated woodpecker bounced along the tree-tops in its characteristic jerky flight.

"As the old saying goes, you ain't seen nothin' yet!" Coley had launched into his natural rhythm, as precise and regular as the heartbeat of a distance runner, the paddle driving silently into the water. Only the small swirls left by Coley's strokes and the faint V of the pirogue's wake marked their passage.

Three hundred yards upriver Coley veered to the left toward a narrow channel opening into the river. Just north of the channel, a huge barge with a dragline parked on its broad deck drifted at its moorings.

Coley pointed with his paddle, the pirogue gliding in a slow curve toward the channel. "You see that? A portent of doom for the Basin."

Lane stared at the massive dragline, rising like some extinct beast above the surface of the barge. "What's it doing out here in the middle of nowhere?"

"They're gonna use it to dig canals back into the swamps," Coley explained, resting his paddle across the sides of the pirogue. "So they can get the drilling rigs back in there to dig the oil and gas wells—and lay the pipelines."

They entered into the narrow channel next to the overhanging winter-bare limbs of a black willow, with Coley moving them along at a slower pace.

Suddenly Lane felt he had been catapulted back through time into a primordial forest. Towering above him, the overhanging branches of the giant tupelo, cypress, and sycamore formed a natural tunnel through which they glided in their frail craft to the soft gurgling of the paddle.

Pale striated light filtering down through a maze of bare limbs gave an impression of perpetual twilight. Damp and heavy, the air took on a close quality. Lane could smell the green lichen on the bark of the trees, the dry scent of the moss, and the wet, rich scent of decaying limbs and leaves that lay in abundance on the forest floor. The mild February weather seemed to amplify all the smells of the swamp.

Lane tried to imagine what lurked in the dark shadows beyond the massive trunks of the trees lining the edge of the channel. He thought of men wearing rough animal skins and carrying weapons of wood and stone as they stalked their prey—animals he could not summon up shapes for with eyes that blazed with a fierce yellow light in the darkness.

"You're mighty quiet."

Lane jerked at the sound of Coley's voice, almost as sudden as a gunshot in the stillness. "I never would have thought anything like this place existed."

"Enjoy it while you can." Coley gazed upward toward the patches of pale blue through the crowns of the trees. "It probably *won't* exist much longer."

"I can't believe that," Lane almost whispered, as though he were obligated to preserve the serenity. "Nobody could change all this. It's too—big, too beautiful."

"I'm afraid you underestimate your fellowman's capacity for destruction—and greed." Coley's voice carried a tone of weariness as he spoke.

Directly ahead the gloom seemed to lift. Then they slipped out of the trees into the glassy surface of the lake. In the shape of a rough oval a hundred yards across, it ran to the south for a quarter of a mile. The forest closed it in on all sides. It was here that the virgin cypress grew, towering more than a hundred feet into the sky and down into the mirrored surface of the lake. Cypress knees stood like jagged brown teeth in

245

the shallows along the banks where willows crowded the water.

Coley grabbed on to a limb extending out over the water, holding them steady. "What do you think?"

Staring in rapt fascination, Lane didn't hear him. He had never seen any place as serene and peaceful as this. As he took it all in, three fleecy clouds sailed above him in a sky growing brighter as the sun began its journey across the Atchafalaya.

"You like my hideaway?"

Lane smiled back at Coley. "Peaceful. That's a word I don't have much use for anymore, but it's the only one I can think of to describe it."

Coley leaned easily back against the pirogue, holding it motionless with the paddle. "I truly wanted you to see this place before the government 'improves' it."

Lane merely nodded, surveying the scene as the light fell into the clearing like soft yellow rain. Glancing down at the tea-colored water, he went suddenly rigid. Alongside the boat, no more than two feet beneath the surface, lay the same monster he had seen in the Mississippi River near Jackson Square. He could have reached down and touched its slimy mottled-green body. Shuddering at the thought, Lane saw that the creature's ponderous torpedo-shaped body, with its rounded snout and tapered tail, was almost as long as the pirogue.

Seeing Lane's reaction, Coley glanced down into the water. "Alligator gar."

Lane continued to stare at the monster, its fins moving lazily to maintain its position.

"Don't worry. It's not dangerous," Coley assured him. "Unless you get between it and something it wants to eat."

"Thanks for the update, Coley," Lane mumbled,

afraid to budge for fear of disturbing the leviathan that had haunted his dreams from time to time. "I feel so much better now."

"I know you hate to leave your buddy down there, Lane, but time's a wastin'. " Coley pushed off from the limb. "We'll come back over here and wet our lines after we grab a bite of breakfast and stow the gear. There's usually some bass stirring around where this little chute comes into the lake."

Lane watched the gar closely as they moved away. With a slow movement of its thick tail, the alligator glided downward, disappearing into the depths of the lake.

"You get a different perspective on life out here." Coley sounded cheerful as he paddled across the lake no more than thirty feet from the north shore. "Things that seem important in the city don't amount to a hill of beans here in the swamp."

Lane stared directly ahead. A tiny cabin with a gallery across the front nestled in the shadow of the giant cypress. Constructed of rough-cut logs, it rested on pilings seven feet above the shallows and forty feet out from the swampy shore. A set of steps ran down the side of the gallery to a small pier made of the same kind of logs. It stood no more than two feet above the surface of the lake.

Glancing back at Coley, Lane announced, "Now that's what I call a hideaway!"

"Elton and I built it when we were kids."

"You mean the Elton in prison?"

"I told you we went back a long way." Coley's gaze turned inward as he remembered those long ago days. "We rigged up a little barge and hauled everything back in here on it. Nails, lumber, windows—cut the logs back in the woods."

Lane gazed at the little cabin, hidden like a welcome haven in the vastness of the great swamp. Although he had never seen it before, he felt almost as
though he were going home. "I'm glad you talked me
into this, Coley."

★ ★ ★

Lane balanced himself in the bottom of the pirogue, casting his Hawaiian Wiggler lure with its red
and white skirt toward the end of a treetop that had
lain for years in the edge of the lake. It provided the
perfect cover for bass, red-ear bream, and crappie
(called sac-a-lait by the Cajuns). Letting the lure sink
a few feet, he began cranking it in on his Shakespeare
reel, taking up the black nylon line with an occasional
jerk on the rod.

The bass hit hard, the line cutting through the water above him as he headed for the bottom. Lane kept
the tip of the square-shaped steel rod high, playing
him. As the drag sang in protest, the bass stole more
line, fighting against the springy pull of the rod.

"Don't let him make it to that brush pile," Coley
shouted. "You'll lose him for sure."

Lane pulled hard on the rod, reeling for all he was
worth. His face was a perfect mixture of the thrill of
the contest and pure pleasure. "That's it. Stopped
him!"

The bass turned and shot toward the surface,
breaking through with a flash of sunlight on its shiny
dark back and gleaming belly. It shook its body furi-
ously to free the hook, tail-danced on the surface, and
splashed back into the lake.

Lane's face broke into a huge grin. "What a bass.
He must be five pounds at least."

When he had finally worn the fish down, Lane

boated him, hooking him on the metal stringer next to Coley's smaller one. Coley frowned when Lane held them up side by side and returned to his casting.

Thirty minutes later, with three good-sized black bass on the stringer in the bottom of the pirogue, Coley leaned into his paddle and sent them gliding across the still water. Fifty yards from the cabin, he tapped Lane on the shoulder, pointing to the north shore. Four mallards paddled about, contentedly feeding on watermeal, rootless plants that were no more than tiny green dots floating on the surface.

Coley's sharp eyes were not the only ones to have spotted the mallards. A thirteen-foot bull alligator, cruising the lake just below the surface had risen silently and heard the noise of their feeding. Then he submerged, his heavy tail sweeping back and forth in powerful surges that drove him at remarkable speed toward his quarry.

Surfacing only once more to get his bearings with only his walnut-shell eyes and the tips of his nostrils visible, the beast failed to see the two men in their small, silent craft. Intent on the mallards, he sped beneath the water on a collision course with the pirogue.

At first Lane thought they had struck a log. A split second later, the pirogue lifted beneath him and he felt himself catapulted upward. In a dreamlike state, Lane saw the broad, smoothly rounded snout of the alligator gape open as the beast exploded out of the lake in geysers of white water. Huge, conical and slightly yellow teeth lined the upper and lower jaw. A great hissing bellow erupted from the alligator, its jaws snapping shut with a sound like the crack of a rifle as it crashed back into the lake.

Lane caught a fleeting glance of the pirogue turn-

ing end-over-end—and Coley, still gripping his paddle, splashing into the water on his back.

Suddenly silence descended on the lake, except for
the soft gurgling swirl of the surface where the alligator's massive tail churned the water, propelling him
beneath the surface toward the mallards.

But today the mallards would escape the crushing
jaws of the alligator. Hearing the bellow as he collided
with the pirogue, they spread their wings, setting
them into blinding motion as they took a few quick
steps across the surface of the lake and swiftly flew
above the treetops.

Glancing about to get his bearings, Lane swam toward the spot where he had seen Coley splash beneath
the surface. Just before he reached it, Coley rose
slowly out of the water, shaking his head, his dark hair
plastered to his face.

Lane grabbed him under the shoulder. "You okay?"

"A little damp." Coley looked at the clumps of cattails lining the edge of the lake twenty yards away.
"You get the pirogue. I can make the shore."

Swimming over to the upside-down pirogue
nearby, Lane righted it, glad that it weighed so little.
The three bass splashed frantically trying to free
themselves from the stringer, still fastened to a metal
ring in the gunwale. He grabbed the hemp bowline
with his left hand and sidestroked toward the tops of
the cattails, pale against the darkness of the woods.

Coley backstroked several yards ahead of Lane, his
arms moving smoothly while his legs, hanging downward in the water until his tennis shoes were out of
sight, trailed limply along behind him. When he
reached the shallows he sat on the bottom, dragging
himself farther toward the bank with his hands sinking into the rich dark "gumbo" mud.

Lane, breathing heavily now from exertion as well as fear, caught up and sat next to Coley in the shallow water. The cattails waved gently around them. A terrible roaring bellow sounded from down the shoreline where the bull alligator had surfaced. With its vicious mouth opening and snapping shut, it thrashed wildly about in the reeds where the ducks had been feeding. The long, powerful tail cut wide swaths through the thick vegetation like a heavy ridged scythe.

"Sounds like he's not too happy about missing his breakfast," Coley remarked as though he had just taken a dip in the neighborhood swimming pool.

"That thing might decide to head down here," Lane said apprehensively, watching the beast vent his rage on the lily pads and reeds.

Coley watched the alligator churn through the shallows on its stumpy legs and plunge beneath the black water, leaving nothing but a momentary gurgling on the surface. "Nah. He's had enough for now. I'm sure glad we ran into such a single-minded gator, though. All he could think about was getting to those mallards as fast as he could." Shivering in the chest-deep water, Coley added, "What worries me is pneumonia—not that gator."

"Let's get out of here, then." Lane turned the pirogue on its side, dumping the water out. "Well, everything's gone. Rods, reel, tackle box—all of 'em on the bottom of the lake."

"Look on the bright side. None of our body parts are at the bottom of that gator's *belly*." Coley grinned weakly, pulling himself up straight in the water. "And we've still got our supper dangling from that stringer."

★   ★   ★

The eastern sky was streaked with magenta as the

sun slipped down beyond the bayous, swamps, willow
islands, and heavy hardwood forests of the Atchafalaya wilderness. From above the tallest tupelo and cypress, a great blue heron sailed over the dark, mirror-
smooth surface of the lake, its wings glinting like gun-
metal in the fading sunlight. Cicadas droned back in
the deep shadows of the trees.

Lane sat in a ladderback chair on the gallery of the
little cabin, his feet propped on the railing. The evening air was cool and moist on his face and it carried
the rich, earthy smells of the swamp. "Best fish I ever
ate."

"Naturally. I cooked 'em." Coley sat in his wheelchair next to Lane, hands clasped behind his head.

Rubbing his hand lightly across his stomach, Lane
thought with pleasure of the flaky, golden-brown bass
fillets, French fries, and the fried hush puppies heavily seasoned with shallots and red pepper. "I think I
could get used to this place."

"Does that mean you like it."

"Maybe. I'd hate to commit myself on the first
trip." Lane glanced in Coley's direction. "Probably
take thirty or forty before I make up my mind."

Just out from the gallery, an alligator snapping
turtle rose slowly to the surface next to a cypress knee.
He was three feet in diameter and weighed almost 300
pounds. In the purple twilight, with his high-ridged
shell cloaked in mosslike green algae, he was almost
invisible. Opening his huge beaked mouth, he gulped
in air with a faint hissing sound, then drifted back
down into the murky depths.

Coley grinned as he watched the turtle. He had
been around so long it was almost like seeing an old
friend. "You oughta bring your daddy down here
sometime. You say he likes the woods and the water."

"I just might do that. He'd love this place." Lane let his eyes take in the dark expanse of the lake and the towering wall of darkness that the woods had become. "You know, I never hear you talk about your mama and daddy much, Coley." It suddenly occurred to Lane that the few times Coley had mentioned them, it had always concerned events that had happened years before. When he saw the look on Coley's face, he knew why.

Coley sat up straight, clasped his hands in front of his chest and rested his chin on them. "They're buried in a little cemetery down in Napoleonville."

Lane remained silent, wishing he hadn't mentioned Coley's parents.

"It happened right before I graduated from high school." Coley's voice was as soft as the breeze rustling through the reeds near the lakeshore. "The house was torn apart. I found them out back behind the smokehouse. We never found out who did it—but all they got was seven or eight dollars cash and Daddy's gold watch that his daddy had given him."

Lane broke the silence in a few minutes. "I'm glad you didn't bring me out here to preach to me, Coley."

"I'm not a preacher." Coley's voice seemed as natural and as unaffected as the sounds of the swamp. "Sometimes I think of myself as a Western Union boy for Jesus. All I do is deliver the message."

Lane thought that he may never have another friend like Coley Thibodeaux.

"I just believe you need to be alone with God for a little while. Let Him deal with your heart." Coley stretched and yawned. "Think I'm going to bed. Playing leapfrog with that gator wore me out. Goodnight." He turned his chair around, opened the screen door, and wheeled into the little cabin.

"Good-night, Coley." Lane listened to the frogs croaking on the far side of the lake. The soft hoo-hooing of an owl drifted on the evening air.

As Lane thought of Catherine and his children, the dusky image of Bonnie Catelon seemed to haunt him like a half-forgotten dream. He called to mind his meeting with the senator and all that it portended. Coley's words, "Let Him deal with your heart," returned to him so plainly that Lane glanced around, thinking he had come back out on the little gallery.

Lane felt a battle raging so strongly within that fear rose in him—the kind he had known in the steamy jungles of Guadalcanal with artillery thundering in the distance and machine-gun bullets whining over his head like angry hornets. He mopped the cold sweat from his brow. *Just this one deal. Then I'll tell them all goodbye.*

On the north shore of the lake, as twilight gave way to the night, a bobcat appeared on a low, grassy bank next to a lofty tupelo. Her tawny spotted fur rendered her almost invisible against the thick brush. Sniffing the air, her sharp ears thrust forward, she carefully studied the area. Satisfied, she bent down to the water and began drinking.

Almost immediately four kittens wobbled out of the underbrush and over to their mother's side. After drinking their fill, the kittens rolled and tumbled and pawed one another under the watchful eye of their mother. She drank briefly once more, then ushered her brood back into the safety of the woods as darkness settled over the Atchafalaya.

★ ★ ★

*The waves of Sealark Channel whispered softly against the beach. Lane stepped alone from the jungle to face the Japanese officer standing in the surf. Blackened and wounded, his uniform in rags, he gripped his Samarai sword with both hands. Lane noticed that five men instead of two knelt before him in the surf, their faces obscured as though a dark veil had been drawn over them.*

*Turning back to the officer, Lane pointed his .45 directly at the man's chest. Now beneath the tattered officer's cap, the fleshy face of Andre Catelon glared defiantly out at him. His flat dark eyes held a malignant glint as he slowly raised the sword above his head.*

*Lane squeezed the trigger—nothing happened. Horrified, he tried again with all his might, but it was as though it had been welded to the guard. He tried to scream, but no sound came; tried to throw himself on the officer, but could not move.*

*Catelon gave Lane a malicious smile. Then he turned away, his sword flashing in the sunlight as he moved deliberately and efficiently into his bloody work.*

Lane clambered slowly up out of the dream, feeling as empty and drained as if he had been in combat. Sitting up and throwing his legs over the side of the bunk, he rubbed his face with both hands. Across the tiny cabin from him, Coley breathed softly in his sleep.

Slipping into his khakis, Lane walked barefoot out onto the gallery. A deep, rose-colored glow filled the morning. Mist floated over the water, hanging like wet cotton in the willows and cypress knees.

Lane sat in the ladder-back chair, the dream still strong in his memory. He thought of Catherine and his children, of Bonnie and of the insidious slide of his ethics. Suddenly a chill swept over him and he felt as though something hard and scaly had brushed against his soul. Staring across the lake at the dark treeline, he wondered if the war would ever end.

★ ★ ★

The clamor down below in the street sounded like a thousand New Year's Eve parties at the stroke of midnight. People in outlandish, garish, and glittering costumes with spectacular headdresses sparkling with sequins or huge ruffle-skirted gowns dripping lace—cowboys, clowns, gangsters, white-fanged Draculas, one hairy-headed Wolfman, and a balloon vendor towing his wares overhead like a rainbow-colored cloud—Superman and Lois Lane and Little Bo Peep complete with sheep—people in every conceivable type of costume, or in no costume at all, thronged Bourbon Street from sidewalk to sidewalk.

"Throw me something, mister!"

Lane had come out on the balcony to escape the smoky din of the party inside the apartment. He stared down at the boy in jeans and black jacket who waved his arms frantically for beads. Wearing an identical jacket, his frail-looking girlfriend clung wearily to his arm.

"Throw me something, mister!" the boy shouted again.

Andre Catelon stood on the other end of the balcony from Lane, directly above the couple. He held a short, heavy glass of Scotch in one hand and a fistful of beads in the other. Clinking his glass down on a wrought iron table, he stripped off a strand of cheap glass beads and dangled them teasingly above the boy's head. Soon a small band of revelers, all screaming "Throw me something, mister!" gathered around the boy.

Lane stared at Catelon's face. It was twisted with drink and the power he exercised over the people below him with his cheap glass beads. He suddenly sailed a glittering strand far out into the crowd.

The boy's face took on a look of betrayal. He glared up at Catelon, put his arm around his girlfriend, and walked dejectedly away into the crowd.

Before the boy had gone ten feet, Catelon tossed the whole knot of beads at him, striking him on the back. He turned quickly around, but several in the crowd had seen the beads fall to the street and dived for them. The boy fell among the others, all of them fighting, kicking and cursing in a desperate struggle for the twenty-five-cent bundle of beads.

Catelon roared with laughter at the brawling down below, holding on to the scrolled iron rail with both hands. Picking up his drink, he finished it in one gulp and disappeared through the French doors into the apartment.

Clutching his tweed sport jacket around his chest, Lane shivered slightly in the late February chill. The warm weather he and Coley had enjoyed during their two days in the Atchafalaya Basin was being pushed back into the Gulf by another cold front moving inexorably down from Minnesota.

Lane watched the garish neon signs of Bourbon Street as they glowed and winked and sparkled above the crowd. Jazz blared out of the open doors of the clubs. Men in straw bowlers and bright blazers stood in other doors hawking the unbridled, on-stage charms of Stormy or Misty or Cherie to the passersby. Lane wondered if anyone would pay admission to see someone named Gladys or Mable.

Bonnie stepped out onto the balcony next to Lane. She wore a Little Bo Peep costume—white frilly dress with red sash and bow, a red silk purse, white stockings, and black patent leather shoes with narrow straps across the instep. A shepherd's crook taller than she completed her outfit. "You look like a little lost sheep," she said. "Too much Mardi Gras getting you down?"

"I guess so," Lane smiled wearily. "After all, how much fun can one man stand?"

"You're right." Bonnie slipped her shepherd's crook around the back of Lane's neck, pulling him gently toward her. She kissed him slowly, drawing back with that peculiar smoky look in her green eyes. "I enjoyed our one day together before everyone else came down—much, much better than all this pandemonium."

Lane took the shepherd's crook from his neck, held it by the shaft, and leaned back against the railing.

"I've got something for you," Bonnie confessed, staring toward the sky, invisible in the glare of neon. "I had a hard time getting up enough courage to give it to you, but here goes." She reached inside her purse and handed Lane a folded sheet of pale green writing paper.

Lane opened it, gazing at the neat swirls and angled lines of Bonnie's handwriting:

Lane,

A cloudless day holds no promise,
All earth etched in transient clarity.
Night gives a glimpse of eternity,
Bright and pure existence
Beyond the touch of time.
Rain, my truest friend here,
Turns back demands of day,
Whispers peace with its cool, gray breath.
You are the night.
You are the rain.

Bonnie

Folding the paper and slipping it into his inside jacket pocket, Lane stared at Bonnie. She looked almost like a child in her costume. Parted in the middle, her soft dark hair was plaited in two pigtails that hung down onto the bodice of her dress.

Lane suddenly felt trapped between the clamor rising up from the street and the din of the party coming through the open French doors onto the balcony. "Let's get out of here."

"I can't think of anything I'd rather do," Bonnie agreed. "We'll spend the day at the Pentagon apartment. Daddy will be down here all day tomorrow recovering from Mardi Gras. But you're going to take a little nap before we leave."

"I really need to get back home. I can't stretch this alleged business trip out more than two days." Lane felt a pang of guilt in his chest. "Besides, I don't want Catherine worrying."

Bonnie took Lane by the arm, leading him from the balcony. "Let her eat cake."

# FIFTEEN

# ROOM 503

★ ★ ★

Ash Wednesday dawned under heavy gray skies. By eight o'clock a slow, chill February rain began to fall on the city. Umbrellas sprouted shiny and black above the heads of the latecomers to work, scurrying along the sidewalks, and the patrons of the early cafes and drugstore soda fountains.

Catherine had asked Mrs. LeJeune to stay with Cassidy and dropped the other children off at school. Then she drove downtown, parking on a side street, her black Chrysler partially hidden by azalea bushes. Across the parking lot, the Pentagon Barracks gleamed dully in the misty, pewter-colored light. This was the second time she had seen Lane's Ford parked in the same place since that day on the ferry with her mother. Wearing the leather jacket Lane had given her, she sat in the car and waited.

Thirty minutes later, a red MG convertible pulled into the space next to Lane's car. The passenger door opened. Lane unfolded from the seat holding an umbrella above his head, walked around the car, and held it above Bonnie Catelon. Still dressed in her Mardi Gras outfit, she held a gray raincoat across her arm, huddling close to Lane as they hurried up the stairs.

Catherine gazed at them, her vision blurred by the rain streaking the windshield and by the tears slowly welling up from the sharp pain in her breast.

Numb, she watched as they reached the second-floor gallery. Lane closed the umbrella, leaned it against the wall, and inserted a key into the door. Bonnie went up on tiptoe and put her arms around Lane's neck, entwining her fingers through the back of his hair. He bent down, his arms encircling Bonnie's waist as he lifted her off the floor, pressing her close.

As they kissed, Catherine shut her eyes tightly and bowed her head. Hugging herself with both arms, she felt unable to stand the pain . . . thought that it must surely burst her chest open. She rocked slowly back and forth in the seat of the car, a low moaning sound escaping from deep inside her.

"Oh, Lane! How could you? How could you?" The hoarsely whispered words sounded to her as though they were being spoken by a stranger. Catherine had always considered her marriage inviolate. No matter how bad things got, it was the one constant in her life. She thought she could never lose it. Lane would always remain faithful to her and she to him. She had believed that since, as a girl, she had first met him. The two of them would grow old together in that safe and comforting knowledge.

Catherine felt engulfed in a terrible, cold darkness, and inside the darkness there was no hope—only unrelenting, grinding pain. It seemed that her life had ended, that it had been only a long ago, half-forgotten dream. She felt so alone that there seemed to be no possibility of anyone else existing in this dark new world that she found herself in.

The rain drummed steadily on the roof of the Chrysler and dented the surface of the river beyond the Pentagon. A tugboat moaned far out on the water, churning its way upriver behind a long line of barges.

For a long time Catherine sat in her car, unaware of the time or the place. She tried to recall memories of her childhood, her husband, her children, but they were all burned away by the image of Lane holding someone else in his arms.

With fingers that seemed numbed as if by cold, she turned the key in the ignition. The engine roared to life. With a last look at that unbearable place on the upstairs gallery, she put the car in gear and drove slowly away toward the river.

Turning left on Lafayette Street, she passed the brick buildings complete with iron columns and grill-work that had given the street its name. Stopping at a red light in the next block, she found herself in front of the Heidelberg Hotel. She could almost see Lane with his arm around her as they entered the hotel on that first night they stayed in Baton Rouge.

Suddenly she knew exactly how to escape this new world where nothing was real but the ceaseless, unforgiving pain. Crossing the intersection, she pulled into the parking garage, left the car with the attendant, and walked back to the hotel.

Inside, the slim, dark-haired man behind the desk greeted her cordially, pushing the register around for her to sign. "Shall I have someone get your luggage?"

"No—thank you." Catherine felt strange talking to the man, as though she hadn't spoken for years.

The man gave her a skeptical look. "And how long will you be staying?"

Catherine glanced up from the register. "Just one night. I'd like room 503 please."

Glancing around at the rows of pigeonholes behind him, the man's eyes narrowed. "How will you be paying, ma'am?"

Catherine reached into her purse, took out a fifty-dollar bill, and dropped it on the desk.

The man's face brightened as he began to make change.

"Don't bother," Catherine remarked absently. "I'll stop by when I leave."

"As you wish." He pointed to the elevators. "Turn left and the room's the last one on the right. I think you'll find it has a beautiful view of the river."

"Yes, it does. Thank you."

Catherine walked across the wine-colored carpet of the lobby to the elevator. Everything looked the same way it had when she and Lane had been there together. This puzzled her because everything else in her world had changed so drastically. As she waited for the elevator, she turned and looked around again, shaking her head slowly.

As Catherine stepped inside the elevator, pushing the button for the fifth floor, she remembered her last trip in it so vividly that she wondered if what she had seen at the Pentagon was a dream. In her memory she felt Lane's arms around her, his lips on hers as they rode up to the fifth floor. Surprised by the swishing sound of the doors opening, they had seen an elderly couple smiling at them as they stood waiting in the hall.

When Catherine got off the elevator this time, no one waited—and no one stood next to her. Walking down the silent hall, she saw the rain falling steadily and the rain-streaked window brimming with heavy gray light.

A radio carried the distinctive sound of Walter Winchell broadcasting the news as Catherine entered the room, but it was merely a noise drowned in a sea of noises to her, along with the sound of the rain outside the window and the muted traffic noises coming up from the streets below.

The room looked exactly the same to Catherine as when she and Lane had stayed there: the slate-blue carpet, the blue-flowered bedspread and curtains, the lamps and chairs, and the gleaming white ceramic tile bath.

She walked over to the corner window, opened it, and gazed out to the tiny Lafayette Park with its curving walkways, benches made of wrought iron and wood, and the bare glistening limbs of the trees, silhouetted like black filigree against the late winter sky.

In the background, the news continued:

*Tax reduction is voted over Truman veto . . . Russia bans all land traffic to Berlin. The West is formulating plans to airlift supplies into the besieged city. . . .*

Catherine let her gaze follow Convention Street as it ran alongside the park, sloping down to the River Road and the levee. Beyond the levee, a smoky white mist covered the surface of the river like a layer of clouds seen from an airplane.

Down below the window, cars hissed along the mirrored streets. Catherine stared at the tops of umbrellas as people hurried along the sidewalks. She stood there gazing down through the rain-streaked window and felt as cold and empty and alone as the tiny park, abandoned in the winter rain.

★ ★ ★

*This is my story, this is my song. . . .*

The sound of music and singing from the radio stirred Catherine from her somber trance. She had no idea how long she had been standing there, locked in her melancholy reverie. The rain had stopped, but the world looked as gray as ashes. With no hesitation, she bent down, unlocked the window, and pushed it up. It stuck three inches above the sill. *I can't even do this right!*

Frustrated and angry, Catherine pushed with all her might, but the window wouldn't budge. She stormed about the room looking for a way to pry the window open. As she entered the bathroom, she caught a glimpse of herself in the mirror. Her pale blond hair looked matted and stringy. She thought of the past two sleepless nights she had spent with Lane away and of how she had let her appearance go in recent weeks.

Suddenly she saw an image of herself sprawled down below the window on the sidewalk with her hair spread lifeless and dull and dirty about her face. She remembered how Lane had always loved her hair, had complimented her countless times on how soft and shiny it was as he caressed it with his fingertips. *I won't end it all looking like this!*

Noticing the shampoo and other bathroom articles lined up neatly on the counter, Catherine took off her jacket and blue sweater and turned the water on in the tub. After washing and rinsing her hair, she sat on the bed toweling it dry.

*Jesus loves you.*

Catherine heard the voice from the radio as though from some great distance. It was like a small light shining in the terrible, cold darkness that seemed to engulf her. She remembered the vivid colors of the Bible pictures on the wall and the bright room where she had gone to Sunday school as a child—and Mrs. King, the soft-spoken, gray-haired lady who smelled like flowers and who told her about Moses and King David and Jesus. And she could almost hear the voices of the children as they all sang their favorite song. "Jesus loves me, this I know."

*And He knows what you're going through—the heartaches, the pain, and the feeling that you're all alone in this world. For you see, He was once a child just like you were. He skinned His knees and cut His finger—and He cried just like you did, and He ran to His mother, just like you did.*

*The Bible tells us that it pleased Jesus to be made like us so that "He might be a merciful and faithful high priest." He loves you so much that He went to Calvary for you. And when He hung on that cross with nails driven through His hands and feet He, too, was all alone in the world—separated from the Father because He took all the sin of the world on himself—including yours.*

*And they took Him down from that cross after He died and they laid Him in a tomb. And on the third day He rose from the dead, and in His victory over death there is eternal life for us all. "For God so loved the world, that he gave his only begotten Son, that whosoever believeth in him should not perish, but have everlasting life."*

Catherine listened to every word now and the words seemed to comfort her.

*Listen now to the words of Jesus. He's talking to you. "Come unto me, all ye that labour and are heavy laden, and I will give you rest. Take my yoke upon you, and learn of me; for I am meek and lowly in heart: and ye shall find rest unto your souls."*

*Come to Jesus now. He loves you so very much.*

Falling slowly to her knees by the side of the bed, Catherine clutched the towel to her breast. "Oh, Jesus! I hurt so bad. Please help me!"

Catherine felt the tears begin and as she sobbed there in the hotel room on her knees, she could sense all the pain and grief and terrible darkness being washed away. It was as though a great stone had been lifted from her heart.

*I will give you rest.* The words kept repeating themselves in her mind. *I will give you rest.* She spoke them aloud and found a great joy in the sound of them: "I will give you rest."

Catherine was smiling now. "Precious Jesus! I've made such a mess of my life. I need your rest. I give myself—all that I have, all that I am—to you. Please change this selfish heart of mine."

With tears running down her cheeks, Catherine lifted her face toward heaven, "Thank you, Jesus! Thank you!"

★ ★ ★

When Catherine left the elevator, walking across the lobby to the desk, the slim clerk approached with his most winning smile. "Yes, may I help you?"

"Yes, you may," Catherine smiled back. "I'd like to check out, please."

The clerk took her name and found it in his register. He glanced up, a surprised expression on his face. "But—you just checked in four hours ago!"

"Yes, I know."

A glimmer of recognition crossed the man's face; then he recalled the incident. "I remember now. You gave me fifty dollars, but I hardly recognize you. You don't look like the same woman."

"I'm not." Catherine's smile was so broad that she felt the skin tightening at the corners of her mouth.

With a puzzled expression, the clerk unlocked the cash drawer and began counting out Catherine's change. "Here you are," he said, holding the money out to her.

"You can keep it."

"But—but it's almost thirty dollars!" the clerk sputtered, still holding the money out.

"Take your wife out to dinner," Catherine told him. She laughed as she kissed the wad of bills and stuffed them in his inside jacket pocket.

He waved at Catherine as she went through the front door. "Thank you!"

After getting her car out of the parking garage, Catherine drove back across town to pick the children up. She parked under a spreading live oak in the graveled area at the side of the street that separated the high school from the elementary.

Wearing her blue jacket with the pearl buttons, Sharon waited for her mother on a concrete bench, her face buried in a book. She recognized the sound of the car and, without putting the book down, walked over and climbed in.

Noticing the car, Dalton faked right and dribbled left past the boy guarding him. Making an easy lay-up that ringed the hoop and dropped in, he picked up his books from the edge of the cement basketball court and ran to the Chrysler.

After her usual two minutes of pretending that she hadn't seen her mother arrive, Jessie left the small group of boys and girls standing under the portico, walked over nonchalantly, and got into the backseat with Dalton.

Catherine greeted her children with a cheerfulness and enthusiasm that surprised even her. Jessie gave her a suspicious glance. Dalton stared out the back window at the basketball game he had just left.

"Who wants to go to Hopper's?" Catherine beamed at the children.

"Me!" Dalton shouted, bouncing up and down on the backseat. "I want a strawberry malt!"

Jessie pushed him over to his side of the seat. "Get away from me, you little heathen!"

"That's no way to talk to your brother, Jessie," Catherine said calmly. "You could use a little of his energy. Sometimes I think you're an old lady in disguise."

Jessie failed to see the humor in her mother's remark and stared out the window at a tall crew-cut boy in a maroon football letter-jacket.

Sitting next to her mother, Sharon put her book down, leaned over and whispered, "You look real pretty today, Mama. Your eyes are all shiny."

Catherine pulled up at a stop sign, gazing down at Sharon's big blue eyes behind the gold frames of her glasses. "Thank you, baby. I *feel* real pretty too." She placed her hand on Sharon's cheek, leaned over and kissed her.

After picking up Cassidy and Mrs. LeJeune, Catherine drove back to the drive-in, parking in the same spot she had the day she first met Gene Duhon.

As the car pulled in, Gene hurried out the side door, stopping cold when he saw the big Chrysler. Remembering Jessie's remarks about her mother's opinion of him, he strolled reluctantly over to the car.

Catherine gave Gene a big smile when he stooped

down with his pencil and pad. After taking all the orders, Gene left the car wondering if Jessie could have been wrong about her mother.

"Were you a good boy for Mrs. LeJeune today, Cassidy?" Catherine held him, sitting sideways and wriggling in her lap, behind the steering wheel.

"I'm always good." Cassidy took off his cowboy hat, swatting Sharon on the head with it.

"Mama, make him stop!"

"Oh, don't be such an old maid, Sharon! He's just playing." Catherine held Cassidy's arms pinned to his sides, tickling him as he giggled and squirmed to get free. "You little rascal. Let's see you pick on somebody your own size."

Mrs. LeJeune, in the usual black cardigan she had worn for winters beyond memory, watched Catherine playing and laughing with her children, thinking it had been a long time since she had seen her friend in such a good mood. "You're certainly a cheerful soul today, Catherine."

"Yes, ma'am. I've never felt better." Catherine thought she would burst with happiness, wanting to gather all four of her children in her arms and hug them for hours. She had a consuming desire to shout to the world what had happened to her in that hotel room such a short time ago, but she had no idea how to begin telling such a marvelous story.

Gene returned with the orders, hooking the heavy tray onto the window. When the ice cream and malts and one cherry Coke had been handed around, Gene turned to leave.

"May I speak with you a moment, Gene?" Catherine set her malt glass back on the tray.

"Uh—yes, ma'am." He held the tray in place against the door as Catherine got out of the car.

Hearing her mother speak to Gene and staring wide-eyed as she left the car, Jessie could only imagine that this would surely end Gene's friendship. She watched Catherine walk slowly toward the building with him, talk for a short time outside the door, and return to the car. Oddly enough Gene's expression had been one of pleasant surprise.

"What did you tell him?" Jessie leaned forward in her seat as Catherine got back into the car.

"I told him to come to our house for supper one night," Catherine replied, closing the car door carefully.

"You didn't! Why?"

"If you're determined to see this boy, then you can do it in your own home. That way you won't have to sneak around." Catherine took a swallow of the malt directly from the tall, heavy glass. "Hmmm. That's *so* good!"

In a state of mild shock, Jessie sat in the backseat sipping her cherry Coke. She wondered if her mother had suddenly gone insane. She pictured two burly men in white coats carrying Catherine away in a straitjacket. *Poor Mama! And I'll have to do all the cooking and cleaning!*

When everyone had finished, Catherine drove Mrs. LeJeune home, parking at the curb in front of her house.

Marie LeJeune knew exactly what had happened to Catherine—she had seen this change in people before. She walked around the car, stopping at Catherine's window.

Catherine rolled down the glass. "Thanks again for taking care of Cassidy."

"Always my pleasure." Marie's gray eyes shone with joy. "And Catherine . . ."

"Yes?"

"Welcome home."

★  ★  ★

"Lane Temple speaking." Lane continued to read the fine print in the Louisiana Title Fourteen Revised Statutes as he answered the telephone.

Cradling the telephone on her shoulder, Catherine stood at the kitchen counter, slicing onions into fine wet slivers on her cutting board. "I'm fixing shrimp creole tonight. It's Mrs. LeJeune's recipe—your favorite."

Lane stared out the window across three narrow alleys to the back entrance of the Hotel Bruin. A gangly dark-skinned man with an apron tied around his narrow waist and a white hat on his small head washed down the concrete with a water hose. "Sorry, honey. I've got to get ready for that aggravated battery trial. I'm first on the docket Monday—probably have to work all night."

"You'll do it tomorrow, then," Catherine said with the finality of a judge's gavel striking the bench. "I'll feed the kids and have them all in bed by nine. See you then."

Lane found himself listening to the dial tone. He never remembered Catherine speaking this way before. Staring again at the rear alley of the Bruin, he suddenly knew that he would go home at nine o'clock exactly as Catherine had said—felt that he had no more control over the matter than the broom had over the man he watched pushing it.

*I wonder what this is all about? Trouble with Jessie? Maybe Catherine's overdrawn at the bank.* But deep inside Lane knew it was neither of those things.

At the other end of the phone line, Catherine finished chopping the onion and bell peppers. Using Lou Ana oil and flour, she made a roux in a deep black iron pot with a lid, then added the peppers and onions, sauteing them until they were slightly brown.

Catherine felt a comfortable warmth settle over her as she listened to the sounds of her children upstairs getting ready for bed. Even preparing the meal seemed something to savor. She finally added the shrimp and lemons, put the cover on, and washed her hands. Feeling thankful for all that had been given her, Catherine went upstairs for bedtime prayer with her children.

# SIXTEEN

# SOMEONE TO LOVE ME

★ ★ ★

As soon as he opened the back door, Lane smelled the spicy aroma of the shrimp creole. "Hmmm, I certainly did come to the right place. If that tastes half as good as it smells, I just might give the cook a raise."

Her hands in a sinkful of suds, Catherine turned to Lane, blowing a wispy tendril of hair back out of her eyes. She wore a simple blue dress with tiny white flowers on it. "You can go wash up. Everything's ready."

Taking his tan raincoat off and loosening his tie, Lane hung the coat on a peg next to the back door and walked over to Catherine. "You smell better than the supper. Is that a new shampoo?" he whispered, his lips next to her ear as he put his hands around her waist.

"Yes." Catherine turned away slightly, remembering that she had washed her hair at the Heidelberg only that morning. It seemed to her a lifetime ago. "Hurry now. It won't be good if you let it get cold."

"Yes, ma'am." Lane left the kitchen, taking the stairs up to their bedroom two at the time.

Catherine put the finishing touches on the dining room table, then returned to the kitchen. Taking two large shallow bowls over to the stove, she spooned in generous portions of fluffy white rice. Next she covered the rice liberally with the thick, dark-red creole sauce, filled with plump shrimp.

Lane came in just as she set his food on the table. He had changed into khakis, a blue chambray shirt, and brown loafers. "Why are we eating at opposite ends of the table?" He glanced around. "And why are the lights so bright?" Switching the overhead light off, he turned on a floor lamp.

Sitting down at her end of the table, Catherine spoke in a level voice. "Sit down, Lane. Your supper's getting cold."

"Fine. I can see the conversation's not going to be as good as the food is tonight." Confused by Catherine's seemingly contradictory behavior, Lane sat down and prepared to attack the shrimp creole.

"Why don't you say grace like you used to?" Catherine sat serenely with her hands in her lap.

"Uh—sure. All right." Lane bowed his head, mouthing a few words. He was beginning to feel uneasy. Something had changed about Catherine that he couldn't figure out.

Catherine ate slowly, savoring the rich, spicy food. It tasted better than any meal she had eaten in months. "Did you get your case ready for Monday?"

"Huh? Oh, yeah, not much to it."

"You said earlier you'd have to work all night." Catherine dreaded what she had to do, but was eager to get things settled at the same time. She knew that before today she would never have had the courage to face up to it.

"I did? Well, it wasn't as bad as I thought it'd be." Lane found himself losing his appetite, but continued to eat steadily.

Pointing to a small platter piled with hot, crispy-chewy French bread spread with a mixture of garlic juice and butter, Catherine remarked, "You're not eating the bread. I think it's almost as good as the creole."

Lane broke a piece off, chewing it with relish. "You're right. How'd you learn to fix it this way?"

"Something I thought of myself, believe it or not," Catherine answered, her placid gaze on Lane.

After they had finished the creole and all but one piece of bread, Catherine served freshly dripped coffee and praline cheesecake for dessert.

"I believe this is the best meal I've ever eaten," Lane mumbled through his cheesecake.

"You've said that about a hundred times since I married you." Catherine had to admit it was one of her best efforts.

Lane sipped the rich, dark coffee. "Well, I guess you just keep getting better and better. And this coffee's perfect. I'm sure glad you let Coley talk you into getting a drip pot."

With the meal finished, Catherine cleared the table and poured fresh cups of coffee.

For the first time since they sat down to eat, Lane gazed thoughtfully at his wife. He had never seen her look more lovely. Her only makeup was a touch of lipstick, but her skin seemed to emit a warm glow all its own; and her hair, lambent in the dim room, shimmered like pale moonlight.

"Lane, what are you staring at?"

"You. I sometimes forget how beautiful you are."

Lane moved his chair back to get up.

"No! We have to talk."

Lane eased his chair back to the table. Picking up his cup, he glanced uneasily at Catherine and sipped the hot coffee just for something to do, hardly tasting it.

Catherine rested her elbows on the arms of her chair, her hands pressed together, fingertips pointing toward the ceiling. "I haven't been much of a wife since we moved down here. Maybe even before that."

"That's not true, Cath—"

"No! Let me finish!" With a deep breath she continued. "And the children have suffered because I've neglected them. Especially Jessie. She's at such a difficult time in a girl's life—a time when she needs a mother's understanding, a mother's friendship. I just hope I haven't waited too long to make things right with her."

Lane's chair scraped on the floor as he started to get up again. "You're being too hard on—"

Catherine stopped him with her eyes. "I need to tell you these things, Lane."

Giving her a sheepish look, Lane conceded. "Okay. I'll keep my mouth shut."

Catherine got up and walked to the tall window, pulled back the flowered drape, and gazed out into the night. A big yellow cat, seeing the movement in the window, froze in its path across the side yard. Sensing no danger, it waved its long tail, leaped to the top of a wood fence, and disappeared.

Catherine turned around and walked directly over to Lane's end of the table. Pulling out a chair, she sat next to him, her hands clasped together demurely in her lap. "You're going to stop seeing her, Lane."

"What do you mean? Who?" The words came out

as flat and dead as the look Lane had glimpsed for a fleeting moment in Andre Catelon's eyes.

Ignoring the response they both knew was a lie, Catherine continued. "I blame myself, but I'm through doing anything else to blame myself for, Lane."

Lane started to speak, but somehow there seemed to be absolutely nothing left for him to say.

"And I'm through *crying* over this." Catherine's eyes grew dark briefly, like a fleeting cloud passing over the sun. "I've no tears left to shed. What I found out is that I was only crying for *myself* anyway—for the things I was doing to myself." Suddenly the light was back in Catherine's eyes as quickly as it had left. "I think that was the whole problem. All I could think about was *myself*—and that's a terrible way to live."

"I don't know what to say." Lane stared down at the white starched tablecloth.

Catherine smiled serenely at her husband. "You don't have to say anything."

Lane looked up.

"I love you very much, Lane. I can't even remember what it's *like* not to love you."

Lane reached across the table for her hand.

Catherine closed her eyes, holding her hand palm out toward him. "No. Not now."

Lane felt sick to his stomach at the thought of Catherine not wanting him. He considered the fact that she might leave him and found it unbearable—unthinkable. "When?"

"I don't know."

They sat in silence for several minutes, Lane nervously sipping his coffee with occasional glances at his wife. Catherine merely waited, knowing that he would eventually tell her what was on his heart.

In the quiet house, the distant, tinny sound of Jessie's radio floated down the stairs. The haunting, bittersweet melody of "I'll Be Seeing You" was unmistakable.

Lane stared at the table, his voice cracked and brittle as he spoke. "I'm so *sorry*, Catherine. I—I never thought anything like this would happen."

Catherine thought of the night Lane took her to his senior prom and of how proud she was to be seen with him. Exactly two years later they were married.

"I'll do *anything* to make it up to you." Lane's voice held the dread he felt at the thought of losing Catherine.

"You don't have to make anything up to me, Lane. You only have to end it with . . ."

Lane stared at Catherine in disbelief. He had expected demands, ultimatums—had expected her to beat him with his own infidelity. "Don't worry—I will."

"I'm not worried."

Catherine's calm voice was like a balm to the fear Lane felt burning inside him. He continued hesitantly. "You're—you're not going to leave me?"

"No."

Lane began to gain control of his emotions. "Catherine, I *promise* I'll be a new man! You'll see. We'll spend more time together—take the kids on a long vacation."

Smiling, Catherine brushed a lock of hair back from her forehead. "I think we've had enough revelations about each other for one night—almost. There's only one more thing I want to tell you."

"Anything."

"Today I accepted Jesus as my Savior." Catherine's face held the serenity of old paintings and she spoke almost as if no one else were in the room with her. "I was listening to Billy Graham on the radio and—"

"But you've always gone to church—that is, until the last year or so."

"That's not what I'm talking about, Lane. It takes place in the heart. Jesus wants more than two hours on Sunday morning. He wants all of you—your whole life."

Lane suddenly knew why Catherine seemed like a different woman. She was experiencing the same depth of faith that Coley talked about.

"Oh—but what He gives in return! It's marvelous beyond anything I can tell you. There's such peace— such . . ." Catherine let her voice trail off, unable to continue.

"I'm glad for you, Catherine. Glad you're so happy," Lane insisted, shifting nervously about in his chair. He truly meant his words, but wished that she would quit talking about what had happened.

Catherine almost started quoting scripture to Lane, but something stopped her. Somehow she knew that his seeing this miraculous change in her life would be enough for now.

Standing up from the table, Lane stretched and yawned. "I think I'll turn in. You coming, sweetheart?"

"Later. I'm going to clean up first." Catherine picked up their cups and saucers.

"Aw, leave 'em till tomorrow! Let's go to bed." Lane held his hand out to her.

Catherine gazed directly into Lane's eyes, speaking with a calm assurance. "It's going to take a while, Lane. You go on ahead and get your rest."

Lane got the message. He kissed her tenderly on the cheek and went upstairs.

Catherine took the cups and saucers into the kitchen and began washing the last of the dishes.

Standing at the sink in her own kitchen, she felt better than she ever had in her whole life. Remembering what she had seen that morning at the Pentagon and what had happened to her in that hotel room, she suddenly realized what a great miracle she had received.

Joy seemed to flow through Catherine like warm, soothing oil, washing away all the hurt and all the tears. A song from her childhood came back to her like a visit from an old and dear friend. She began to sing softly as she washed the dishes.

> I am Thine, O Lord, I have heard Thy voice,
> And it told Thy love to me;
> But I long to rise in the arms of faith,
> And be closer drawn to Thee.
>
> Draw me nearer, nearer, blessed Lord,
> To the cross where Thou hast died. . . .

Catherine continued to sing the old song as she finished the dishes, put them away, and turned out the lights. Then she left the kitchen, went through the dining room and past the yellow shine of the stairwell to Lane's study. Taking her Bible down from the bookshelf, she turned on the lamp and sat down at his desk. After a few minutes, she looked up, a smile on her face, realizing that for the first time in her life she knew the Author of the book she was reading.

★ ★ ★

The March wind whipped through the front door of the building as Bonnie entered the dimly lit hallway. Coley shivered slightly as the chill entered his office door. Looking up from his work, he saw her walk past, wearing rose-colored slacks and a black sweater, heard the sound of her heels clicking on the wooden stairs as she climbed to the second floor. She entered Lane's office without knocking.

"I told you not to come here, Bonnie!" Lane glanced wearily up from the bulky law book.

Bonnie's face was pale. The delicate skin beneath her eyes had taken on a purplish hue. Her dark hair was tousled from the wind. "I had to see you, Lane."

"It's over between us and that's all there is to it," Lane declared bluntly.

"You wouldn't return my calls. You wouldn't answer my letters."

Letting his breath out heavily, Lane closed the book. "I love Catherine. I never should have let this happen. And now it's got to end."

Bonnie almost collapsed into the heavy wood chair in front of the desk. "I can't stand not being with you!"

Lane rubbed his eyes with both hands, then stood up and walked around the desk. "Let's be honest about this whole thing, Bonnie. Your job was to persuade me to come in on your daddy's oil and gas deal."

"Y—yes. That's how it got started," Bonnie replied, her voice quavering. "But that's got nothing to do with why I have to see you now."

"Look, I'm not blaming you. I'm a grown man." Lane sat on the edge of the desk. "You didn't force me to do anything."

"Oh, Lane, I don't want to talk about any of that!" Bonnie's eyes had a look of desperation. "I don't care about who's to blame anymore! I just miss you so much."

Lane felt sick in the pit of his stomach as he witnessed the results of his callous decision. And he thought how much worse it must have been for Catherine. "I cared about you too, Bonnie, but what we had was wrong. We're kidding ourselves if we try to make something decent out of it."

"It's not wrong to love someone. I can't let myself believe that."

"It's wrong to hurt other people—to be so selfish you don't even consider them." As Lane watched Bonnie's anguish, saw the grief in her shadowed eyes, he pictured how he would feel if Catherine ever left him. What he saw was a world of gloom, a world where he rose alone each morning to plod mechanically through day after dreary day.

"I can't think about this anymore. Nothing makes sense to me." Bonnie put her face in her hands. "I only know I want to be with you."

Lane stepped closer to Bonnie, reached his hand out to touch her on the shoulder, then quickly drew it back. "We have to end this right now, Bonnie."

Her reaction was startling. "No!" Bonnie jumped from the chair and began pounding on Lane's chest with both hands. "No! No! You can't do this to me!"

Grabbing her by the wrists, Lane held her at arms' length. "Bonnie! Settle down!"

Bonnie began kicking at Lane, connecting on his shin with a hard leather sole. With a cry of pain, Lane let go of her wrists and moved back. Bonnie grabbed a heavy glass ashtray from his desk, flinging it at him with all her might. Lane leaped aside, but the ashtray caught him a glancing blow on the left temple, its sharp corner gashing the skin.

"Oh, Lane! I'm so sorry!" Bonnie put her left hand to her breast, watching the bright flow down the side of Lane's face. "Are you all right?"

Lane took a white handkerchief out of his inside jacket pocket, holding it against his head to staunch the blood. Feeling dizzy, he walked unsteadily over to the chair Bonnie had been using and slumped into it.

Bonnie knelt beside him, leaning over to look at his head. "Does it hurt badly?"

His vision blurred, Lane gazed at Bonnie. "A Jap bullet hurts worse." He pressed the handkerchief tighter to his head. "But I could shoot back at them."

Taking the handkerchief from his hand, Bonnie held it away from his head, staring at the cut. "It looks bad. I'd better take you to the hospital."

"No!"

"Lane, you need stitches." Bonnie dabbed at the flow of blood, slowing now as it began to coagulate.

"I'm fine."

Dropping Lane's handkerchief on the floor, Bonnie picked up her purse and went into the half bath connected to Lane's office. In a few seconds she came back out with a fine linen handkerchief she had wet and began to clean the wound on Lane's head. "Hold still now."

Still feeling slightly dizzy, Lane winced as the cold water touched the cut.

When she had finished, Bonnie folded the handkerchief, pressing it against the side of his head. "I wish you'd let me take you to the hospital."

"No. It'll be all right." Lane sat up straight, his head beginning to clear.

Bonnie knelt down beside the chair. "Lane, forgive me. I don't know how I could have done that."

"It's not your fault. You're just a girl." Lane glanced at her, shaking his head sadly.

"I'm twenty-two years old." An edge of indignation crept into Bonnie's voice. "I'm *not* a girl!"

Lane stood up, walked to his desk and sat on the side of it. "Yes, you are. I knew that it had to end like this, and I let it happen anyway."

Bonnie stood up. The light through the tall windows striking the dark tangle of her hair cast her face into shadow. She stood staring at Lane like a child preparing to ask permission to play outside a while longer.

Before she could speak, Lane said solemnly, "I've *always* loved Catherine, Bonnie." His eyes held the unmistakable gleam of truth. "I always will. I can't imagine living without her. I don't know that I'd even *want* to live without her."

A single tear glistened on Bonnie's shadowed face as she stood perfectly still.

Lane continued as though speaking the words was a sacred quest entrusted to him. "I don't know *why* I let this happen between us." Lane paused, his brow seamed with thought. "Pride maybe. The idea that someone as young and pretty as you would be attracted to me. I don't know. Sometimes I think men are the dumbest creatures on this earth."

Bonnie had remained perfectly still while Lane spoke, as though there were a precipice on either side of her. "Couldn't we—just be friends?"

Staring at the floor, Lane shook his head sadly.

"I—I won't be able to see you anymore—ever?"

Lane didn't move, leaning against his desk and holding Bonnie's handkerchief pressed against his head.

"I don't know what to do. I'm afraid to leave, Lane. Afraid to go back to the way things were before. . . ." Bonnie glanced back at the door that led out onto the landing and the stairs as though it intended to harm her. "If only—if only I could find someone to love me the way you love Catherine."

Hearing the quiet desperation in her voice, Lane wanted to embrace her and tell her everything would be all right. But he knew that it would be the worst thing he could do—that it would only prolong the hurt and the sorrow. "You *will* find someone, Bonnie," Lane murmured, unable to look at her.

Bonnie had begun to cry softly.

"And he'll treat you far better than I've treated either you or Catherine," Lane added, hoping it was the truth.

Without looking at Lane, Bonnie turned slowly and left the office, the door closing after her with a soft click like the lock on an old chest.

Lane heard her footsteps in faint retreat on the stairs, then the sound of the hallway door closing. His head had begun to throb painfully, but as he looked at Bonnie's handkerchief, he saw that the bleeding had stopped.

# SEVENTEEN

# LANE'S SLINGSHOT

★ ★ ★

"Lane!"

Stirring at the sound of his name, Lane dropped the bloodstained handkerchief on his desk and walked over to the door. Opening it, he glanced at his watch and saw that it had been only a few minutes since Bonnie had left. Stepping out onto the narrow landing, he saw Coley at the bottom of the stairs.

"Come on down."

"Be right with you."

Coley nodded, spun the chair around smoothly, and wheeled back into his office.

Lane tossed Bonnie's bloodstained handkerchief into an open desk drawer, picked up his own from the floor, and went into the little half bath. The wound on his temple was an inch-and-a-half long and deeper than he thought it would be. He cleaned it again, dried it with a hand towel, and put on a Band-Aid. It left the ragged ends of the cut uncovered.

Staring into the mirror to check his medical

handiwork, Lane noticed for the first time the dull glimmerings of age that had crept into his eyes.

Going downstairs, he entered Coley's office just as he was pouring fresh coffee into two heavy white mugs, chipped and stained from constant use.

Lane sat in his usual chair next to the window. "I can really use a cup of that."

Maneuvering his wheelchair into place, Coley glanced at the bandage on Lane's head. "That must have been some ruckus upstairs."

"Worse than it sounded." Lane's eyes were drawn as always to the sign above Coley's desk.

"I assume that means it's over between you and Bonnie," Coley said solemnly.

Lane looked away from the sign, nodded his head, and took a sip of coffee.

"I saw her come by the office on the way out. That girl's in bad shape."

"I don't know what to do for her."

Coley took a deep breath. Using his elbows as braces, he pulled himself up straighter in his chair. "Exactly what you're doing now—leave her alone."

"How did things go so wrong?"

Coley didn't bother to answer, knowing that Lane had the answer before he asked the question. "If you're waiting for me to say, 'Don't worry about it, everybody makes mistakes,' or 'You didn't do anything everyone else isn't doing,' forget it. I'm all out of platitudes."

Lane held Coley's steady gaze with his own. "I guess I *was* waiting for that, wasn't I? I should have known you're too good a friend to let me get by that easy."

"What's past is past as far as Bonnie's concerned. She'll pull through it all right." Coley's face held the hint of a smile. He was glad that Lane hadn't whined or tried to hide behind a wall of excuses. "Anybody who can survive growing up with Andre Catelon for a father has to have a special kind of strength."

Lane thought of the look in Bonnie's shadowed eyes as she poured out her grief to him, heard again the desperation in her voice and wondered what had gone on in all those days and nights she had spent as a child in the house of Andre Catelon. "I went to see him last week."

"I know."

"You know?" Lane's eyebrows raised slightly; then a look of resignation crossed his face. "Sure you do. Why does that surprise me?"

Coley chuckled softly.

"I want to get my life straightened out, Coley." Lane stared at the cup in his hand. "I owe it to Catherine and my children. They deserve a better husband and father than I've been."

Coley remained silent, knowing that Lane needed to get it all out in the open. "I told Catelon that I was through—that I wanted no part of what he and Walker were doing."

"I'm sure he graciously consented to grant *whatever* you wanted."

"You think this is funny?"

"I find it mildly amusing." Coley stared at Lane with an elfish gleam in his eyes.

Lane couldn't figure out Coley's attitude about the situation, knowing that it could mean his disbarment. "Catelon told me they had my name on the contract to handle the state lease deal for Pelican Oil and if I tried to back out now he'd see I went to jail for fraud, violating the public bid laws, and conspiracy to bribe a public official."

"Sounds serious."

"He'll never force me to go through with it!" Lane snapped, angry at Catelon, at himself for his stupidity, and at Coley for his apparent lack of concern.

"You're not?"

"No!" Lane felt like taking a swing at Coley. "I'd rather be in jail than under Catelon's thumb."

"Now that shows good sense," Coley remarked casually. "Once you owe a debt to a politician, you're theirs for life. There's nothing you can do to get out."

Lane felt trapped and helpless.

"Except to beat them at their own game." Coley stared over his coffee cup, waiting for Lane's reaction.

It came a few seconds later, when Lane realized that Coley's words carried an offer. "You're kidding. I can't go up against Catelon. He's got the whole state government on his side. What have I got?"

Coley merely smiled serenely.

"Why, it'd be like David going against Goliath—without his slingshot."

Reaching into the side pocket of his wheelchair, Coley took out a heavy brown envelope and dropped it on the table. "Here's *your* slingshot."

Finding himself unable to follow the workings of Coley's mind, Lane opened the envelope, dumping the contents out. As he examined them he realized that they were copies of the official bid forms of all the oil companies. Still puzzled, he asked, "What good will this do?"

"Crooks, especially political crooks, handle the big things well," he replied enigmatically. "It's the little things they pay no attention to—just like they pay no attention to the little people."

Lane shrugged, waiting for Coley to get to the point in his convoluted fashion.

"Look at the date and time stamps on the bids."

Lane did just that, noticing that they were all stamped between 4 P.M. and 5 P.M. on the day the bids were closed. He knew that all the companies turned their bids in at the last minute by means of a messenger service to ensure the least possible chance of someone finding out what the amount was.

"Now take a look at this." Coley reached back into the pocket of his chair, took out a final bid, and tossed it on the table with the others.

This time Lane knew immediately what Coley had accomplished. The Pelican Oil bid wasn't received until the next day—stamped and dated exactly seventeen hours and six minutes after the bidding was officially closed.

"That's all you need." Coley began collecting the bid forms and stuffing them back into the envelope. "If he tries to give the leases to Pelican Oil, you can send him to prison. Of course, if he thinks you're just bluffing and does it anyway, you'll go right along with him—but he won't do it."

"How can you be so sure?"

"Because he won't do anything to risk losing that title *Honorable* before his name. The *Honorable* Andre Catelon, senator from the Parish of Orleans."

Lane settled back for a taste of Coleyan philosophy.

"Catelon is *addicted* to politics—and he's by no means in the minority. His just happens to be an extreme case."

"Addicted?"

"Precisely. He needs his political office like a dope addict needs a fix. It's the most important thing in his life." Coley's eyes narrowed in concentration. "The power, the money, the yes-men around him all fawn-

ing and truckling to his every whim. All the lobby-
ists—I think *bribe-ists* is a better word for most of
them—wining and dining him. A few years of this and
he can never handle a real job again. Don't worry
about Catelon taking a chance on losing his office for
the sake of these leases—he'll do *anything* to keep it."

"I believe you. One thing I don't understand." Lane
pointed his finger at Coley's thin chest. "You're a politician! Nobody truckles to you, you don't go to the
fancy parties, and you spend *all* your time with the
little people, as you call them."

Coley merely shrugged the way he did often, as
though he didn't consider himself a part of the world,
much less a part of the political scene. "I guess I'll find
out when I see if I can walk away from it or not."

"I don't even think you want any part of it now,"
Lane ventured. "Whatever the reason you're in office,
it's not because you enjoy it."

Coley ignored Lane's opinion. "One other thing
you should know."

Lane waited.

"Once you make Catelon your enemy, there's no
going back. He'll carry the vendetta for the rest of his
life, no matter what you do. It's the way the game's
played."

"That's a comforting thought, Coley," Lane said
wearily. "I'm so glad you told me."

"This is serious, Lane. You'll have to watch your
back with him from now on."

"I will."

"And most of the others will be on his side. In their
perverted sense of morality, *you're* the traitor."

"Any more encouraging words?"

"Just want you to know the facts before you make
your decision."

"Doesn't change a thing."

"Good for you."

★ ★ ★

Lane parked on the street in front of the Capitol building between the statue of Huey Long and the Grand Staircase. He sat for a moment with his hands on the steering wheel of the '39 Ford. Thinking of the new Cadillac he had looked at in the showroom only two weeks ago, he glanced around at the shabby interior of the coupe. "Well, when I get finished in there today," he said aloud, "we'll be spending a few *more* years together."

Stepping out of the car, the brown envelope dangling from his left hand, Lane stared up at the limestone structure that rose in front of him. It gleamed faintly in the bright morning sunshine. He walked around to the left of the Grand Staircase, past a cluster of statues representing some historical moment, and through a side door into a lofty, dimly lit corridor beneath the main entrance.

"Moanin', Mr. Temple," Nathan Shropshire grinned brightly. Wearing a starched white shirt, neatly pressed khakis, and black oxfords that shone like new pennies, he sat in one of the two old theater seats he used for his shoeshine stand. His tan skin was speckled with faint brown dots, and gray hair fringed his bald head. Just under six feet tall, he weighed in at 140 if he carried his wooden brush-and-polish box onto the scales with him.

"Hey, Nat. How's it going?"

"A whole lot better'n I deserve. Dat's for sho'." From years of habit, Nathan glanced down at Lane's shoes. "Look like you could stand a little touch-up."

Lane somehow felt completely at ease as he stood

talking with Nathan, a comfortable kind of feeling he only had with his family and Coley Thibodeaux. "I guess so, but I've got some business to take care of inside first."

Nathan noticed that Lane had lost weight over the past few weeks and when the anemic light in the corridor hit his face just right, the man could see the first faint signs of age around Lane's eyes. "Well, don't you go lettin' them business deals get the best of you, Mr. Lane. Some folks I seed gets so busy tryin' to make a killin', dey plumb forgets to make a livin'."

Lane smiled. "I think you just might be on to something there, Nat."

"How yo' family doin'?"

"They're doing real good. And yours?"

Nathan chuckled softly from deep inside his blade-thin frame. "Fat and fine. Leola so big now it take me a day-and-a-half jes' to walk around her."

"I think you're just about the happiest man that I know, Nathan," Lane observed good-naturedly, "except maybe for Coley Thibodeaux."

"Mr. Coley's my good buddy. Ain't many in dis place take up time wid' a ol' colored shoeshine man, but Mr. Coley, he got plenty of time for ever'body."

Lane felt he had just learned something very important but, as was the case with such things, he knew it would take a while for it to incubate into something whole and alive that he could make some sense of. "I'll stop by on the way out, Nat."

"Sho', Mr. Lane."

★ ★ ★

"Well, it's good to see you again, Lane. I knew you'd come to your senses." Catelon, wearing his best election-year smile, walked around from behind his desk.

Lane stuck Coley's heavy brown envelope into Catelon's extended hand.

"What's this?" Catelon took the envelope, hefting it in both hands. "Not the contracts already? I haven't even called the press conference yet to announce the company that won the public bidding."

"Just as well," Lane said flatly.

Catelon's smile began to fade as he walked back around his desk and opened the envelope. He dumped the contents out and began to sort through them, searching each document for some clue as to why Lane had come back to see him. Then his face clouded over, his eyes taking on the flat, hard look Lane had seen before as it suddenly hit him. "This doesn't change anything. You won't open your mouth about this or you'll go to prison."

But Lane had seen the brief flicker of doubt in Catelon's eyes. "Try me."

"You don't have the guts for it." Catelon's face twisted in rage. "You're a nickel-and-dime nobody who hasn't got sense enough to see a good thing when it's dumped in his lap."

"Maybe we'll be cellmates." Lane held Catelon's gaze until the man glanced out the window and sat down in his chair. "I figure by the time the trial's over, they ought to be bringing the crops in up at Angola. You'd look good dragging a cotton sack down one of those half-mile-long rows."

Catelon's face seemed to relax and he broke into a smile, except for the dark void of his eyes. "I don't think you understand the magnitude of what you're doing, Temple."

"Probably not."

"There's more to it than just the money you're throwing away on this one deal."

Lane didn't reply, knowing that Catelon was beaten or he would have ended their meeting by now.

"If you persist in this, there's not a company or client worth doing business with that'll touch you." Catelon leaned forward on his elbows. "*I'll* see to that."

"Well, it doesn't take much for us nickel-and-dime nobodys to get by anyway," Lane smiled. "There's probably enough other *nobodys* out there who won't mind doing business with me."

Catelon leaned back in his chair, his feet three inches from the floor. "This is your last chance. If you walk out that door, you're as good as dead in this town."

"You could be right." Lane stared into Catelon's eyes. "But if I don't, I end up like you—*dead* wherever I am."

Catelon's eyes blazed with fury as he stood up. "You'll regret this, Temple!"

As he turned to leave, Lane glanced back over his shoulder. "By the way, you can keep those bid forms with my compliments. I've got the originals."

Lane felt the hot blast of Catelon's obscenities on his back as he left, but he held no anger toward him— it was somehow swallowed up by his deep feeling of gratitude that, after all he had done, Catherine hadn't left him.

On the way out of the Capitol, Lane stopped and visited with Nat for a while, thinking how strange the world was that Nat should have a shoeshine stand and a man like Catelon should have a plush office and power.

Walking out into the April morning, Lane noticed that the azaleas lining the paths in the formal garden were in full bloom—ablaze in bright shades of purple and white and pink. He didn't remember seeing them at all when he got out of the car.

★ ★ ★

Wearing a lavender dress, Catherine sat with her family in a high-backed oak pew midway down the aisle. Dressed in their Easter finery, they were all together in church for the first time in more than a year.

As the announcements were read, Catherine watched the motes drifting like tiny flecks of gold in the light streaming through the high windows. A sense of peace and belonging filled her that seemed as radiant and as constant as the sunlight.

On the podium the song leader, dressed in a tan suit and bright red tie, announced the page number and raised his arms. The congregation stood up, their voices lifted in song above the sounds of the piano and organ.

> Blessed assurance, Jesus is mine!
> O what a foretaste of glory divine!
> Heir of salvation, purchase of God,
> Born of His Spirit, washed in His blood.

Catherine sang the old song without looking at the open hymnal in her hands. Standing next to her, Jessie glanced about in an obvious state of boredom. Noticing her, Catherine pointed to the hymnal, holding it in front of her. Jessie shook her head, but on the next verse began to sing from memory, her voice as clear and pure as a mountain stream.

As they were finishing the last chorus to a final flourish of the piano, Catherine thought of that chilly, rainy day in February when she had heard the song on the radio. Closing her eyes, she gave thanks for the grace that had snatched her from the brink of eternity.

> This is my story, this is my song,
> Praising my Savior all the day long.

When the service was over, they went to the Piccadilly Cafeteria where they stood in line with roughly half of the Sunday morning churchgoers in Baton Rouge before they could eat. Afterward, at home, Catherine and Lane hid Easter eggs for the three younger children. Jessie, feeling that she had paid her dues to the family by going to church *and* out to eat with them, went upstairs to her room.

"It's been a lovely day." Watching her children at play, Catherine sat next to Lane as they drifted languidly in the porch swing on the back gallery.

"Ummm," Lane nodded, using one foot to keep the swing in motion.

Hoping she wouldn't disturb the peaceful mood that had settled about them, Catherine felt she had to speak what had been on her mind for weeks. "Do you think we should stay in Baton Rouge—after what happened with Catelon?"

"Why not?"

"He'll try to hurt you for not going through with that oil and gas deal. I heard Coley say he's not the type to forgive and forget."

"That's his problem."

"You sure you'll be all right?"

"Sweetheart, I survived three years of Jap bullets and bombs and seventeen years of marriage with you—I can handle Catelon."

Catherine punched him in the stomach. "You think that's funny?"

Lane flinched, grabbing her arm as she drew back

to hit him again. "Hey, you pack a pretty good wallop for such a little girl."

"Mama, look what Cassidy's doing now." Holding her wicker Easter basket of colored eggs, Sharon looked up through the gallery railing.

Catherine pulled free and saw Cassidy hanging on to the first limb of the fig tree at the rear of the yard, scrambling for a hold with his feet. "Cassidy, you get down from there right now," she yelled instinctively, turning to Dalton to tell him to go get his brother out of the tree.

"Yes, ma'am." Cassidy let go of the limb, dropping to the ground. With a sheepish grin on his face and a slight rip in his Gene Autry shirt, he walked slowly back to join the other children.

Catherine and Lane stared at each other dumb-founded.

"It's an Easter miracle," Lane announced, glancing toward heaven.

Laughing softly, Catherine moved closer to Lane and laid her head on his shoulder. "You have any plans for tonight?"

Glancing down at her, Lane saw the tranquil smile on Catherine's face. "None I couldn't change."

"I thought we might spend some time together."

"My place or yours?"

"Mine."

As the swing moved with a drowsy motion, Catherine watched the honey bees lifting off the clover blossoms. The soft, heavy air carried the scent of jasmine and roses and damp, rich earth bursting with new life. Sunlight fell warmly on her back as it slanted across the open lawn and splashed the tops of the live oaks with pale yellow light.